Cuno's N

The rancher turned to hi
Suddenly, he blinked, and recognition returned to his gaze. He removed his pipe from his teeth, knocked the dottle onto the wide-boarded floor, and lifted the coffee mug from the table.

"What would you say to hitchin' up one of your wagons and getting my daughter and the Lassiter kids the hell out of here?"

"Out of here?" Cuno almost laughed. The man really was crazier than a tree full of owls. "You're hemmed in by Indians on three sides, might even be some behind the house. Even if you aren't totally surrounded, in case you haven't checked recently, you've got one hell of a high granite ridge behind you. The only way outta here is to fly, and my wagons haven't sprouted any wings."

PRAISE FOR PETER BRANDVOLD AND HIS NOVELS:

"Brandvold creates a fast-paced, action-packed novel."

—James Reasoner

"Action-packed . . . for fans of traditional Westerns."

—*Booklist*

"Recommended to anyone who loves the West as I do."

—Jack Ballas

"A writer to watch."

—Jory Sherman, author of *The Savage Curse*

"A natural born storyteller who knows the West."

—Bill Brooks, author of *Vengeance Trail*

Berkley titles by Peter Brandvold

The .45-Caliber Series
.45-CALIBER FIREBRAND
.45-CALIBER WIDOW MAKER
.45-CALIBER DEATHTRAP
.45-CALIBER MANHUNT
.45-CALIBER FURY
.45-CALIBER REVENGE

The Sheriff Ben Stillman Series
HELL ON WHEELS
ONCE LATE WITH A .38
ONCE UPON A DEAD MAN
ONCE A RENEGADE
ONCE HELL FREEZES OVER
ONCE A LAWMAN
ONCE MORE WITH A .44
ONCE A MARSHAL

The Rogue Lawman Series
BULLETS OVER BEDLAM
COLD CORPSE, HOT TRAIL
DEADLY PREY
ROGUE LAWMAN

The Bounty Hunter Lou Prophet Series
THE GRAVES AT SEVEN DEVILS
THE DEVIL'S LAIR
STARING DOWN THE DEVIL
THE DEVIL GETS HIS DUE
RIDING WITH THE DEVIL'S MISTRESS
DEALT THE DEVIL'S HAND
THE DEVIL AND LOU PROPHET

Other titles
BLOOD MOUNTAIN

.45-CALIBER FIREBRAND

PETER BRANDVOLD

BERKLEY BOOKS, NEW YORK

THE BERKLEY PUBLISHING GROUP
Published by the Penguin Group
Penguin Group (USA) Inc.
375 Hudson Street, New York, New York 10014, USA
Penguin Group (Canada), 90 Eglinton Avenue East, Suite 700, Toronto, Ontario M4P 2Y3, Canada
(a division of Pearson Penguin Canada Inc.)
Penguin Books Ltd., 80 Strand, London WC2R 0RL, England
Penguin Group Ireland, 25 St. Stephen's Green, Dublin 2, Ireland (a division of Penguin Books Ltd.)
Penguin Group (Australia), 250 Camberwell Road, Camberwell, Victoria 3124, Australia
(a division of Pearson Australia Group Pty. Ltd.)
Penguin Books India Pvt. Ltd., 11 Community Centre, Panchsheel Park, New Delhi—110 017, India
Penguin Group (NZ), 67 Apollo Drive, Rosedale, North Shore 0632, New Zealand
(a division of Pearson New Zealand Ltd.)
Penguin Books (South Africa) (Pty.) Ltd., 24 Sturdee Avenue, Rosebank, Johannesburg 2196,
South Africa

Penguin Books Ltd., Registered Offices: 80 Strand, London WC2R 0RL, England

.45-CALIBER FIREBRAND

A Berkley Book / published by arrangement with the author

PRINTING HISTORY
Berkley edition / September 2009

Cover illustration by Bruce Emmett.

ISBN: 978-0-425-23018-3

BERKLEY®
Berkley Books are published by The Berkley Publishing Group,
a division of Penguin Group (USA) Inc.,
375 Hudson Street, New York, New York 10014.
BERKLEY® is a registered trademark of Penguin Group (USA) Inc.
The "B" design is a trademark of Penguin Group (USA) Inc.

PRINTED IN THE UNITED STATES OF AMERICA

10 9 8 7 6 5 4 3 2 1

For mi amigos in the
Fort Collins Comics Collective:

Mike Baron
Scott Beiser
Kevin Caron
Jeremy de le Garza
Gabe Eltaeb
Lee Oaks
Nick Runge
Scorpio

1

CUNO MASSEY SAW the Indian a quarter second before the arrow careened toward him from a snag of brush and sun-bleached rocks. The razor-edged, strap-iron blade flashed wickedly in the high-altitude sunlight, moaning like a bobcat cub in a spring thunderstorm.

The Ute was hunkered down between two sun-blasted boulders, scowling, his face a russet, brown-eyed, war-painted oval. As he loosed the arrow, his right hand snapped back sharply from the bow. He gritted his teeth and pinched his coffee-colored eyes with fury.

The arrow traversed the thirty yards between Cuno and the Indian so quickly that Cuno had no time to do anything but wince as the feathered projectile seared a shallow trough along his left cheek before clattering and breaking against the rock scarp behind him. He'd been holding his cocked Winchester across his saddlebows. Now he raised the gun and squeezed off a shot toward the Indian.

At the same time, his skewbald paint, Renegade, startled by the clatter of the missile and the Indian's raucous yowl, skitter-stepped sideways. The sudden lurch threw Cuno's shot two feet wide of the still-howling Ute, who was thrusting a hand into the quiver down his back, reloading.

Another arrow whooshed past Cuno's ear to slice into the orange sand and gravel near the paint's right rear hoof, and a second brave loosed a savage howl behind him.

Renegade squealed and bucked. Cuno reached for the saddle horn, missed it, and holding his Winchester in his right hand, flew back over the paint's lurching hip.

He turned a somersault in midair as two more arrows whistled around him, one clipping his right calf with a searing burn. Then he was on the ground, rolling, dust from his own fall and from his horse's scissoring hooves wafting around him.

He rolled off his barking shoulder and, racking a fresh shell into the rifle's breech, swung toward the first Indian and fired three shots, shooting and levering quickly, the whip-cracks of the .44-44 echoing off the rocky scarps looming around him. Amidst the chipping rocks and powder smoke, the Indian's painted face disappeared.

Levering another round, Cuno wheeled. The Indian behind him was in midair, leaping straight down from the top of the northern scarp. He hit the ground on both moccasined feet, screeching like a demented brush wolf, then bounded toward Cuno, a stone club in one hand, his bow in the other.

Cuno aimed and fired. His slug sliced across the top of the Ute's right ear exposed by his back-buffeting, chocolate mane.

The Indian didn't blink. Raising the club, he lunged toward Cuno. The stocky blond freighter grabbed his rifle with both hands, set his feet, and smashed the Winchester's barrel against the brave's red-and-white-striped forehead with a dull smack.

The blow stopped the brave in his tracks. The ear-rattling war cry died on his lips, and he stumbled sideways, dropping his chin and dragging his toes, knees slackening.

The brave's cry was replaced by a low, eerie mewling, and the growing thunder of horse hooves. Cuno wheeled to his right. Beyond the near rocks and cedars, clay-colored dust rose in the waning afternoon sunlight. Cuno levered a fresh shell into the Winchester's breech and bounded toward the oncoming rider, leaping rocks and shrubs and wincing at the hitch in his shoulder.

He ran thirty yards and stopped.

A long-haired horseback rider in calico and deerhide appeared above the cedars and willows. The mewling rose into a deep-throated war cry as the brave, clad in a wolf-head cape, a medicine pouch dangling down his chest, aimed an old Springfield rifle straight out from his left shoulder. The brave's entire face, beneath the wolf snout atop his head, was painted the color of a Colorado sunset, the black eyes like chunks of coal beneath two bands of solid blue.

As the head of the brave's horse appeared above the brush and thickets, the rifle belched smoke and fire. The heavy slug thumped into a rock behind Cuno. The Indian's cry grew shrill and, stretching his lips back from his teeth, he reined his big Appaloosa toward Cuno, intending to run him down.

Heart thudding, feeling the throb of the pounding hooves in the ground beneath his boots, Cuno held his ground. He snapped his Winchester to his shoulder and drew a bead on the Indian's chest, just above the big stallion's bobbing, wide-eyed head and buffeting mane.

The horse was ten feet in front of Cuno when Cuno squeezed the Winchester's trigger and drilled a quarter-sized hole through the brave's breastbone. The horse screamed, drowning the Ute's grunt as he flipped straight back off the horse's rump, disappearing into the dust and cedars behind the horse's flying hooves.

At the same time, Cuno leapt off his boot heels, pivoting and diving left.

The horse's broad chest smacked his right airborne boot, twisting him slightly in the air just before he hit the ground on the same shoulder he'd landed on before, and he rolled. Looking back, he saw the stallion lunge on past him, reins trailing from the braided halter, leaping shrubs and boulders and disappearing behind a cabin-sized lump of black lava rock.

The horse's thudding hooves and angry whinnies dwindled into the distance. The dust sifted slowly.

Cuno looked in the direction the last brave had fallen. He saw only an indistinct hump in the brush, unmoving.

Cursing under his breath, he rolled onto a hip and climbed to a knee, the movement of his foot oddly restricted, though in all the excitement, he hadn't noticed it before.

A blue ash–wood arrow trailed from his right deerskin legging, the strap-iron head touched with blood. Cuno reached down, worked the arrow back out of the cuff—it had gone through two layers of deerskin—then snapped it in half and tossed it into the brush. Now he could feel the strangely chill blood dribbling down his calf, but the ache was only slightly worse than that of a deerfly bite.

Holding his right arm stiffly against his side, he heaved himself to his feet and swung the arm up beside him, balling his cheeks as the ache in his shoulder bit him.

The shoulder didn't seem broken or separated. A bad bruise. He'd live. He picked up his rifle, dusted it off, and, thumbing cartridges from his shell belt and into the Winchester's loading gate, tramped slowly back to the scene of the ambush.

He'd ridden up here, away from the freight wagons that he and his partner, Serenity Parker, were trailing up from Crow Feather to the base of the Rawhide Range, to scout the movement in the hills that old Serenity had glassed from his wagon seat. They'd spied Indian sign—unshod hoof tracks and the body of a woodcutter pinned to his wagon with arrows and a feathered war lance—along the trail from Rawlins, two days back.

The Utes weren't supposed to be making war in this neck of the woods. Why they'd been shadowing the wagons, and ambushed him up here, he had no idea. But something cold had dropped deep inside him, and he had a bad feeling the last twenty miles to the Trent ranch headquarters, at the southwestern base of the Rawhide Range, wasn't going to be half as smooth as the first hundred and fifty.

At the edge of the slight clearing in the rocks, he stopped. The Indian he'd clubbed had disappeared. He saw the two round indentations in the sand where the brave had dropped to his knees. Scuff marks and blood drops led off between two large boulders at the edge of the clearing.

Slowly, licking his chapped lips and holding the cocked Winchester straight out from his right hip, Cuno followed the trail. He pushed through the thick cedars, meandered around the buck brush and sage, raking his gaze from left to right before him.

He stopped.

Just ahead and left, the brave was down on his hands and knees, crawling feebly away, head down. Low groans rose above the rasp of the Ute's beaded moccasins carving twin lines in the sand behind him.

Cuno lowered the Winchester and looked around. Neither hearing or seeing any more attackers, he continued toward the brave. Spying Cuno's broad shadow in the sage beside him, the warrior stopped and whipped around so quickly that he lost his balance and fell backward onto his elbows.

His bony chest rising and falling sharply, he glared up at Cuno, his coffee-colored eyes blazing. Blood dribbled from the deep gash in his right temple, just below his hairline.

He was a wiry, muscular warrior, with several old knife scars in his cheeks and one just above his nose. He couldn't have been much over seventeen, but his eyes blazed and his chest heaved with a grown man's fury. Like the Sioux and the Crows, Ute boys were taught to fight with knives at a very young age, bound to their opponents with a five-foot length of rawhide clamped between their jaws.

Cuno whipped his left arm out angrily. "Why?" At Fort Dixon, where he'd been fulfilling a freighting contract since May, he'd picked up a little Ute. He translated his question, sweeping his arm out once more for emphasis.

He wasn't sure if the brave understood. The younker only flicked his eyes across Cuno's Winchester '73, a faint yearning showing there, before he snapped his head sharply right.

Cuno had heard it, too—the erratic pop of rifle fire and the unmistakable screech of attacking Indians. The young freighter's heart turned a somersault in his chest.

The wagons!

He glanced back at the brave. The kid had found the strength to drag a knife out from the sheath strapped behind his back. With a cunning light in his eyes and a dimpling hardness in his jaws, he flicked the blade straight up to his shoulder, preparing for a killing toss.

Cuno shot him twice through the chest. The kid's head slammed back as the knife clattered into the gravel beside him. Blood pumped from the twin holes in his calico- and wolf-skin-clad torso, glistening in the angling sunlight. His legs quivered and his hands clutched at the gravel.

Cuno whistled shrilly through his teeth, calling his horse, as he ran at a slant down slope toward a jumble of sandstone rocks and boulders. He bounded up the scarp on his muscular, powerful legs, ignoring the hitch in his calf.

At the top he cast his dread-filled gaze southward, and his heart leapt once more.

His three wagons—manned by Serenity Parker and two other men he'd hired in Crow Feather—were inching along the off-white trail, heading to Cuno's left. They were little larger than brown ants from this distance of a half mile, and the trail they were following was a faint line through the scrub and cedars and occasional sandstone boulders littering the broad, bowl-shaped valley.

The Indians—five dusky figures on paint horses—were galloping along the trail behind them, within fifty yards and closing. One was extending a rifle in one arm while the others raised bows, quivers jostling down their fur-clad backs.

Cuno whistled again as with shaking hands he replaced the spent cartridges in his Winchester's breech. Hooves thumped and a horse blew and he raked his eyes away from the Indians attacking his freight-heavy wagons to see Renegade bound out from behind a larger hump of gray-and-red-banded rock.

The horse's silky dun mane billowed in the wind, his reins bouncing along the ground to both sides.

"Come on, boy!"

As the horse approached the base of the scarp, Cuno clambered along the curved side, stepped off a protruding thumb, and dropped into his saddle. Sliding his Winchester into its boot jutting over the right stirrup, he leaned forward, grabbed the reins, and wheeled the horse sharply.

In a second, horse and rider were plunging down the rocky, cedar-stippled slope, angling east toward the wagons, the big horse's iron-shod hooves raising a veritable thunder, heavy dust rising behind the mount's arched tail.

At the base of the slope, Cuno slipped his Winchester from the boot, cocked it one-handed, and gritted his teeth. "Here we go!"

2

CUNO CROUCHED LOW over his saddle horn as Renegade raced through the high-desert scrub. As he topped a low rise, he saw the Indians moving in a right-to-left line before him, loosing arrows at the dust-obscured wagons while the brave with the carbine triggered sporadic rounds over his piebald's head.

A hundred yards from the trail, Cuno dropped over a low rise and checked the skewbald down, peering ahead through the rocks and shrubs for a new fix on his position.

The Indians were whooping and yelling, their horses thudding along the hard-packed trail, slower than before because of the freighters' crackling rifle fire, but still overtaking the wagons. Ahead of the galloping warriors, the Conestogas were raising a raucous clatter. Serenity and the other two drivers were shouting and triggering lead behind them, and the frightened mules were braying loudly.

Cuno reined Renegade sharply left and pressed his knees against his saddle—all the signal the well-trained skewbald paint needed to lurch forward into another ground-chewing gallop. Cuno intended to cut the Indians off from the wagons, buy some time for Serenity, Dallas Snowberger, and

Dutch Rasmussen to fort up and return fire. In their lumbering wagons, jerking along too crazily for accurate shooting, they were easy pickings.

Horse and rider dropped into a depression behind a high, shelving dike. When they came out the other side, an arrow cut the air a foot in front of Cuno's head—so close he could hear the windy buzz. Renegade whinnied.

Cuno looked in the direction from which the arrow had careened and saw one of the braves angling toward him at breakneck speed. Cuno swung his rifle at the oncoming buck and triggered an errant shot.

As he jacked another round one-handed and kept Renegade chewing up the terrain before him, angling toward the trail and the wagons, the Indian nocked another arrow. The tall, war-painted brave aimed and let go.

Cuno timed his duck just in time. The arrow cleaved the air where his head had been. Probably would have drilled him through his ear. These warriors were more accustomed to shooting from a moving mount than Cuno was.

Cuno took his reins in his teeth and raised the Winchester to his right shoulder. He planted the rifle's bobbing sights in the middle of the brave's jostling form. Their horses were on an interception course. The brave reached behind for another arrow.

Cuno fired. The brave jerked his head up as though startled. Cuno cocked and fired again.

The brave threw his arms out to his sides, tossing the arrow out in one direction, the bow out in the other as he flew back off his brown-and-white paint's lurching right hip. As the horse continued forward, Cuno saw the brave bounce off a boulder and hit the ground rolling in a broiling dust cloud.

Lowering the Winchester, Cuno hauled back sharply on his reins. Renegade whinnied again and sank back on his haunches, rear hooves skidding and kicking up dust and bits of sage and juniper. The Indian's paint raced past, a foot in front of Renegade's nose, and continued on up the slope toward the rocky northern ridge.

Cuno dropped into another depression. When he came out of it again, he glanced toward the trail. Two of the three Conestoga freighters, with Philadelphia sheeting drawn across their high-sided beds, had pulled off into the brush on the far side of the trail. Behind them, four Indians were milling, no longer closing the gap between them and the wagons but continuing to yowl and loose arrows at the already pincushioned oak sideboards.

Cuno slowed Renegade to a fast trot and glanced back along the dusty trace.

The third wagon, driven by Dutch Rasmussen, had disappeared amidst the gently rolling, boulder-pocked scrub. Gunshots rose from that direction—no doubt Rasmussen himself trying to hold off one or more of the braves who'd likely driven him off the road.

"Shit!" Cuno headed Renegade straight for the two wagons, raising his Winchester to dispatch one of the harassing braves and silently cursing his fate. He and his men had come within twenty miles of the Trent headquarters to get hornswoggled and tail-knotted by a half dozen mooncalf Ute younkers likely out on a whiskey-inspired tear.

Cuno had a thousand dollars tied up in those wagons, mules, and in the freight—a winter's worth of food and dry goods—intended for Logan Trent's Double-Horseshoe Ranch at the base of the Rawhide Range. He and Serenity had had too good a year of freight hauling for Fort Dixon and local ranches to lose it all here at the start of winter. They needed the Trent payout to get them through the snow months, without having to swamp Denver saloons, which he and Serenity had been forced to do last winter while building up a stake for wagons and freight.

Cuno triggered his Winchester over Renegade's head.

An Indian who'd just loosed an arrow at Serenity's wagon jerked and sagged sideways in his saddle. Two rifles spoke around the wagons, the twin powder puffs rising nearly simultaneously, and the brave was punched straight back off his saddle blanket to pile up in the rocks and brush, unmoving.

Two more Indians were milling in the tall shrubs thirty yards west of the Conestogas. They were still howling above the blasts of Serenity and Dallas Snowberger's rifle fire, but without their previous fervor.

Serenity was hunkered beneath the end of his Conestoga while Snowberger was shooting from amongst the jumbled black rocks on the other side of the wagons, no doubt trying to detract fire from the bellowing mules.

Cuno leapt down from Renegade's back. Racking a live round into his Winchester, he ran crouching behind a low shelf of sand, rock, and spindly cedars toward the wagons. As the dusty Philadelphia sheeting of the first wagon rose on his right, he dashed up from behind the shelf and ran toward the wagon beneath which Serenity was still triggering his Winchester.

He dove beneath the high bed in a spray of dust and gravel, pushed up on his elbows, and raised his Winchester toward one of the painted figures still jostling around behind their screen of shagbark and cedars.

Serenity whipped his wizened, gray-bearded face toward him, deep-set gray-blue eyes bright with surprise as he began whipping his rifle around. "Cuno . . . jumpin' Jehoshaphat!"

Cuno triggered a shot. His bullet clipped a rock and ricocheted into the scrub, trimming limbs.

"I seen a long blond scalp hangin' from one o' them red devil's loincloths and thought it was yours!"

"Not yet." Cuno triggered another round. He jerked his cocking lever down, and the smoking shell arced over his right shoulder. "You see what happened to Dutch?"

"Took an arrow." Lying belly flat, Serenity was sighting down the Winchester. "I seen him tumble outta the driver's box. You get a fix on how many're out here?"

Serenity fired, his rifle screeching. An enraged cry rose from behind the screening brush. "*Got* you, you son of a *bitch*!"

Snowberger's rifle roared twice from the rocks on the

other side of his wagon, and there was another groan and the thud of a brave hitting the ground.

"Dallas, hold your fire!"

Cuno scrambled out from under Serenity's wagon, leapt a rock, and holding his cocked rifle up high across his chest, bulled through the scrub cedars. On the other side, he aimed the Winchester straight out from his shoulder and looked around.

To his left, one of the braves was down on one knee behind a boulder, clutching his shoulder and groaning. Blood dribbled from a gash in his forehead. His horse was galloping off to the south, trailing its hemp reins.

Another horse trotted southeast from the wagons, the brave on its back crouched forward over the animal's neck and holding both arms across his belly.

"I hit this son of a bitch." It was Snowberger, walking up on Cuno's right and angling toward the groaning Indian whose hand kept swiping feebly at the war club thonged on his hip. His tightly wrapped and feather-trimmed braids were caked with sand-colored dust and bristling with cactus thorns.

The thirty-year-old freighter—clad in checked wool trousers and suspenders and a blue wool shirt under a shabby suit coat—aimed his Henry repeater at the Indian's forehead and gritted his teeth. "Bastard damn near took my eye out."

The brave glanced up, saw the barrel aimed at his head, and screamed. Snowberger calmly clipped the scream with a round through the brave's temple.

Cuno saw the brave slump down, quivering, in the periphery of his vision as he stole forward, swinging his rifle from right to left, looking for more warriors. Serenity came up through the cedars behind him, breathing hard and thumbing fresh shells from the bandoliers crossed on his scrawny chest clad in twenty-year-old, fringed buckskin.

"They get any of the mules?"

Serenity had a raspy voice as pinched up as his bearded

face. "One took an arrow in his rump but not deep. He'll last to the Trent headquarters . . . if *we* do."

"How 'bout yours, Dallas?"

"Nah." Snowberger tossed the Indian's tomahawk into the brush and moved up left of Cuno, ten yards away, brushing at an arrow graze under his left eye. He peered around warily from beneath the brim of his soiled, tan hat. Cuno had hired the man out of a Crow Feather saloon, when Serenity had convinced him they needed a spare driver and an extra gun in this apron land west of the Great Divide, where renegades from the mining camps were known to harass freight trains.

Snowberger had proven a capable driver and handy with a sidearm. Two days ago he'd shot a sand rattler about to strike one of the mules—a single, clean shot through the neck with a nondescript Schofield .44. Now it looked like he could hold his own with an old, beat-up Henry sixteen-shooter, as well.

They'd suspected they might attract trouble with white men. But not from the area's Indian tribes—the Utes, Crows, and Southern Utes—most of whom were said to have been peacefully minding their own business for the past year or so in the wake of Custer's demise at the Little Bighorn in Montana.

Snowberger wiped blood on his pants. "They came up on us from both sides of the trail, not long after you pulled off to scout the ridge."

"Told ya I smelled the red devils," Serenity said.

Cuno, convinced they were alone here, was lengthening his stride and lowering his rifle, heading west toward where the third wagon had disappeared.

"Poor old Dutch," Serenity said, breathing hard as he walk-jogged to keep up with Cuno, who, at five-ten and a hundred and ninety pounds, most of it hard muscle, had a good three inches and fifty pounds on the graybeard. "Got a bad feelin' about the ole boy."

Cuno glanced over his shoulder at the dark-eyed Snowberger. "Dallas, stay with the wagons. We're gonna see about Dutch."

Snowberger was a grim, silent man, but he didn't balk at taking orders from one nearly ten years his junior. He brushed at his cheek again and stopped, cradling the Henry in his arms and staring west with that dark, pensive gaze beneath ridged, black brows. He obviously didn't feel any more optimistic than Serenity about Dutch Rasmussen's fate.

Cuno and Serenity had walked fifty yards beyond Snowberger when, beginning to climb a low, rocky hogback liberally pocked with dried cow plop, both men stopped suddenly. Serenity sucked a breath through his teeth.

Black smoke ribboned up from the other side of the hogback, swirling gently. There was the spine-rippling scream of a mule and the sudden thud of horse hooves.

Cuno lurched forward, breaking into a run and leaving Serenity behind as he sprinted up over the top of the hogback and down the other side. He could see the wagon now, angled off the trail and piled up on its side in rocks and brush.

Most of the mules were down and unmoving. One wheeler and a leader thrashed in their traces, trying to stand in spite of the horribly tangled chains and leather ribbons. Behind them, flames leapt up from the wagon's rear, growing and spreading quickly, black smoke broiling.

Cuno dug his heels in. Holding the Winchester in one hand, he pumped with his free arm and his knees, chin up, teeth gritted. His hat blew off and drifted back behind him.

He had to get to the wagon, put the fire out before it consumed his entire load and the precious Conestoga itself.

Beyond the smoking, flaming wagon, a cream horse and dusky-skinned rider galloped west, away from the Conestoga—long hair bouncing down the brave's broad back.

As Cuno approached the wagon, which lay a good fifty yards south of the trail, he slowed to a stop, breath raking in and out of his tired lungs, arms dropping to his sides. Futility bit him deep. The entire top of the sheeted load was involved now, and the flames were curling up over the driver's box. The two surviving mules screamed and thrashed, both bristling with fletched, red arrows.

Cuno looked around for Dutch Rasmussen. The big Swede was nowhere in sight. Behind Cuno, boots thudded, spurs sang, and breath rasped harshly in and out of tired, old lungs.

"Shoot those mules!" Cuno yelled over his shoulder as Serenity ran up behind him, the graybeard's face creased with misery.

He could hear the old man cursing behind him as he ran around the wagon and swept the sage-and-juniper-pocked terrain with his eyes, looking for Rasmussen. Serenity had just silenced the second mule with a shot to the head when Cuno spied the freighter lying up near the trail.

A big, blond Scandinavian with a red face and bulbous nose bright from too much hooch, the old mule skinner lay on his back across a pinyon pine sapling, one tall black boot, crusted with old mule manure, propped on a mossy rock.

Two arrows protruded from Rasmussen's hard, swollen belly clad in a bright red calico shirt and a smoked elk-skin vest, another from the side of his hatless head. One, shot into his lower back, had been broken off in his tumble from the wagon. Blood pooled out from the wound to stain the wiry brown grass beneath him.

Cuno dropped to a knee beside the big man—a good freighter no less reliable for Cuno's having to drag him out of a Crow Feather brothel the morning they were to hit the trail for the Trent Double-Horseshoe.

Cuno tugged at a dry grass clump as he stared down at Rasmussen's inert face and scrubbed at his own forehead angrily with a sleeve of his fringed buckskin tunic. He looked toward the burning wagon. Serenity was moving toward him, silhouetted against the leaping flames and broiling smoke behind him.

"Is that Dutch?" Serenity called when he was within twenty yards, squinting his deep-set eyes.

Cuno stood, nodding grimly. "I'll get a shovel."

Just then there was a cannon-like roar that made the ground leap beneath Cuno's boots. He stopped dead in his tracks as the burning wagon exploded in an expanding orange ball, stabbing flames and jets of white smoke in all directions. Wood chunks and slivers from crates and barrels were tossed high, and airtight tins and burlap food bags were launched in lazy arcs high above the wreck.

Cuno stood, hang-jawed, as several of the tins and torn, burning food pouches thumped down around him, a couple of cans clanging off rocks.

At the same time, there was the ear-wrenching pop of ignited cartridge rounds. Several rounds whistled through the air around Cuno's head, more plunking up dust and grass before him, a couple sending up the angry whines of ricochets.

Cuno wheeled toward Serenity, who stood sideways, lower jaw hanging, blue eyes bright with shock. *"Cover!"*

Cuno grabbed the old man's tunic and half carried, half dragged the stove-up oldster, heavy from the brass-filled bandoliers on his chest, behind a boulder flanked with pines. They dropped to their knees and bowed their heads as the cacophony of exploding rounds crackled like Mexican fireworks on All Saints' Day.

The cannonade continued for nearly a minute, then died off gradually.

When Cuno looked up, Serenity Parker was scowling down at him from his craggy, bearded face. "Damnit, ya young firebrand—why didn't you tell me we was haulin' enough ammo to take on the whole Sioux Nation?"

Cuno's jaws were hard, his clean-shaven face red with fury, his words pinched down to a taut rasp. "Took the words right out of my mouth, you old bastard!"

3

CUNO MASSEY AND Serenity Parker—a young, muscular man and a bandy-legged oldster in ragged buckskins and a bullet-crowned sombrero—walked out from behind the boulder to mosey toward the burning Conestoga and its spilled freight. In the aftermath of the explosion, it was impossible to tell that the burning mass had even been a wagon, so little of it remained.

The smoke boiling up into the clear, western sky was rife with the acrid odor of burning mule and gunpowder.

"If you didn't know we was haulin' ammo," Serenity said, blinking owlishly as he regarded the fire, "how in the hell did it get aboard that wagon? Certain-sure old Dutch didn't put it there without tellin' us about it."

Cuno bent to snuff a patch of burning sod and a burlap scrap marked with the first three letters of COFFEE. There were a dozen other such fires but a recent October rain had dampened the ground enough to prevent a wildfire. Not far from the burlap scrap, a chunk of smooth, dark wood lay against a rock.

Cuno walked over and picked it up. It was a broken rifle

stock. The varnish glistening across the smooth, walnut wood marked it as relatively new.

Cuno showed the wood to Serenity, who tugged on his beard. "Didn't know you was haulin' rifles, neither."

Cuno tossed the stock away with a curse.

Putting out more small fires with their hats, he and Serenity continued on past the burning wagon, which had burned so suddenly and so hotly that it was burning down now for lack of fuel. They found several more bits and pieces of Winchester rifles—some swaddled in charred burlap dusted with wheat flour—and part of a leather pouch marked with the large, red numerals .44-40.

Dallas Snowberger had led the two remaining wagon teams onto leveler ground and had adjusted the harness ribbons and chains, some of which had gotten tangled in the frenzied run from the Utes. But he was standing behind and between the wagons as Cuno and Serenity marched up, his rifle resting on his shoulder, an incredulous expression on his dark-eyed features.

"We haulin' ammunition?" he asked.

"Help me get this sheet off here," Cuno ordered.

When they had the canvas free of the metal tie rings fixed to the outside of the wagon panels and had rolled it up against the back of the driver's box, Cuno lowered the end gate and leapt up into the freight box. He shifted crates and sacks around until he'd exposed one of the big Colefax & Co. ground-wheat barrels.

When he'd pried the top of the barrel up with a claw hammer, he removed his gloves and sank his hands into the brown-speckled flour. Leaning forward, he sank them wrist-deep. He felt something that wasn't flour. Wrapping his hands around the object, he pulled it up, spewing flour around the barrel.

He held up the long, burlap-wrapped object and tossed it to Serenity. He dug another one out of the barrel, tossed it to Dallas Snowberger, who'd been regarding his silent industry with grim skepticism. Cuno dug two more similar objects out of the barrel, tossed one onto the freight efficiently packed around him, and jerked the leather ties from both ends of the other one.

He pulled the flour-dusted burlap back from what he already knew would be a rifle. Specifically, it was a .44-40 Winchester Model 1878 with a smooth, varnished walnut stock and blue-steel receiver. It was so new that Cuno could smell the oil, the wood, and the freshly milled iron. Nothing fancy about the carbine. Nothing distinctive about it. It was like the ten thousand other saddle guns that Winchester had built that same year.

Except for the fact it had been loaded onto Cuno's wagon without his knowing about it. Or, he thought, loaded into flour barrels that he himself, Serenity, Snowberger, and Rasmussen had loaded into the wagons back at the trailhead in Crow Feather, off the wagons of another supply train fresh in from the railroad line at Ute.

"That skunk!" Serenity said, hefting his rifle in his hands and glaring at Cuno. "Trent didn't tell you nothin' about haulin' guns and ammo for him?"

"If you're haulin' ammo," observed Dallas Snowberger, setting his Winchester and its burlap wrapping onto the wagon's tailgate, "you sure wanna know about it. An' get paid for it."

Cuno hammered the lid back on the flour barrel. He jumped down off the Conestoga and grabbed a shovel from the supply box under the driver's seat. "I'm gonna go down and bury Dutch. Then we're gonna find out what these hidden rifles are about."

Cuno whistled for his horse and started walking back toward the burning wagon. The blaze had died down to the size of a large cookfire, the charred scrub around it still smoking. When he'd walked forty yards, Renegade came running in from the south, trailing his reins, his eyes jittery from all the shooting, the explosion, and the popping ammo.

Cuno swung up into the leather and galloped over the low hills to where a good man lay dead along the trail.

* * *

When Cuno had buried Dutch under some cedars along the northern slope, Serenity said a few words over the rock-covered grave, his sombrero in his hands. Then he and Snowberger climbed into the wagons, got their ribbons straightened out, and muscled the heavy oak handles back, releasing the wooden wheel brakes.

The mules blew and the wheelers swished their tails with anticipation. A few brayed raucously. The teams didn't like the smell of smoke and the heavy death fetor of their own.

Cuno mounted his skewbald, glancing once more at Dutch's grave humping against the slope, marked with a crude wooden cross. He lifted his gaze to the ridge beyond and then along the trail behind.

No movement out there. But that didn't mean more Utes weren't near.

Cuno gigged Renegade forward, ahead of the wagons, and Serenity and Snowberger whipped up their teams, and they started east once more, the wagons thundering along the rutted trail. The pale, two-track trace wound into the Rawhide Range hulking blue-green in the distance, more green than blue now with the sun angling down in the west.

The fir-clad slopes were mottled here and there with thick groves of aspen, their leaves a rich October gold. The lower slopes were rusty with wild mahogany, chokecherry, and rabbit brush. The air cooled gradually and acquired a cinnamon tang touched with juniper and running pine sap.

Cuno scouted the slopes on either side of the trail, ahead of and behind the rattling wagons and the chuffing, braying teams. He was glad to see mule deer and a few elk grazing the high parks between sprawling forests. That meant no Indians were skulking about, preparing another ambush. He even spotted a brown bear rambling across a slope, stopping every now and then to grab a snootful of gooseberries before continuing his lazy, uncaring stroll toward a bowl-shaped beaver meadow.

He'd spied a few cattle here and there over the last two days of travel, but as he and the wagons continued deeper into the shelving slopes and shallow valleys along the western Rawhides, small, scattered herds appeared. Cuno didn't know much about cattle, but those he saw appeared to have been bred up from longhorns. Big, rangy beasts with red-and-white coats shagging up for winter and wearing plenty of tallow.

The sun had just fallen when they dropped into a broad valley of breeze-brushed buffalo grass and sage, pooling with cool, blue shadows. A couple of riders appeared on their right—white men in cowhide vests and Ute chaps. They jogged down out of the pines of the higher slopes, six-shooters jutting from soft, worn holsters on their hips.

Cuno, riding ahead of the wagons now, as he figured they were close to the Trent headquarters, held up his hand for Serenity and Snowberger to halt their teams. He watched the armed riders come on across the valley bottom on their deep-barreled, stout-legged cow ponies.

"Freight for the Trent ranch?" one of them asked as they checked their horses down along the trail. He was a stone-faced hombre with gray eyes beneath the funneled brim of his weather-stained Stetson. A matchstick poked out from one corner of his mouth. He and the other man both carried Spencer repeaters in saddle boots.

"That's right."

"Thought there were supposed to be three wagons."

"There were . . . until about two hours ago."

The gray-eyed hombre glanced at his partner, a blue-eyed, dark-haired man with a jagged scar across his nose. "Follow us."

The riders spurred their ponies onto the trail ahead of Cuno and followed the bending trail along the valley's broad bottom, heading northeast. The caravan traveled for fifteen more minutes before the trail curved more east than north, and there, straight ahead, hunkered at the base of a hulking, gray ridge, lay a collection of log and adobe-brick dwellings, a couple of big hay barns, and several hitch-and-rail corrals amidst scattered cottonwoods and sycamores.

The Trent headquarters looked stark and insignificant at

the side of that broad valley, under that hogback mountain. The kind of man who'd carved a home for himself here—just himself, God, and the coyotes—was a man born with the bark on.

Either that or he was as crazy as a tree full of owls.

Cuno had never met Trent, only his foreman. Whoever the man was, and however tough or crazy he was, he had some questions to answer about those rifles and about the Indians Cuno should have been told about. The young freighter had been hornswoggled crossways, and Trent had cost him a good man, a wagon, and five hundred dollars worth of freight.

Followed by the rattling wagons, Renegade clomped under the Trent Double-Horseshoe portal and over split pine logs bridging a broad, stony stream curving through yellow-leafed cottonwoods and aspens. The water, sprinkled with fallen leaves and pine needles, was rolling fast out of the mountains, which were no doubt getting hammered every afternoon with chill autumn rains.

In a few weeks, the rains would become snow. Soon, this ranchstead would be socked in tight as a drum. Cuno was glad he, Serenity, and Snowberger would be heading back out to Crow Feather after a two-day layover to rest the mules. He'd already decided to spend the winter in southern New Mexico, where he'd rustle up another freighting contract in warm-weather country.

As Cuno jogged past a couple of corrals and cattle chutes, he saw a small fire in the middle of one corral, and a half dozen men gathered around a bawling calf. Fall branding, no doubt, in the wake of the autumn gather. Most of the cows would have been brought down from the summer pastures by now.

A springhouse and windmill angled past on Cuno's left, and then the two lead drovers swung right around an adobe-brick, brush-roofed toolshed and blacksmith shop, heading toward a long, low bunkhouse at the south end of the hard-packed yard.

As they did, Cuno looked up the 5 percent grade, toward

the main lodge standing a hundred yards away. Flanked with cottonwoods and ash buffering it from the steep mountain wall behind, it was a big, sprawling, two-and-a-half-story barrack with smoke churning from a large field-stone chimney. The first story was constructed of gray rock with deep-set shuttered windows. The second and third stories were all lodgepole pine, with sashed windows under the broad eaves staring grimly down on the yard. These, too, were outfitted with swung-back shutters notched with rifle slits.

A broad gallery sloped off the house's front wall. From the posts hung at least two dozen deer, elk, and moose antlers, with skulls of the same as well as bears, horses, cows, and a few other animals Cuno couldn't identify. Three shaggy, ash-colored wolf pelts hung from a rope stretched between two front gallery posts, ruffling in the crisp breeze and ever darkening as the light bled from the vast, empty sky.

Bringing his eyes back forward as he approached the bunkhouse, Cuno turned them sharply left again, to where a slender figure in a buffalo robe stood outside a horse stable. It was a girl, he realized after closer inspection, with long, silky blond hair falling from under a low-crowned sombrero.

The girl was holding a charcoal-colored kitten on her shoulder. She and the kitten were both staring warily toward Cuno and the wagons. The kitten dug its claws into the girl's shoulder, humping its back and curling its tail angrily at the rattling wagons and the clomping, blowing mules.

The girl was backing toward the house flanking her, the wind blowing her hair as she tried pulling the kitten down off her shoulder and into her arms. She stumbled slightly on a rock, and Cuno saw tan, doeskin moccasins beneath her ankle-length robe. As she wrestled the kitten into her arms, she turned her back to the yard and continued up the grade toward the house, lowering her head to the cat, her silky hair blowing out behind her in the wind.

Cuno turned to the bunkhouse, where three men in heavy coats milled, smoking coffee mugs in their hands. As the two lead drovers swung down from their saddles, one said, "Freight from Crow Feather, Boss."

One of the men leaning against the bunkhouse wall straightened slowly and moved forward, scowling up at Cuno and the wagons. He was a slightly built man with big, round blue eyes under a single, black brow and longish, dark brown hair curling over his ears. Something in his face—the perpetually belligerent eyes, the big, white front teeth and flared nostrils—reminded Cuno of a badger.

"Thought there was s'posed to be three wagons."

"There were!" Serenity and Snowberger barked at the same time, beating Cuno to the punch.

Badger looked over the wagons.

The gray-eyed gent who'd let the caravan into the yard growled, "Injuns, Quirt."

Quirt settled his malevolent gaze on Cuno, tossing his head toward a large, windowless log building mounted on six-foot stilts beyond the cookhouse, the area beneath the floor jammed tight with unsplit pine logs. A block and tackle rigged with a stout iron hook hung down over the raised loading dock. "Take it on over to the supply shed. I'll send a couple men over to help you unload. Coulda gotten here sooner. It's almost chow time."

Cuno nodded to Serenity and Snowberger, and as the men hoorahed the teams into motion once more, Cuno put his horse up to the bunkhouse's raised porch. Quirt had just tossed his coffee over the rail and had turned to enter the bunkhouse.

"I wanna talk to Trent," Cuno said, sitting straight-backed in his saddle. "He up at the main house?"

Quirt turned, a frown wrinkling his single black brow. "You don't talk to Trent. Only Kuttner talks to Trent. Kuttner's the ramrod."

Quirt thumbed his chest clad in a collarless, black-and-white calico shirt under a fringed, deerskin jacket. "I'm the *segundo*. Freighters deal with me. When I've checked off your freight, made sure everything's here we ordered and paid for—minus, of course, what you lost to the Injuns—then I send up to the house fer a check. And Kuttner brings it down."

Cuno saw no reason to waste time on this badger-faced lackey. He reined Renegade around and nudged the horse with his knees, heading toward the house.

"Hey!" Quirt cried. "Don't you understand *English*?"

Cuno kept going. A big man in soiled buckskins, a long rat-hair coat, and a wool cap had led a tall, black horse from the stable on the right.

Behind Cuno, Quirt shouted, "Hahnsbach, stop that son of a bitch!"

The big man dropped the black's reins and, as Cuno was about to round the stable's front corner, bolted out in front of Renegade and grabbed the skewbald's bridle. He wore a thick, curly brown beard and a patch over one eye.

"Where you think you're going, amigo?" he said in a faint German accent.

"Let go my horse, friend," Cuno said mildly, concentrating on not letting his right hand slide toward the grips of his ivory-gripped .45. He wanted an explanation from the head honcho, not a lead swap with the man's cow nurses.

The man held Renegade's bit firm in his big hand as Quirt came stomping across the yard toward Cuno, spurs chinging angrily, batwing chaps whipping back against his legs. "I don't like it when folks don't listen to me, see? Now, I told you, no one talks to Trent but Kuttner. If you got a burr under your tail—"

Quirt cut himself off as Cuno, unable to control his fury anymore, removed his boot from his right stirrup, set the sole of the same boot flat against Hahnsbach's chest, and kicked it forward hard. The assault took the big German by surprise, and he jerked straight backward, releasing Renegade's bridle bit and, with an indignant grunt, fell on his broad ass in the dirt.

"Goddamnit!" Quirt cried.

The badger-faced *segundo* bounded forward and grabbed

Cuno's right arm. Cuno tried to jerk himself free, but the ramrod was stronger than he looked.

Growling and mewling with exasperation, he ground his fingers into Cuno's arms as he flung his other hand toward the reins held taut in Cuno's left fist. Accidentally, Cuno gouged Renegade's ribs with his spurs, and the horse pitched suddenly, loosing a shrill whinny.

Cuno tried to grab the horn, but Quirt's own flailing hand was in the way. Before he knew it, the burly young freighter was tumbling off Renegade's side and barreling into Quirt.

Ah shit, Cuno thought. *Here we go . . .*

4

QUIRT SCREAMED WITH fury as he and Cuno piled up in the dirt together.

Through the wafting dust, Cuno saw the other two, eager-eyed waddies leaping over the bunkhouse's porch rail, while a stocky Chinaman in a long white apron and a wolf hat with earflaps came running out of the cookhouse wielding a spatula in one hand, a cast-iron skillet in the other.

"It's a fight, boys!" the Chinaman bellowed.

Cuno pushed up on his knees. Rage surged in him. As Quirt lifted his head from the dirt, Cuno rammed his right fist into the *segundo*'s broad cheek. Quirt's head snapped back, and he cursed shrilly, spittle frothing on his lips.

Cuno gained his feet and stepped back, realizing his mistake when he saw the other two drovers closing on him, grinning malevolently, crouching and balling their hands at their sides. He'd forgotten about the German until he backed into a stout, yielding object that smelled like rancid sweat and chewing tobacco.

Hahnsbach grabbed him with a savage grunt and pinned his arms behind his back.

Quirt grinned as he pushed off his knees, his longish

brown hair blowing around his head, his leather hat having piled up against the horse stables. "Hold him, Fred."

Quirt moved toward Cuno. Behind the ramrod, Serenity and Snowberger, having scrambled down from their wagons at the first sign of trouble, were jogging toward the melee in front of the stables, Serenity flanking the Chinaman, and Snowberger moving up behind the two grinning waddies from the bunkhouse porch.

Cuno tried jerking his arms free of the German's grip, but there was no doing. The big man had him firm.

Quirt strode up with a wolfish grin on his thick lips and buried his right fist in Cuno's solar plexus. Cuno's knees buckled and he went down, the German still holding his arms behind his back.

Sucking air into his lungs, he heard Serenity Parker give a shrill, Indian-like war cry, and in the upper periphery of his vision he saw the bandy-legged graybeard, minus his bandoliers now, leap onto the squat Chinaman's back and snake his mule-eared boots around the stout man's waist. The Chinaman bellowed furiously as the two went down in a limb-flinging pile, the Chinaman trying to brain the old graybeard with his spatula and Serenity howling like a trapped lobo.

At the same time, one of the other two waddies wheeled. Snowberger coldcocked him. The dark-eyed freighter was about to belt the second waddie when Cuno, his gut on fire, jerked his arms free of the German's grip.

Bounding off his knee, he delivered a whistling roundhouse to Quirt's jaw. The ramrod stumbled back, groaning and lifting a hand toward his face. Before the ramrod could touch his jaw, Cuno punched him again, knuckles out. The man's nose exploded like a ripe tomato, turning his cheeks red.

As Quirt dropped to his knees, bellowing like a poleaxed bull and clapping both hands over his nose, Cuno glanced behind him. A huge, red fist at the end of a bulging arm the size of a fencepost was blurring toward his head.

Cuno ducked. The fist and arm whistled over his head.

Hahnsbach grunted as, propelled by his own momentum, he wheeled sharply to one side. Cuno hammered his fist against the side of the man's stout head. He'd brought his fist back to deliver another enraged blow, when thunder boomed suddenly, making the ground rock and echoing off the stables like something solid before flatting off over the valley.

The report was still being swallowed up by the near mountains and the green-dark sky when Cuno saw the source of the thunder. A big man stood thirty yards up the grade toward the house, his hip cocked, boots spread. He was a hatless, bearded gent in whipcord trousers and a sheepskin vest over a black shirt with pearl buttons.

He wore two pistols in soft leather holsters high on his lean hips, and a bone-handled bowie knife jutted from a deerskin sheath crowding his left-side gun. Smoke licked from the sawed-off, double-barreled shotgun that he held straight up in his left hand. The gut shredder's brown leather lanyard hung down around his thigh.

His short, curly, pewter-colored hair lifted in the breeze around his head. His face was expressionless, his eyes shaded by his mantling brow.

"Cuno Massey?" he barked.

Serenity, Snowberger, the Chinese cook, and the two other waddies were all frozen in mid-motion.

Cuno stood, feet spread, fists balled, his chest rising and falling heavily. Before him, on one knee, Hahnsbach grunted a German epithet.

Cuno regarded the shotgun-wielding newcomer skeptically, haltingly, half expecting a pumpkin-sized mass of double-aught buck to be blasted through his belly. "Who're you?"

"I'm the one with the shotgun. Mr. Trent wants you up at the house."

Cuno unclenched his fists and looked around. Behind him, Serenity and the Chinaman lay on their sides, their fists full of the other man's shirt, grimaces frozen on their cheeks. Snowberger stood crouched, fists clenched, like a boxer. The other two waddies were on their knees, twisted around toward Cuno and the man with the shotgun.

Closer by, Quirt was down on all fours, watching the ground as blood from his nose stained it. "You son of a bitch," he grunted, keeping his head down. "Broke my fuckin' nose!"

Cuno walked around the grunting Hahnsbach and picked up his hat. Shaping its crown and setting it on his head, he looked around again until he saw Renegade standing near the stables at the south side of the yard. Several men had spilled out of the branding corral and had apparently been heading over to join the melee when the shotgun had filled them all with doubt.

One of the waddies, a young, long-faced kid in an oversized black hat, held Renegade's reins up close to the bridle and was running a soothing hand down the skewbald's stout neck.

"Stable him for me, will you?" Cuno said to the kid as he began tramping up the grade toward the man with the shotgun. "Plenty of oats after he's warmed down some, and a rubdown if you feel obliged."

The man with the shotgun nodded at the kid, then, resting the barrel of the gut shredder on his shoulder, wheeled and began making for the big house spewing smoke from its chimney at the top of the hill.

Cuno followed several paces behind and kept an eye skinned on the two bores of the gut shredder propped on the shoulder of the man he assumed was the foreman, Kuttner. He wasn't sure what kind of a bailiwick he'd ridden into here. He hoped he wouldn't have to shoot his way out, but he would if he and his men were crowded any more than they already had been.

As he approached the house behind the foreman, he saw a man standing atop the porch, puffing a brass-tipped briar pipe. He was a slender, stoop-shouldered gent in a beat-up opera hat from which a thick mop of silver hair curled.

The man had a long, heavy-boned, craggy face, a broad, pitted nose with a round red tip and a nasty-looking growth to one side of it, up near his right eye and tapering into his cheek that was the color of near-ripe chokecherries. A long, white scar doglegged down over his left jaw from just above a large, red ear.

A clawhammer coat hung off his bony shoulders, and his baggy denims were secured to his equally bony hips with braided rawhide suspenders. Beneath the coat was a soft, doeskin tunic elaborately stitched with red and blue thread. From the breast pocket, another pipe, a notebook, and a pencil stub protruded.

"Trent," Cuno said tightly, mounting the porch steps behind the man with the shotgun, his jaws hard and his cheeks hot, "I wanna know why I was haulin' rifles and ammo without bein' told. And I wanna know why I wasn't told the Utes were on the prod out here."

"Hey!" the foreman barked, wheeling around to stand on the other side of the door from his boss. "Check your tone, button. And it's *Mr.* Trent to you!"

Trent held up a placating hand. "Stand down, Henry. You gotta figure on a torn-up corral when you invite a broomtail maverick into your remuda."

"This broomtail broke Quirt's nose, Mr. Trent."

"It'll mend." The old man looked Cuno up and down while he pensively puffed his pipe. "So you're Cuno Massey. Built like a lumber dray, but I figured you'd be taller."

Cuno's tone was one of barely restrained patience. "You have the advantage here, Mr. Trent. I wouldn't know you from Adam's off-ox. How do you know me?"

"Didn't need to meet personal. I heard about your exploits with your six-gun and fists. Shit, boy, you're legend in these parts—don't you know that?"

"Let's get back to the snubbing post, Mr. Trent."

"We'll get to your business," Trent said, wrinkling his coarse silver brows and spewing pipe smoke from one corner of his mouth. He canted his head toward the door. "Inside. You look like you could use a drink . . . and adequate recompense for your troubles."

Before Cuno could reply, Trent had turned and moved through the open, split-log door, limping deep on one side. Cuno glanced at the foreman. Kuttner's face was expressionless as he stood there, holding his gut shredder on his shoulder and resting one hand on the walnut grips of the big Remington jutting from a cross-draw holster angled high on his left hip.

Cuno moved through the door and followed Trent's vague, limping figure through the smoky shadows that permeated the lodge, his boots sounding inordinately loud on the scuffed board floors. The place smelled gamey and smoky, with the tang of kerosene and candles.

As Cuno moved through a hall that seemed to split the big, silent, ship-like house in two, he glanced into several rooms furnished with heavy, wooden cabinets and ornate, brocade-upholstered chairs and leather couches. Charcoal or wood-chip braziers glowed. Game trophies loomed on the walls, and hide rugs were stretched upon the floors.

At one point, the ceiling creaked, and there was the guttural tone of an Indian speaking his mother tongue somewhere in the second story, beneath the sound of water poured from a bucket. Cuno thought he heard a softer girl's voice, too, but maybe it was just the wind, which was making the house shift and groan like a ship at anchor.

Uneasily, he followed Trent through an open door, with Henry Kuttner clomping lazily along behind him.

"Come in, young Massey," Trent said, moving around behind a heavy oak desk easily the size of a freight wagon's bed. Trent squawked down into a deep chair upholstered in mountain goat and boasting ram horns for arms.

As Trent threw open a large checkbook and reached into a pocket of his frock coat, he said, "Henry, pour Mr. Massey a drink, will you? I had that cognac shipped all the way from San Francisco nearly a year ago—six bottles. Still have two in the cellar. I'm more of a whiskey man, myself."

Cuno stood halfway between the desk and the door. He hadn't taken his hat off. "I don't drink the hard stuff."

"Oh?" Trent looked him up and down. "That strikes me as odd. Most pistoleros go in for hard hooch and easy cooch. I should know—I've met a passel."

"Look, Mr. Trent, I'm sorry if I spoil all your notions about pistoleros. I'm just a hardworking freighter who lost a good man about three hours ago—on Double-Horseshoe range, I might add—because you didn't warn me about the Ute trouble."

"Oh?" Trent had donned a pair of silver-rimmed spectacles that looked too small and delicate atop that big, red nose. "How is that my fault? I gave no assurances that your journey would be free of the usual hazards."

"Utes aren't a usual hazard. Haven't been for a couple of years. If they had been, I'd have hired extra men. And you'd have paid for 'em." Cuno moved forward and sat at the edge of the guest chair angled before the desk and rested his elbows on his knees. "Now, about the rifles and ammo I didn't know I was carryin'. That's dealin' from the bottom of the deck, Mr. Trent."

Trent set his pen down, removed his glasses, and sagged back in his chair. "That, I admit, wasn't entirely honest."

Cuno chuffed a caustic laugh. "Entirely? If my man hadn't been dead before the Indians set fire to his wagon, he sure as hell would have been afterward. Lucky there weren't more of us around that wreck when it popped, or—"

"Hold on," Trent said, holding up the hand in which he held his spectacles, beetling those shaggy silver brows. "Let me explain." He looked at Henry Kuttner standing between the door and a large, popping fireplace beneath a snarling bobcat head. "Henry, give him one of those ales from the cellar."

"I don't want an ale," Cuno said, keeping his eyes on the rancher. "I want to know about them rifles."

Trent returned his gaze to Cuno, slitting the gray,

slightly rheumy orbs once more, as though again sizing up the wolf he'd found in his office. "I don't blame you for gettin' your neck up. I'll admit, it was an underhanded thing to do. But I had good reason. A mercenary reason, but a reason nonetheless."

Trent winced as he wrestled up from his chair and, tossing his glasses on the desk, limped over to the fireplace. "A month and a half ago we had trouble out here. A couple of my men—they hadn't worked for me long and I hadn't even met them; it was Quirt that hired 'em—found a Ute girl out alone on one of my creeks."

The stove-up old rancher turned his ass to the fire and stared out the window on the far side of the room. "They raped her. Then they killed her. Said she fell and hit her head on a rock. Well, there's been hell to pay out here ever since . . ."

5

CUNO'S GUT CLENCHED at the story of the Indian girl's rape and murder. He had a feeling he knew where the story was heading from here, but he let the old rancher, warming his bony behind in front of the fire, continue.

"I gave the rapists their wages and sent them packing on the same hosses they rode in on," Logan Trent said, still staring gravely out the ever-darkening window at a large cottonwood in the backyard that was a mess of untrimmed rabbit brush, rocks, gnarled trees, and wheatgrass. "Henry and two other men found them a week later. They hadn't gotten off my range. They'd been hacked to bits no bigger than one of my hands. It was their clothes that identified them."

"Can't blame the Utes for that. Probably would have done the same myself."

"No, you can't blame them," Trent agreed. "But they should have quit there." He swung his grizzled head toward Cuno. "My range riders have been attacked on three occasions. One was killed. Two line shacks have been burned, and fifty head of my prime cattle were run off a ridge. Killed. Wolf and eagle bait."

"Have you talked to the cavalry stationed at the Rogers Outpost?"

"I sent a courier. He came back the next day tied to his saddle and decked out in a Ute war lance."

Trent walked over to a table fronting the window and poured whiskey from a plain brown bottle into a water glass. He held the glass up to the window and studied the amber liquid against the dying light. "You see, young Massey, the girl those two cork-headed lobos raped was Chief Leaping Wolf's youngest daughter. Wasn't right in the head. Often ran off from the lodge to fish or swim on her own."

"How'd you find out who she was?" Cuno asked.

"One of the chief's sons-in-law, a white man named Noah Crawford, rode in and told me. Crawford has a couple of gold diggings on my land. I get a cut if he finds anything. Anyway, Crawford said that Chief Leaping Wolf is so blistering mad that when Crawford tried to get the old man to turn his horns in, to content himself with the fact the rapists had died slow, hideous deaths, Leaping Wolf almost killed him. Had him whipped and staked outside for two nights in spite of the chief's daughter's protests."

Trent sipped the whiskey, balling his cheeks and smacking his lips, then raised the glass again to the light. He laughed but there was no humor in it, only a sad fatalism. "Crawford ain't goin' back to the chief's encampment anytime soon."

Cuno studied the man's profile. Trent's misfortune tempered his anger, but the image of Dutch Rasmussen's arrow-bristling body was still fresh in his mind and the smoke from the burned wagon still lingered in his nostrils and lungs. "Why wasn't I told about this, Mr. Trent?"

"Because I didn't think you'd come. Or might not be able to find enough men to come. It's a gut-wrenching trek through rugged country even without the Indians. You throw them in . . ."

Trent limped back over to his chair and sat down with a squawk. He favored Cuno with an admiring, coyote-like grin. "I knew you'd try to come, given the right pay, and given your reputation for taking on jobs others might shrink from. It was your father and stepmother who were murdered—correct? And you pursued their killers—the notorious Rolf Anderson and Sammy Spoon—all the way up the Bozeman Trail."

Cuno's general annoyance with the man was aggravated by his cunning, arrogant demeanor, as though he was holding a royal flush and he wanted everyone to know well in advance of his throwing down and cashing in. "Where the hell'd you hear about that?"

"Word gets around one watering hole after another. Eventually even makes its way out here." Trent took another drink, shuttered an eye, and pointed at Cuno's chest. "That ain't all I know, neither. You killed Franklin Evans—rancher up around Julesburg."

Stonily, Cuno held the man's gaze. "Trent, you look as happy as a tick on a fat dog."

"Hey!" Kuttner objected. He'd collapsed into a chair by the fire, facing his employer and Cuno.

Unfazed by the remark, Trent merely shook his head and chuckled. "Bastard ran me off my first homestead up in the Antelope Hills, about twenty miles from Evans's headquarters. That's when I headed here, to the backside of the Great Divide. Always meant to go back and beef the bastard myself, but then I started raisin' herds and kids, and the opportunity exhausted itself. Besides, I figured the old rattlesnake had done bit the wrong dog fox and got his head chewed off.

"Yessir, I heard about all that," the old rancher continued. "And then, after this powder keg with Leaping Wolf's daughter exploded, and I found myself in dire need of a supply run to get me through the winter, I heard your name mentioned by a few fellas out on the range. Said they'd seen the brawny blond firebrand who killed Franklin Evans haulin' freight for Fort Dixon."

Trent shrugged his bony shoulders. "So I fired off a telegraph to Dwight Doyle at the mercantile in Crow Feather to hire you on. And I gave him my list to fill."

"But he left out the part listing the rifles—to me, anyways."

"Ah, we're back to the rifles." Suddenly, Trent leaned forward and rammed his fist onto the desktop. His nose swelled with exasperation. "Damnit, with Leaping Wolf runnin' wild across my graze, I needed a good thirty repeaters to get me through the winter. One for every man I got, with plenty ammo for each gun. And by God, I was gonna get it any way I could.

"I knew you could get your wagons through, so I knew you were the one. No, I didn't tell you about the rifles—I didn't tell *anyone* about the rifles except for Doyle—because I didn't want it to get around that Leaping Wolf was on the prod. If that happened, I'd never get anyone to run me freight! If I didn't starve out this winter, I'd be overrun with savages, and old Leaping Wolf's squaws would be mopping out their lodges with my purty silver hair!"

Suddenly, Trent winked as he gazed across the desk at Cuno. "Except you. I knew you'd come. I knew you wouldn't be afraid. Even see it as a challenge. But most of the other freighters I've known are far too concerned about their wagons and their mules—"

"And their men . . ."

"And their *men* . . . for any derring-do!"

"Well, I've got one dead man, a burned wagon, and six dead mules, and if the rest of that ammo had caught fire, I'd be out more wagons and more mules, and I might not be sitting here squawking about it."

Trent donned his glasses, picked up a pen from a holder, and flipped the cap off an ink bottle. He looked at Cuno over his smudged spectacles. "Will a bank draft do?"

"As long as I make it back to Crow Feather to cash it."

Trent dipped the pen in the ink bottle and scribbled out the check. He set the pen aside, ripped the check out of the book, and tossed it across the desk to Cuno.

Cuno picked it up. He'd been prepared to get his tail up all over again, but the amount—two thousand dollars—more than covered the agreed-upon figure as well as an additional amount for the mules and the wagon and for the thirty rifles Cuno had been hauling in ignorance.

"I know there's no covering the cost of a dead man," Trent said, "but it's a tough country. If you look close, you'll see a grave in every wash."

"I'll tell that to Dutch's woman in Crow Feather," Cuno said. Rasmussen had lived with an old whore named Glenda when he wasn't hoorahing mules at the end of a jerkline. Cuno would give Glenda a couple hundred dollars to see her through a couple of years on her own.

Stuffing the folded check in a pocket of his buckskin tunic, Cuno rose from his chair and turned to the door.

Behind him, packing his pipe, Trent said, "I'd like to invite you and your men back to the house for dinner later. Say, around seven o'clock? Give you adequate time for a bath and a change of clothes, if you so desire."

Cuno tramped past the grimly staring Kuttner to the door. "No, thanks."

"I have a wonderful cook. A full-blooded Sioux with a club foot. Ain't much good for anything *but* cooking, and the cooking he does right well. He's preparing an elk roast with a delightful chokecherry sauce." Cuno turned from the office door as the old man sat back in his chair, casually touching a match to his pipe and puffing smoke like an old steam engine on an uphill push.

Trent said, "You and your men are welcome to bed down here in the lodge, as well. I have four empty rooms upstairs."

"We'll dine in the cook shack and throw down with your men in the bunkhouse, Mr. Trent." Cuno drew a deep, weary breath. "Thanks just the same. We'll rest the mules for a day or two, be pullin' out again by Wednesday."

Trent lowered the pipe and stared across the room at Cuno, brows beetled. "Please. It's the least I can do to compensate your men—"

Cuno tapped his breast pocket. "The check will do." He wheeled and tramped back down the dark hall toward the front door.

In the ceiling, he heard the slap-squawk of running, wet feet. The tapping continued beyond him overhead. As he approached the broad foyer of the front door, steps squeaked to his right.

He stopped and turned to see a girl standing halfway down a dark, narrow stairwell—the same long-haired blonde he'd seen in the yard with the cat.

She stood now, dripping wet and holding a buffalo robe around her slender shoulders. With her hair plastered across her head and over the robe's broad collar, she looked like a half-drowned gopher. Only her face was far from gopher-like.

It was, in a word, angelic.

"Mr. Massey?" she said softly, her chest rising and falling heavily beneath the bulky, brown robe.

The robe came down to just below her knees. One bare foot was slightly lifted on one step, while the other had come down sideways on the step below. Her wet calves were peach-pale, smooth, and perfectly sculpted.

Cuno's voice caught in his throat, and he found himself fumbling his hat from his head. "It's Cuno, Miss . . . ?"

"My bathroom is over Father's office, and I heard you talking. I wasn't meaning to eavesdrop." The girl tipped her head to one side and knotted her brows. "Won't you *please* come to supper? We seldom get company out here, and Father gets lonely. He told me all about how you hunted down the killer of your father and stepmother. He's quite the connoisseur of gunslingers, you see, and he's been waiting to meet you."

The pretty, blue-eyed waif bent her knees with beseeching and balled her cheeks, which were mottled red from her hot bath and from chagrin at her half-dressed state. "Won't you *please* join us? It would mean so much to him, and he's ordered a big, elaborate meal in your honor, Mr. Massey."

She fumbled with the robe, which she held from the inside, up close to her throat, with both hands. As she did, the two unbuttoned flaps parted slightly to reveal the deep, inside curves of her creamy breasts. They, too, appeared pink from the hot bath.

The vision bit Cuno deep, and his throat dried. In one fell swoop, his beef with the old, arrogant rancher was gone, and all that remained was this naked, wet vision of young, vibrant femininity clad in a buffalo robe before him.

"I reckon . . . if you think it's that important . . ."

"I do, indeed, Mr. Massey."

"All right, then," he stammered, his eyes roving down her delicate body once more before climbing back to those deep, soulful eyes set wide above a long, fine nose. "I'll be back."

The girl turned suddenly and began padding back up the stairs. "Thank you!"

"Hey, wait a minute."

She stopped, turned. The robe parted even farther, revealing for a split second all of one pink, bud-like nipple. She seemed totally oblivious of her beauty and sensuality, which was somehow enhanced by that bulky, moth-chewed robe.

"What's your name?"

"Oh," she said, smiling, the flush rising in her cheeks. Her eyes flashed in the last of the light emanating from the windows on either side of the lodge's front door. "I'm Michelle Trent. I live here most all the time now."

"You'll be joining us for supper?"

"Of course."

Cuno felt his lips spread with a shit-eating grin, and he was glad Serenity couldn't see him now. "All right, then."

The girl continued up the stairs. Cuno donned his hat and stumbled out the lodge's front door.

6

AS CUNO DESCENDED the grade from the big house toward the bunkhouse and stables, he saw Renegade staring at him from over the corral gate at the yard's western edge. The skewbald whinnied and twitched his ears—little more than a silhouette in the last of the twilight.

"Eat your hay," Cuno said, glancing at the pile of cured timothy mounded at the horse's feet. His mind was on the girl and the flesh peeking out from behind the bulky robe.

The men had disappeared from the branding corral, and buttery light shone in the sashed bunkhouse windows, over the broad porch equipped with a hammock and several stout log chairs as well as a sandbox spittoon. A rumble of conversation emanated from both the bunkhouse and the cook shack, which was still spewing smoke from its fieldstone chimney. The smoke was rife with the aroma of spiced beef and coffee.

The Chinese cook could be heard, berating someone for tracking manure onto his floor then ordering the man outside: "Git! Git! Git!"

A hatted silhouette carrying a plate and a steaming cup of coffee stumbled out the shack's side door, laughing, and mounted the bunkhouse porch. As the waddie pushed into the bunkhouse, Cuno moved up to his two wagons fronting the supply shed's loading dock.

One of the wagons was nearly empty, and Serenity and Dallas Snowberger were winching one of the crates up to the loading dock on the shed's raised platform—raised to keep rodents and other critters from burrowing into the place from under the floor and befouling costly supplies that weren't all that easy to acquire out here.

"You fellas about done?" Cuno said.

"Oh, look who's here!" Serenity said as he turned the winch's squeaky crank atop the loading dock. "Just in time to help us unload the last wagon."

"Quit grousin', you stove-up ole mossy horn." Cuno tapped his tunic pocket as he climbed the ramp angling off the wagon's open tailgate. "I got your money. We'll split it up when we get to Crow Feather. Enough here for a nice, long drunk and carouse in Denver on the way to New Mexico."

"Hazard pay?" asked Snowberger as he headed back to the wagon.

"I reckon."

"Ain't gonna do Dutch much good," the graybeard said as Cuno carried a crate of bagged Arbuckles down the wagon ramp.

"Were you expecting it to?" Cuno set the crate on the ground under the winch hook, wrapped the leather harness around the crate, and set the hook. As Serenity winched up the crate, Cuno looked around. "I thought Quirt was gonna send some of his rannies out to give us a hand."

"That broken nose you gave him changed his mind," Snowberger said, balancing a bag of parched corn on his shoulder. "He decided we could do the unloadin' ourselves."

"Hope there's food left," Serenity said. "The smell o' that beef's been pressin' my belly button ever tighter against my backbone."

"No beef tonight," Cuno said, grunting under the weight

of a parched corn sack that Snowberger handed over the side of the wagon. "Fellas, tonight we're headin' to a fancy sit-down meal up to the main house. Trent's special invitation."

Cuno didn't mention the daughter's fortification of the invitation, but the image of her standing on the narrow, dark stairs, sopping wet under that bulky robe with the partly open front, scampered across his mind again like a mischievous cat, flooding his loins with a young man's keen, hot desire.

"You mean we're gonna sit down to a meal with the man that hornswoggled us into carryin' rifles and ammo he didn't pay us for?"

"He paid us."

"Only after we done carried 'em," Snowberger grunted.

"And Dutch went under on account o' them savages we weren't warned about," Serenity added, angrily cranking the winch. "What'd he have to say about that?"

"Not much," Cuno snapped, annoyed at the question. "He wrote us a check."

He grabbed the last feed sack out of Snowberger's hands and tossed it down beneath the hook. "But I don't think Dutch would mind all that much if we went up to the house and sat down to a meal with the man. At least, I'm gonna go. You two can stay down here and swap big windies with Quirt's boys, if you wanna be rock-headed about it."

"Ah, hell, I'll go," Snowberger said, dropping out of the wagon's empty bed with a grunt. "Like to tell the man where he can go . . . after I've done smoked his cigars and enjoyed his food and liquor."

"Hell, I'll throw in," Serenity said, stomping bandy-legged down the loading dock's board steps. "I wanna tell ole Trent what I think of him up close enough that he can smell my rancid breath!"

"Yeah, well, you're gonna have a bath first," Cuno grouched as he started removing the sheeting from the second wagon. "So you best spend the next hour or so, while we bed the mules down, getting used to the idea."

On the other side of the wagon, Serenity dropped his jaw and widened his eyes, flabbergasted. "A *bath*?"

"You heard me."

"Jesus Christ! Who else the old fucker got dinin' up there—*U. S. Grant*?"

The tips of Cuno's ears warmed, but he kept his mouth shut.

In spite of the dustup earlier in the yard, the Chinaman seemed pleased to oblige Cuno and his men with hot-water baths in the open lean-to shed off the rear of the cook shack.

The stocky son of Han seemed downright eager to do it, in fact, in spite of the twenty men he'd just fed and all the cleanup he had yet to do in the kitchen. The man enjoyed a good row now and then, Cuno figured, as he ran a bar of lye soap across his work-sculpted pecs, and the Chinaman dumped another bucketful of steaming water between his legs. The steam billowed in the cold night air.

The Chinese cook didn't seem to take umbrage with the nick Serenity had given him across his fleshy right cheek, for, as the Chinaman filled the tubs and rummaged for towels, the two got on like old army pals, bantering and joking and wheezing deep laughs, though the Chinaman appeared to understand only about half of all Serenity's raspy, half-shouted words.

As Cuno scrubbed at the grime and mule stench engrained in his brawny hide, Serenity sang as he lathered his bony chest, looking like some scrawny, plucked, bearded chicken in his own corrugated tin tub nearby. Dallas Snowberger, contented to merely soak and let the suds do all the work, hunkered low in his own tub and puffed a long, black cigar from the Chinaman's own personal stash.

Cuno lifted a leg to scrub a foot, unable to extinguish the hauntingly celestial face of Logan Trent's daughter from his mind. A girl like that—all sensuous innocence with a well-filled corset, to boot—could tie a man's loins in knots.

Cuno found himself not as eager as he had been to hightail it back to Crow Feather.

"Come on, fellas," he ordered, rising from the tub, the suds sliding on down his chest and thighs. "Time to haul ass up to the lodge."

Serenity squawked a mocking laugh. "Wouldn't wanna keep ole Trent waitin', now would we?"

"Trent sure got stuck in his craw," Snowberger mused aloud as he slitted an eye at Cuno and continued puffing his cigar.

"Somethin' up there did, anyways," Serenity said, clamping an arthritic hand on each side of his tub and hoisting his bony, pale body up out of the water. "Sorta looks like he seen a ghost, don't he?"

"Or a witch. Maybe one o' them warlocks the Injuns believe in."

"I'm hungry," Cuno growled. "Christ, I haven't eaten since noon, and then it was only a handful of Serenity's overboiled beans."

They dried, then dressed in the only other set of clothes they'd brought along, shivering in the chill night air behind the cook shack, the water still steaming from the tubs, a big moon rising over the high, bulky eastern ridge.

Cuno pulled on a pair of faded denims—old but clean—and a thin doeskin tunic bleached bone-white by countless washings. He knotted a red neckerchief with white polka dots around his neck, stuffed the tails into the tunic, stomped into his boots, strapped on his gun belt, and donned his hat, taking an extra moment to adjust the angle.

He strode back through the cook shack, where the cook was washing dishes on one of the ranges in the back shadows, and singing in his eerie tonal tongue, a cigarette dangling from between his mustached lips. Cuno tossed the man a silver dollar, thanked him for his generous services, and continued on out to the porch.

Impatiently, he waited for his less-eager comrades.

When they both arrived—Serenity wearing buckskins that looked no fresher than the ones he'd worn on the trip and Snowberger in denims, brown shirt, and simple black vest—they began tramping across the dark yard and up the slow grade toward the well-lit house hulking atop the hill.

Near one of the several corrals on the south side of the yard, fronting the creek, three horseback riders sat talking to a man standing before them. Cuno couldn't hear what they were saying, but their tones were grave. It took him a few seconds to realize the man on the ground, clad in a black frock coat, wavy pewter hair glistening with oil and smoking a stout cigar, was the foreman, Henry Kuttner.

The aroma of the man's cigar as well as his musky cologne wafted on the chill, fall breeze.

Beyond the men, on the far side of the creek, running hoof thuds rose. Cuno, Serenity, and Snowberger stopped and turned toward the creek, as did the mounted men and Kuttner.

"Jesus Christ!" one of the waddies said, hipped around in his saddle. "Sounds like those boys got the devil's hounds on their tails!"

"What now?" Kuttner said, removing his cigar from his teeth and squaring his shoulders at the ranch's front portal into which a couple of old bison skulls had been nailed. The portal and the bleached skulls were silhouetted against the starry, moonlit sky.

The jostling shadows of the four riders came on across the sage-tufted flat, galloping hard. They thundered across the bridge and pushed on under the portal, and in seconds they were rounding the far corrals and checking their mounts down as they approached Kuttner and the other mounted waddies.

"Trouble, Boss!" one of the newcomers exclaimed, sliding out of his saddle while his horse skidded to a dust-lifting halt and one of the other horses whinnied angrily behind him. The man scrambled around to one of the other men, who crouched low in his saddle, one hand clamped around the arrow protruding from the side of his neck, just behind his ear. "Blackie took an arrow around Wolf Head Canyon!"

Kuttner stood statue-still, fists on his hips, feet spread. His cigar glowed in his right hand.

"He said there was five of 'em, Boss," one of the other newcomers said, holding the reins of his jittery mount up close to his chest. "Ambushed him at the very bottom of the canyon. Lucky he was on old Tom, or he never woulda made it outta there with his hair!"

"Get him into the bunkhouse," Kuttner said, jerking his head toward the lighted windows behind him. "Have Riker tend him. Any of you other boys see anything?"

"Just sign," said a bulky man in a blanket coat, his collar drawn up to his ears. "And what the magpies left of three more dead cows. But I don't like it, Mr. Kuttner." The man cursed his leaping horse, and when the horse settled some, the man returned his bright-eyed gaze to Kuttner once more. "I got a bad sense o' things. Lots of tracks criss-crossin' the range, every which way. Movin' in closer to the headquarters. You know that big cottonwood tree on that saddleback butte by the Three-Fork range? There was a Ute arrow stickin' out of it. Just the arrow. Nothin' else. They're gettin' set for something—I'll guaran-damn-tee you that!"

"You don't know that, Bill," Kuttner said calmly, just loudly enough for Cuno to hear on the other side of the yard. "Might be they're just tryin' to make us jumpy."

"They done it," Bill said. "Yessir, Mr. Kuttner, I don't mind tellin' you—I'm *damn* jumpy!"

The first rider had eased the wounded man out of his saddle, and as they moved off toward the bunkhouse together, Kuttner tapped ashes from his stogie. "Put your horses up and get some grub, Bill. You, too, Reno. I'll be up at the house. Send someone to fill me in on Blackie's condition after Riker has checked him out."

When Bill and Reno had led their own and the other two

horses off to the stables, Kuttner talked to the four fresh riders for another half minute, then sent them galloping out of the ranch yard. Cuno glanced at Serenity and Snowberger standing beside him. Serenity cocked a brow. Snowberger just looked dark.

Kuttner strode up to them puffing his stogie. He, too, looked dark as he regarded the ground as though he'd dropped a quarter.

"Looks like you got your hands full out here, Kuttner." Cuno jerked his head toward the men just now thundering across the wooden bridge and heading off into the moonlit flats beyond. "Scout riders?"

Kuttner nodded. "Try to keep four out at all times after sunset."

Cuno introduced Serenity and Snowberger to Kuttner, and after a stiff shaking of hands, the four headed up toward the house.

"How many men do you have on the place, Kuttner?" the graybeard asked.

"Nearly twenty. Enough to hold off Leaping Wolf's band. He don't have no more than fifteen or twenty himself, and, from what my scouts tell me, only a handful of rifles."

"Well, you got about twenty brand-new Winchesters, now, don't you, Kuttner?" Snowberger growled as they headed up the house's broad porch steps.

"That we do," the foreman said, opening the front door and waving the others in ahead of him. A frosty smile shone in his eyes. He had a voice like sandpaper raked across a steel file. "All the way back and left, gentlemen. First, don't be offended if I ask you to hang your hats and guns on the pegs just inside the door, and to scrape your boots on the mat."

Serenity snorted. "You wanna check our teeth and peek under our fingernails, too?"

Cuno elbowed the oldster in the ribs.

When they'd hung up their guns and hats, and scraped the dust and dung from their boots, Cuno led the way down the hallway lit by only a couple of guttering candles in wall sconces. He followed the left fork into a broad, arched doorway that let into a dining room in which a large, timbered table stretched and a vast fieldstone hearth popped and sputtered, pushing heat out around it.

Logan Trent himself sat at the table's far end, dressed as before but without his hat and with his thick, silver, curly hair neatly combed back behind his big, red ears. He was slouched in his chair, staring over the top of an old, yellowed newspaper toward the door, his silver spectacles perched low on his big nose.

"Mr. Massey, gentlemen, come in," he said, folding the newspaper, removing the glasses, and rising from his chair. "I just talked to Run, and he said all was ready. He's pulling the elk out of the oven even as we speak. When he's carved it, he'll wheel it in."

Trent tossed his newspaper down on the simple, elegantly appointed table—bone china plates, cups, crystal goblets, and two demijohns of wine but no tablecloth—and limped toward Cuno and the others. After a brief introduction to Serenity and Snowberger, which was as stiff and awkward as the one that had preceded it outside, Trent turned to a stout oak door.

"Run, go ahead and carve the roast! Michelle's not here yet," he added, lifting his chin toward the ceiling and speaking even more loudly, "but if we waited for her, that elk would end up cold as an old maid's heart by the time we served it!"

He wheeled and threw a hand out at the table. "Gentlemen, forgive my manners, but I don't get much company, and my wife's been dead for seventeen years. I'm out of the habit of entertaining."

"I'm out of the habit of bein' entertained," Serenity chuckled, tugging on his damp beard and regarding the table as though it were a coiled rattler he'd just found in his bunk.

"Choose a chair and take a load off, Mr. Parker," Trent said. "Wine's on the table. Pour yourself a glass and throw down a drink. The grub'll be on the table in six jerks of a hangman's noose."

After several years of man hunting as well as of being hunted by other men, Cuno preferred his back to a wall, so he tramped around behind the heavy, varnished pine table and sat down at the far end, to the left of Logan Trent. The gimpy rancher stood, awkwardly formal, behind his own chair, eyes flicking around in their sockets anxiously, as though wondering if he hadn't forgotten something important.

"Mr. Trent," Kuttner said, as he pulled out the chair across from Cuno, "today's four scouts rode in before I sent the others out. Blackie took an arrow in the neck."

The growth along Trent's nose darkened slightly. "Bad?"

Kuttner hiked a shoulder as he shrugged down in his chair. "If they don't have to amputate, I reckon he'll be all right."

"Damn," Trent said, twitching an eye at the table. "Don't wanna lose Blackie. He's the best rifleman we have."

"Well, if he makes it, he's got plenty of rifles to shoot with," Serenity dryly quipped as he dropped into the chair beside Cuno. "Yessir, fourteen purty Winchester repeaters made it through that war dance goin' on out yonder."

"Mr. Parker," Trent said, leaning over his chair back to hammer the graybeard with a hard stare. "Your grievances have adequately been filed by Mr. Massey, to whom I apologized and awarded a sizable check. I know that doesn't bring back your dead driver, but it should give you a new wagon, six new mules, and more whores than you, sir, can possibly fuck over an entire Denver city winter!"

Serenity slammed his fist on the table and started to rise, bellowing, "Well, you, sir, got no idea just how many—"

"Father?" It was a girl's voice—soft, high-pitched, and slightly raspy.

It cut Serenity off like a pistol shot.

Cuno turned his gaze from Serenity to the room's arched

doorway. Michelle stood there, a blond vision in a simple, green velvet dress cut low enough to show off her long, creamy neck and chest and just enough cleavage to start a young mule skinner's heart to turning somersaults in his rib cage.

Her long, honey-colored hair was brushed straight down across her shoulders, the ends curled like a licking tongue. It fairly glowed in the umber light from the popping fire. A pearl necklace lent the girl—seventeen or eighteen at the oldest—an elegant, old-fashioned charm that accentuated her girlish, wholesome allure.

She favored her father with a demure smile as, entwining her hands at her waist, she said, "You know I don't approve of such barn talk, Father." She cast her sparkling glance at the table. "I apologize for my tardiness, gentlemen. I'm Michelle Trent."

Cuno and the other men in the room slid their chairs back and climbed to their feet.

As Logan Trent grumbled and chuffed behind his own chair, Serenity cleared his throat meaningfully and rammed an elbow into Cuno's ribs. He looked up at the brawny young freighter knowingly and winked.

"Forgive me, my dear," Trent growled. "Got my blood up there for a minute. Friendly disagreement, I assure you. Come in and have a seat. Yes, gentlemen, this is my lovely, devoted daughter, Michelle . . ."

Trent let his voice trail off as more footsteps sounded down the hall behind Michelle. They were the tap of light leather shoes set down in a brisk, forthright step. And then, the owner of that step—a tall, ivory-pale lad with a cap of coal-black hair and matching mustache and goatee, and dressed to the nines in a black suit, glowing white shirt, and fawn vest trimmed with a gold watch chain—marched up beside Michelle and placed an arm around her shoulders. He lifted his dimpled chin to the room as though posing for a photograph.

Michelle smiled proudly and reached across her matronly bosom to squeeze the young man's hand.

7

JEDEDIAH H. GALLANTLY marched up to the table in soldierly fashion, still jutting that dimpled jaw, and shook everyone's hand. His hand, Cuno noticed, was as smooth as a baby's rump. It was as pale and waxy as fresh paraffin. The man wore a slim silver ring on his pinky and a giant onyx set in gold on his forefinger.

"Pleased to meet you, gentlemen," the young man said, stepping back to pull a chair out from beside Kuttner for Michelle. "You're the, uh . . . the freighters, isn't that right?"

"That's right," Cuno said, feeling as though he were wearing the tip of a Ute war lance in his belly.

Michelle folded gracefully into her chair, smiling demurely, celestially, her eyes bright but owning a vaguely distracted, bored cast, as well.

Young Gallantly slid her forward, then moved to the chair to her right. "Did the trip go well? No trouble with the Indians?"

"Oh, we had trouble with the Injuns, all right," Snowberger growled, retaking his seat to the right of Serenity Parker.

"Lost a man," Serenity said. "A good one . . ."

"Oh," Gallantly said, frowning, "I'm sorry to hear that." He slid his gaze between the freighters and Trent, as though the freighters' word alone could not be trusted. "Did the rifles make it?"

Trent sagged into his own chair, shaking his head with annoyance. "We've already had this conversation, Jedediah. I'll fill you in later." Glancing at his guests, he said, "Gentlemen, my future son-in-law is of the Gallantly family of St. Louis, Missouri. Bricks is their trade, but young Jedediah's father, Mortimer, has a sizable ranch in Wyoming, as well. Not far from Ute. Jed grew up in St. Louis, but he learned the ranching trade after getting a degree in land and cattle finance back East somewhere . . ."

"Maryland!" Gallantly threw in with a proud grin, filling Michelle's wineglass from a demijohn.

"And he and Michelle are set to take over the place after they're hitched and"—Trent chuckled raspily and threw back a long swallow of his own wine—"after I'm planted in my favorite gooseberry thicket at the foot of Old Stone Face."

"Oh, Father!" Michelle admonished, pooching out her bee-stung lips. "Such talk." She brushed her glance across Cuno, Serenity, and Snowberger. "In truth, gentlemen, Jedediah and I are simply moving onto the ranch to *assist* Father in his later years. Mr. Logan D. Trent, I suspect, will be bouncing around giving the orders until well after all his grandchildren are out riding the range on their own cow ponies!"

Cuno swallowed down the dry knot in his throat and leaned forward, entwining his hands on the table and making an effort to keep his eyes off the girl's pale, swollen bosom enhanced by the pearls. "When will you and Mr. Gallantly be married, Miss Trent?"

"June first," Gallantly answered for his promised bride, locking a faintly challenging gaze with Cuno.

"Ah, a June wedding," Cuno said, spreading a smile that he thought would crack his cheeks and break his molars.

Just then, to Cuno's relief, the stout oak door opened and a big man with long black hair and flat, broad Indian features rolled a cart into the room from the kitchen. He moved with a limp even more severe than Trent's.

"Ah, Run!" the rancher exclaimed, clapping his big hands together. "Not a moment too soon. Michelle was about to lay into us with her wedding plans, and it's far too early in the evening to start yawning!"

Trent's laughter boomed around the room.

"Oh, Father!"

The big Indian in a calico shirt, duck trousers, suspenders, and a brown leather vest wheeled the cart up to the table, between Trent and Kuttner.

Trent said, "Gentlemen, allow me to introduce my cook, Runs-with-the-Ponies. Run has been with me since I first came here—just me, two horses, and a half dozen longhorns, two Durham studs, and a Springfield rifle. Met in the army, we did. Run once cooked for General Sherman. Best damn grub slinger in the West, to my mind. And after you've enjoyed a few bites of this delectable elk, I'm sure you'll agree!"

Somehow, in spite of feeling sick to his stomach, Cuno was hungry. His belly grumbled and his mouth watered as the big Indian produced the platter containing the huge, smoking roast covered with dark red chokecherry sauce and surrounded with steaming potatoes, carrots, and turnips. The Indian never said a word as he dutifully carved up the roast, filled everyone's plate in turn, then shuffled around on his moccasined feet—one of which seemed to be clubbed—and nudged his squeaking cart back into the kitchen, the oak door flapping on its springs behind him.

"Now, he'll get into the chokecherry wine, and we won't see him for the rest of the evening," Trent whispered, holding a hand to his mouth. The old rancher shook his head as he cut into a half-inch-thick wedge of elk, bloodred in the middle, charred around the edges, and sopping with the heavy sauce seasoned with garlic, onions, and several herbs including mint. "I don't begrudge him. His only home is here. We, his only family."

Trent suddenly set down his fork and lifted his wineglass in salute. "Gentlemen, milady," he said with a courtly nod at his daughter, "to warm fires, hot meals, and fascinating company."

After the toast, and favoring Cuno with a soft, blue-eyed glance, Michelle Trent said, "Speaking of fascinating company, Father informs us you've cut quite a path for yourself, Mr. Massey."

Cuno's ears warmed slightly as he impaled a carrot chunk with his fork. "Not sure what you mean, Miss Trent. I've made my way as best I could, I reckon."

"Oh, come now, Cuno," Trent said with a mouthful. "You don't mind if I use your first name, do you? It's such a rare one, indeed!"

"Been called a lot of things, Mr. Trent."

Trent, well into the wine and enjoying himself, laughed overloud. "Come now, Cuno, you mustn't be shy. I've told my daughter, Jedediah, and Mr. Kuttner about your exploits—those I've learned about via the moccasin telegraph, that is, or read about in the papers. They were quite impressed, as was I—a man so young, barely a teenager, taking to the blood trail to avenge his family."

"Blood trail, indeed, Father!" admonished Michelle. "You've read too many dime novels."

Serenity chuckled as he shoveled the delectable food into his mouth.

"I have to agree with your daughter, Mr. Trent. That's gilding the lily just a tad."

"Maybe just a tad."

Trent grunted as he dropped an arm to reach beneath his chair, his broad, bearded face reddening with exertion. When he raised his arm again, he was holding the yellowed newspaper he'd been reading when Cuno and the other men had first entered the room. He tossed it onto the table in front of Cuno.

"But only just a tad," Trent added, "and no more than

Mr. Hiram A. Crutchfield did in his article there in the *Ute Tribune*."

Cuno brushed at his mouth with his cloth napkin and picked up the folded paper open to page five, at the top of which large black letters boldly announced, "Man-Hunting Sprout from Nebraska Powders the Vengeance Trail!" Slightly smaller type continued: "Blood-Hungry Young Mule Skinner Straps on Six-Guns to Hunt the Killers of His Beloved Family." And below that, in type like cursive handwriting and abutted by the sketched likenesses of two crossed Colt pistols: "Notorious Thieves and Killers Rolf Anderson and Sammy Spoon Would Rue the Day They Ruffled the Feathers of Cuno Massey!"

There were sketches of Anderson and Spoon—mouths drawn wide in whooping, kill-crazy laughter—as well as one of Cuno himself, looking grim under his flat-brimmed plainsman hat, his young, grave features framed by his long blond hair. The sketch favored him well enough, though he'd never known himself to narrow his eyes like that, as though he were perpetually staring into the blinding sun. In both of his raised fists, a six-gun blazed.

At the very bottom of the page, beneath four columns of dense text, there was one more sketch—of Cuno standing with his feet spread wide, crouching, his long hair blowing back behind him as he shot down Anderson and Spoon with a smoking pistol in each hand. Both outlaws looked utterly horrified and flabbergasted as Cuno's bullets lifted them off their feet and threw them straight back toward the paper's left fold.

Both men had only begun to raise their own revolvers before the young firebrand, twice as fast as his foes, had triggered lead through their hearts.

"Well, look there," Serenity said, leaning over to peruse the paper in Cuno's hand. "You're fy-muss!"

"Where'd this come from?" Cuno muttered, frowning down at the yellowed paper.

He'd never heard of the writer, Hiram A. Crutchfield. Whoever the scribbler was, he hadn't been with Cuno in that remote range along the Bozeman Trail when Cuno had turned Anderson and Spoon toe down before they could sell rifles to the rampaging plains tribes. The only other person there at the time was the half-breed girl Cuno would later marry, July Summer.

Crutchfield was probably just a Ute newshound who'd heard a few rumors from folks who'd been part of the same wagon train as Cuno that summer, and he'd scribbled out a lascivious tale full of gun smoke and blood, to raise his circulation.

Cuno tossed the paper down with a caustic chuff, took up his knife, and cut into his slab of elk meat. "A Dead-Eye Dick faker," he said. "Nothin' against Mr. Dick. Used to read his books myself . . . back before I found out what life behind the gun was really like. I'd pay no attention, Mr. Trent. There's no way the man could have got it right."

"Do tell, Cuno," Trent urged, chewing a mouthful of meat and potatoes. "I admire nothing more than a young man standing up for himself and his murdered family! For taking his own fledgling gun against those of seasoned killers, and the devil take the hindmost!"

"No," Cuno said, feeling uncomfortable. He hadn't set his hat to become a gunslick—he'd been forced into it by the killings of his father and stepmother—and he wanted nothing more than to put that bloody past behind him. "Not the time or the place, Mr. Trent."

"Tell me, Master Cuno," said Jedediah Gallantly, swabbing up chokecherry sauce with a chunk of elk meat, "how many notches do you have on your gun . . . if you don't mind the question?"

"Jedediah, please," said his betrothed. "You're sounding like Father."

"No, I'd like to know." Gallantly smiled mockingly at Cuno across the table, his pasty cheeks glistening waxlike in the candle- and firelight. "Call it a prurient interest."

"I value my forty-five too highly to carve notches in the handle, Mr. Gallantly."

"Cuno Massey here killed Franklin Evans," Trent said to

Kuttner. "And the notorious bounty hunter Ruben Pacheca at the same time!"

The foreman nodded gravely and raised his eyes from his plate, which he'd already nearly cleaned. "Much obliged, son." His eyes slitted with a devilish grin. "I've got a few enemies need killin', too, if you're interested. Can only pay in hardtack and jerky, of course, but . . ."

"Obliged, Mr. Kuttner. I'll stick with mule skinnin' for now."

"How boring!" said Logan Trent.

"Depends on who you're workin' for," quipped Serenity.

Dallas Snowberger, who'd been eating in customary silence, laughed.

"Do tell me, Mr. Massey." Michelle cleared her throat and frowned down at her still-full plate, as though the words were coming hard for her. "How many men *have* you killed?" She looked up then suddenly, staring at Cuno as though he were a riddle she was having trouble unraveling. "How many lives have you taken?"

Logan Trent chuckled. Jedediah Gallantly looked down at his lovely wife-to-be in bemused surprise.

Her fair cheeks flushing slightly, she hiked a shoulder and rolled a potato around on her plate with a fork.

Cuno felt like a freak at a carnival sideshow. It was his own damn fault, allowing himself to be lured up here by his lust for a wet blonde in a buffalo robe.

Now he wished he were back in his wagon, huddled in his blankets beneath the stars. Or, better yet, on the trail back to Crow Feather. Anywhere but here, where Trent seemed to hold him up as some kind of primitive wild man while his daughter saw him as the essence of pure evil and Jedediah Gallantly passed him off as merely freakish and amusing, when all he'd done was play the cards he'd been dealt the best way he knew how.

He forked food into his mouth as the burn of anger rose up from the base of his spine. He heard himself reply to the girl's question in a flip, mocking tone. "Oh, 'bout fifty.

Maybe sixty. I lost count sometime last summer, after I drilled ole Karl Oldenberg. Blew his lower jaw off, if I remember correct, on the main street of a little Wyoming town called Alfred. Or, was that Colorado Bob?" Cuno laughed. "There's been so many, I forget . . ."

"Good grief!" exclaimed Gallantly. "You blew a man's jaw off?"

"Blew an ear off a half-breed child rapist named Fuego. *Pop!* The man's ear was gone, silver hoop ring and all!"

"Oh!" Michelle put a hand to her mouth and turned her head to one side, as though about to evacuate her delicate little belly.

8

WHEN MICHELLE HAD recovered from nearly regurgitating what little of her meal she'd eaten so far, she turned her now-frosty, incredulous gaze back to Cuno. "You *didn't*? A man's *ear*? *Why*?"

"Michelle, you don't want to know," advised Jedediah Gallantly, wrapping a protective arm around her shoulders.

"'Cause he'd just strangled a deputy United States marshal through the bars of his jail wagon," Cuno said, his calm, offhand manner belying how much he was enjoying himself. "I knew, then, I'd have to pull the jail wagon through the mountains myself, when I had better things to do. Galled me so bad, I wanted to kill ole Fuego, sure enough."

Cuno shoved a forkful of food, which he was now thoroughly enjoying, into his mouth. "Settled for shootin' an ear off."

Beside him, Serenity was jerking with laughter while hiding his face behind his wineglass. Beside Serenity, Snowberger was shoveling food into his mouth as though afraid he'd soon be cut off and shaking his head darkly.

From across the table, Henry Kuttner regarded Cuno as

though he were a problematic steer caught in a bog. The pewter-haired and mustachioed foreman had both his elbows on the table, and his empty fork was sagging in his right hand. His eyes were like dark green marbles set under ridged salt-and-pepper brows.

The rancher, Logan Trent, was chewing slowly while smiling patiently at his daughter and future son-in-law. He appeared a man who'd brought a bear onto the premises to give his loved ones a taste of the wild, to toughen them up a little, and the bear had performed even better than Trent had predicted.

He said nothing.

Michelle stared disgustedly at Cuno, both her delicate, white hands resting on her plate.

"Really, Mr. Massey," objected Jedediah Gallantly. "You do realize there's very little place for that kind of behavior anymore, don't you? The West is filling up with people. The railroad has come through, and spur lines are being laid all over. The law is here and, thus, civilization!"

Chewing slowly, Cuno extended a fork toward the roast sitting on its platter in the middle of the table and glanced at Trent. "Do you mind . . . ?"

"Help yourself!" Trent encouraged, waving a hand at the elk. "Please feel free. Your men, as well!"

"What I'm saying, Mr. Massey," Gallantly continued, as Cuno loaded up the plates of Serenity and Snowberger, "is that there is no longer any place for men who insist on taking the law into their own hands and living by the gun, so to speak! That breed is dying out, and you must conform to the laws of civilized society or end up . . . end up . . . in *jail*! Or be *hanged*!"

Cuno dropped a thick wedge of elk onto his plate, then poked his fork at Trent, then at Michelle. "What if someone came in here one night and killed your father-in-law and raped your wife and then killed her, too? What would you do about it?"

"Why, I'd send the law after them!"

"Out here?"

"I'd ride to the army outpost and notify the authorities. I'd send soldiers after the killers. They'd be run down, given a proper trial, and hanged!"

"By the time you got to the fort, those men would be halfway to Mexico. Your wife and father-in-law would die unavenged. And those savages would be free to wreak the same havoc on others."

"All right, that's enough!" ordered Michelle Trent, putting some hard steel into her voice, her face flushed with anger. "We get your point, Mr. Massey. We're deeply sorry for what happened to your family, but you must know that civilized men do not live for revenge. Only barbarians live for revenge."

"But men—and women—are basically barbarians," Cuno said. "From what I've seen and experienced, I firmly believe we're all savages. Some more than others. And you're right—the West *is* filling up . . . with savages. They outnumber the lawmen and the folks trying to keep a leash on their own inner savage about a hundred to one. And the only way to fight savages who've turned their horns on you or your family is to become one yourself."

Trent cocked an eyebrow, fascinated. "To let yourself become who you—or *we*—really are. To let your true nature take over . . ."

"That's how I see it," Cuno said, slicing his second helping of elk.

"I guess we'll just have to agree to disagree, Mr. Massey," Gallantly said tonelessly.

Trent suddenly pounded his fist on the table and leaned forward, pinning his future son-in-law to his chair with a vicious stare. "He's right, don't you see, Jedediah? You and Michelle were both educated back East. Yes, there's law in the East. Plenty of savages there, too, but there's some semblance of law and order." He shook his head slowly, darkly. "But not out here. If you two are gonna live here at the base of Old Stone Face and raise your family amongst the savages—and I want that very much; my daughter is all the family I have left—you've got to be ready to defend what's yours!"

"If you think I'm going to lynch squatters and rustlers, Mr. Trent . . ."

Cuno said, "Squatters and rustlers are the least of your worries at the moment, Gallantly."

Silence fell like a burial shroud. Both Michelle and her betrothed shuttled questioning frowns between Cuno and Trent, who colored slightly and tried to cover it with his wineglass.

"Father said the Indians have become a nuisance, yes, but they're not posing any *real* danger."

Serenity snorted. "Tell that to Dutch Rasmussen!"

"Who's Dutch Ras—" Michelle's frown cut deep lines into her forehead as both she and Gallantly looked at Trent. "Father, what's going on?"

Trent didn't meet his daughter's gaze as he forked a small chunk of gravy-drenched potato into his mouth and growled sheepishly, "The freighters were attacked by a small party of bronco Utes. One took an arrow."

"They turned him into a human pincushion, Mr. Trent," Serenity said, slamming his own bony fist on the table. "Make no mistake!"

Michelle jerked back in her chair, dropping her fork with a loud clang and slapping her hand to her heaving bosom. "What's made them so angry, Father?"

Trent looked for a moment like he had a chunk of meat caught in his windpipe. His furtive gaze flickered toward Cuno, and then he busied himself with brushing his napkin across his beard, loudly clearing his throat, and sliding his chair back from the table. "Like I told you, Daughter, they've been aroused by the army somehow."

The old rancher gained his feet and raised his voice, changing the subject abruptly. "Since Run has no doubt retired for the evening, Michelle and I shall cut the pie. You men look like you're ready for dessert and coffee—a little cognac, perchance?"

Cuno wiped his mouth with his own napkin and, bored and disgusted by the conversation as well as the company, including that of the spoiled, judgmental Michelle and her oily eyed beau, he slid his own chair back and stood. "Much obliged, Mr. Trent. It was a long pull from Crow Feather, and I think I'll call it a night."

"Me, too," Serenity said. "That elk didn't leave much room in my belly for pie."

"But this isn't just any pie, Mr. Parker," bellowed Trent, swaying a little on his feet, glassy-eyed from the wine. "This is pie from the peaches off Run's own tree in the backyard!"

Cuno made his way around the table, followed by his men. He stopped beside Michelle's chair and extended his hand to her. "Miss Trent, it's been a pleasure."

"The pleasure's been mine, Mr. Massey," she said, her blue eyes again politely demure though her tone was coolly disapproving.

Cuno released the girl's tender hand and shook that of Jedediah Gallantly, who stood, knocked his heels together like a Russian soldier, and dipped his chin in a courtly half bow.

"You're certainly welcome to the beds upstairs," Trent told Cuno as the rancher shook his hand. "Like I said, I've plenty of room."

"The bunkhouse will do just fine, Mr. Trent. Thanks again for your hospitality."

"Kuttner will see you out," the rancher said to Cuno's back.

"We know the way."

Once outside, still buckling or adjusting their gun belts or donning their hats, the three freighters stepped off the porch into the dark, silent yard in which scurried an icy breeze touched with the fragrance of mountain pines.

"I've had better sit-downs in a dentist's chair," Serenity grouched as they began moseying down the grade toward the bunkhouse, its windows the only lights in the yard.

"The elk was a mite stringy," Snowberger said, plucking

a sliver of meat from between his teeth. "That big Injun would do better to shoot a younger critter next time."

"Me, I prefer beef," Serenity said. "They got enough of 'em around here."

Snowberger snorted. "Less'n the Injuns took more than their snare."

Cuno walked in brooding silence with Serenity and Snowberger to the middle of the yard. Then, as the other two continued toward the freight wagons for their bedrolls and war bags, he angled left toward the stables.

"Gonna check on the mules before I call it a night," he said.

The other two, yawning and moving sluggishly with all that Trent food in their bellies, bid the younger man good night and continued tramping off to the wagons. "Hope there's a couple o' free bunks in there," he heard Serenity say as the two silhouettes dwindled against the bunkhouse lights. "I'd like to sleep warm tonight. I ain't as young as I used to be, and my bursertitus is actin' up. Must be the altitude . . ."

Their voices and foot thuds faded. Cuno paused at one set of stable doors. Something caused him to look back toward the big house looming, its lower windows glowing, against the black velvet mountain wall behind it.

Smoke from the big fieldstone hearth unspooled from the chimney, like gray gauze. Cuno's mind was a mix of confused emotions, but at the heart of it lay the image of the girl's eyes regarding him with her cool, faintly mocking, vaguely horrified reproof.

Who the hell was Michelle Trent to judge him? Had she lived his life?

Hell, she'd spent most of her years being educated at some fancy finishing school back East, swapping dry smooches in a city park with the pasty-faced privy snipe, Jedediah Gallantly, whose family cooked bricks for a living without, no doubt, having ever touched a single one.

What really frustrated Cuno was that, when he'd first discovered her sopping wet and only half clothed on the dark stairs, he'd seen something in her eyes that had intrigued him and had compelled him to want to know her better, only to discover that she was someone else entirely.

A pretty shell.

Just another rich man's spoiled girl corrupted by privilege and easy prejudices.

Not that it mattered. She belonged to Jedediah Gallantly, and he could have her. They deserved each other.

Voices rose from Cuno's right. He turned to see Serenity and Snowberger again, heading back toward the bunkhouse with their gear on their shoulders, rifles in their hands—a bandy-legged little man limping along beside a taller, stoop-shouldered gent, both men speaking in desultory, tired tones as they mounted the bunkhouse porch. Their boots clomped dully and out of sync.

Serenity pulled the door open and there was a moment of good-natured gibing as they skirmished over who should enter first. Then, chuckling, Serenity followed Snowberger inside and closed the door behind him.

Cuno pulled one of the stable's two sliding doors open and slipped inside. He closed the door, fumbled around in the dark to light a lamp, then tramped down the broad, straw-strewn alley toward the back, where his twelve mules stood, two to a stall, on either side of the alley.

"Hello there, fellas. Ladies. How're you doin' this evenin'? Those Double-Horseshoe oats go down all right, did they?"

Cuno chuckled to himself. If he wasn't careful, he'd end up growing old alone; horses, mules, and dogs were the only folks he ever felt truly comfortable around.

He hung the lantern on a post and entered one of the stalls, giving the mules a closer inspection than what he'd had time for earlier. A half hour later, after having reset two shoes, pried gravel out of a couple of frogs, and given one more of the beasts a thorough curry, combing out its burr-laden tail, he checked their water and headed for the door.

He glanced back once more at the mules standing in the rear shadows, blowing softly or shifting their hooves, the one called Samson giving his head a weary shake. Yep, Cuno felt closer to his mules than to most people—other than Serenity, that was. He considered the old graybeard family. Aside from him, his life—after so much had come to pass—was all mules and wagons.

Not his gun.

No, not his gun.

He'd lived by his gun in the past only when he'd been forced to. But he was trying as hard as he could to live only by his wagons, his mules, and his horse. Someday, when the frontier became as friendly and as civilized as Michelle Trent and Jedediah Gallantly believed, wrongly, that it already was, he'd give up his gun for good and live the life he'd intended for himself way back before Anderson and Spoon had murdered his father and stepmother . . . back before Franklin Evans's bounty hunters had killed his pregnant wife, July.

In other words, he'd suppress his own inner savage.

"Have a good one, mules," he said, then blew out the lamp, replaced it on the hook by the door, and went outside.

He retrieved his bedroll, rifle, and red-and-black wool mackinaw from one of the wagons and headed for the bunkhouse to scrounge up an empty bunk for a warm night's sleep. He mounted the porch steps and stopped suddenly.

Through the low, sashed window right of the door, he could see a half dozen men, including Serenity, playing cards at a long table about halfway across the lantern-lit room. Someone slapped pasteboards down, and a low roar went up. A glass slid off the table and hit the floor with a glassy thump.

"Ah, dang ye, Gristle!" someone bellowed. "You spilled my whiskey, and that was the last o' that good bottle I got from the sutler's store over to the Rogers Outpost!"

Cuno compressed his lips. Suddenly, the mules looked even better than before, and the silent stables beckoned.

He wheeled, retraced his steps to the stock barn, and jerked the door open. This time, he didn't bother with the lantern. He threw his gear down in the first empty stall he came to, doffed his hat, and kicked out of his boots. Dropping into his blankets and burrowing deep in the straw, he sighed and closed his eyes.

Michelle Trent stared at him disapprovingly from the twilight fog of early slumber.

"Really, Mr. Massey!" chortled her betrothed.

"Kiss my ass," Cuno grumbled and went to sleep.

He had no idea how much time had passed before he woke with a start and reached for his .45.

All he grabbed was leather. The .45 was gone.

Someone laughed.

Another, nasal voice said, "You broke my nose, you son of a bitch!"

9

CUNO LOOKED UP. Three men stood outside the stall, staring over the partition at him.

They were blurred figures in the barn's dim light, breath puffing around their hatted heads. He recognized the *segundo*, Quirt, by the red-spotted white bandage taped over his nose.

Cuno blinked sleep from his eyes and narrowed one lid. "If I don't get my pistol back in about three seconds, you're gonna be pinin' for the time you only had a broken nose."

Quirt jerked forward and held up Cuno's ivory-gripped Colt Frontier, showing it off. "Come out and get it, mule skinner!"

Cuno scrambled to his feet, anger burning at the back of his neck. No one trifled with his guns if they knew what was good for them. Quirt and the other two men—one on each side of the ugly *segundo*, both about three inches taller than Quirt, and broader—stepped back away from the stall partition, swaggering, one rolling his shoulders, loosening the joints.

Cuno pushed through the stall door. Quirt backed up,

twirling Cuno's gun on his finger and grinning, showing his white teeth below the white bandage on his narrow, horsy face.

The freighter nodded at the two big men who shuffled up in front of him, between him and Quirt. All three men were wearing heavy coats against the penetrating morning cold. "Who're they?"

"Friends of mine," Quirt said. "Paid 'em four dollars each to break your nose . . . and whatever else they get around to breakin'."

Cuno slid his gaze from one brute to the other. "Four dollars ain't much for gettin' the holy shit kicked out of you, friends."

Quirt chuckled. "You ain't gonna kick the holy shit outta these hombres, mule skinner. Why, these boys pull fence posts outta the frozen ground with their *hands*."

"They're gonna have a hard time doing that with *broken* hands." Cuno lifted his chin at Quirt. "Beat it, fellas. Quirt's the one with the beef . . . and my gun. Let's not turn this into a rodeo."

Quirt laughed. With his broken nose, he sounded like a magpie.

The brutes grinned.

While Quirt hiked a hip on a water barrel and continued playing with Cuno's .45, the brute on Cuno's left shrugged out of his coat and hung it on a nearby nail from which harnesses drooped. Staring menacingly at Cuno, he slid his suspenders off his shoulders, jerked his shirttails out of his pants, and unbuttoned and removed his shirt.

He didn't stop until he was out of his grimy undershirt. Then he stood before Cuno—a big, broad, hairless mountain of a muscle-bound man, pocked and lashed here and there with knife scars. His smile, missing two front teeth, was like a giant rattler's.

The other brute stayed in his coat and hat. He had one wandering eye. That and his leering half smile made him look drunk. He was growling deep in his throat as the other man stepped forward, chin down, drawing his bunched left fist back and widening his eyes.

Shorter than the bare-chested brute, and lighter on his feet, Cuno sprang forward and, before the man could swing his left haymaker forward, Cuno punched him twice in the gut hard. It surprised the brute as well as twisted him around and threw him back into a stall partition with an enraged "Whufff!"

The other brute shuffled forward. Cuno wheeled toward him. The man grunted as he swung a roundhouse right, which glanced painfully off Cuno's upper right cheek. Shaking off the blow, Cuno ducked to avoid the next one, then stepped forward and buried his own right fist in the brute's gut.

As the man chuffed and dropped his head slightly, Cuno delivered two savage jabs to the man's face. The man's nose gave beneath Cuno's big fist like a bladder flask of blood, and the man was suddenly looking a lot more like Quirt.

"Ah, come on, Deuce!" Quirt complained. "That ain't what I paid ya for!"

Deuce loosed a shrill curse and blinked through the blood in his eyes, gritting his teeth and balling his fists with rage.

Cuno didn't step back before the bare-chested gent was on him, hammering his jaws with two quick jabs. He stumbled back, hearing bells toll in his head. Setting his feet, he blocked another punch with one arm, turning the bare-chested brute slightly, and then twice he rammed his left fist against the man's right ear.

As the man twisted to Cuno's right, Cuno hammered him with a right crosscut, jerking his face back around toward the freighter, his bloody lips glistening in the growing light from a window and his brown eyes snapping wide with fury. Cuno was beside the brute now, spreading his feet and preparing another couple of jabs to the dazed man's face.

To his left, he saw the other man stumble toward him,

raising a long hickory ax handle in his right hand. *"Ahhhhhhh!"* the brute bellowed, swinging the handle forward in a broad arc.

"Just fists, Deuce!" Quirt yelled from the rain barrel.

Cuno ducked as the ax handle curved toward his head, and the mallet whistled as it cut the air unimpeded. Deuce grunted with exertion. There was a solid, bony smack and another, louder grunt. Still crouching, Cuno turned as the bare-chested brute froze suddenly, blinking slowly, eyes losing focus.

"Oh, Jesus, Bill!" Deuce cried, dropping the ax handle down by his side and regarding his partner with exasperation. "I didn't mean . . ."

Bill's head wobbled. His jaw hung askew and blood ran in twin streams down the side of his head and neck and down his shoulder. He dropped to his knees and, unblinking, fell straight forward onto his face.

"Deuce, damnit!" Quirt cried, dropping down off the rain barrel. "I told you—only your fists! Is he *dead*?"

Breathing heavily, keeping his fists balled, Cuno backed away from Bill, who was moving his feet from side to side and shuttling his glance between Deuce and Quirt.

"Don't think he's dead," Deuce said, suddenly raising the ax handle once more and glaring glassy-eyed at Cuno, "but this son of a bitch sure—"

There was a tinkle, like a spoon tapped against a wineglass. And then, suddenly, Deuce's head jerked slightly, and the muscles in his face planed out.

He looked at Cuno with faint blame in his eyes.

Cuno blinked his own eyes as if to clear them, slow to understand that the fletched end of a Ute arrow was protruding from the right side of Deuce's head, while the sharpened strap-iron end poked out of the other side, just above Deuce's left ear.

The blade was sheathed in thick, red blood speckled with white bone and brain matter.

Deuce feebly raised his right hand, almost as though he were waving, then dropped it down his side. At the same time, Cuno jerked his gaze toward the broken window and, seeing movement in the murky dawn shadows of the ranch yard, heard the rising thunder of approaching hooves and the growing cacophony of mewling warriors.

In the periphery of his vision, as he bolted toward Quirt, Cuno saw Deuce tumble over Bill. Quirt was staring toward the window through which the arrow had sliced into the stable.

"Is that . . . ?"

"Who do you think it is?" Cuno grabbed his .45 out of Quirt's hand. "Too early for Santa Claus!"

Quirt shouted an epithet and clawed his own pistol from its holster. Cuno quickly stomped into his boots and slid his Winchester from its leather sheath.

Quirt was moving stiffly toward the barn doors, shoulders raised, gun held low by his side.

"What the hell you waiting for?" Cuno yelled as he ran past the *segundo* and heaved one of the doors open. "I don't think they're here bearing peace offerings."

Arrows thumped into the stable's logs walls. Hooves thundered. The Indians' war cries were now so loud that they covered the stable door's rasp along its metal track. Cuno had thrown the door three feet wide when an arrow smashed into it, reverberating like a ricochet.

Three war-painted Utes galloped past him, heading for the bunkhouse. Men were spilling from the bunkhouse in various stages of dress, some wearing only their longhandles and socks. One man tripped over his own pants and tumbled down the porch steps with an angry yell.

The three braves bore down on them, loosing arrows quickly and expertly, throwing two drovers back against the bunkhouse wall while one took an arrow through his calf as he came off the porch.

Cuno racked a shell into his Winchester's breech, aimed quickly, and fired. The Indian he'd drawn the bead on turned, and the bullet careened wide. He nocked an arrow, howling like a mad coyote, and, putting his paint horse into a gallop toward Cuno, let fly.

Cuno jerked his head down and to one side. The arrow buzzed by like a bee, nearly taking out his right eye, before it slammed into the stable door behind him.

Cuno levered his Winchester and fired as the brave swung his horse to Cuno's left. The Winchester's round slammed into the brave's deerskin-clad arm, and the brave howled even louder than before, throwing his head back on his shoulders, then sagging forward in his blanket saddle as his horse galloped westward.

"Holy Christ!" Quirt cried as he bounded through the door and dropped to a knee beside Cuno. "More comin' up from the creek!"

Cuno could see more braves rushing up from the south, several peeling off from the main group and galloping toward the main house at the top of the hill. What had captured the brunt of his attention, however, were the two braves that had climbed atop the bunkhouse's shake roof from the rear and were scampering up toward the front, one nocking an arrow while another held a Spencer repeater with a leather lanyard.

They were both looking down at the cowboys and Serenity and Snowberger still stumbling bleary-eyed out the bunkhouse's front door. A couple of the drovers were triggering pistols or rifles, but the sudden attack had caught them by surprise. Their bullets so far had grazed only one warrior who, turning his pinto in tight circles, triggered arrow after arrow at the yowling, cursing drovers.

While Quirt triggered his Schofield .44 at the Indians galloping up from the creek, Cuno shouted, "Serenity! Behind you!"

Cuno aimed and fired. One of the Indians was punched back off his feet. He hit the shake-shingled bunkhouse roof on his back, then rolled down over the eave and hit the porch in a dust puff between Henry Kuttner and a bearded drover wearing only longjohns and an open buffalo robe.

Both men, shooting the new Winchesters Cuno's train had brought to the Double-Horseshoe, paused to glance down at the bleeding Indian who tried to climb onto his hands and knees. While Kuttner drilled a round through the wounded Ute's head, Cuno fired three more rounds toward the bunkhouse roof.

Serenity, wearing only his boots, long johns, and beat-up sombrero, fired his Colt Navy, and one Ute was thrown down the backside of the roof while another dropped to his butt.

Blood leaking from the seated brave's belly, the warrior tried to bring his Spencer carbine to bear. A drover on the porch, wielding a sawed-off shotgun in one hand and a Colt in the other, fed the brave double rounds of buckshot and a .44 slug, turning his head to pulp.

Arrows whizzed around Cuno's head, punching into the stable wall behind him. Levering a fresh round, he fired at the Indians streaming in from the creek.

They galloped in a shaggy line past the corral to the bunkhouse, loosed a couple of arrows at the drovers now holed up behind rain barrels or stock troughs or kneeling behind the porch rail, then galloped back westward past the stables before which Cuno and Quirt knelt, blinking against the broiling dust as they fired into the horde.

The Indians yowled like wolves on the trail of a bison herd. The drovers cursed and shouted. The arrows made whipping sounds as they caromed through the air, then barked loudly as they slammed into the log walls of the bunkhouse and the stables or clattered through windows.

Rifles whip-cracked, echoing around the yard, and pistols popped. There were the intermittent, thundering blasts of the bearded man's sawed-off gut shredder.

As the drovers got oriented, Indians began to drop, screaming. One splashed into a stock trough in front of the bunkhouse, and the drover crouching behind it backed up, spitting water from his mouth and firing wildly into the trough until the thrashing brave stopped thrashing and sank.

Quirt had emptied his second six-shooter when, on one knee to Cuno's right, his hammer clicked, empty.

"Shit!"

He lowered the gun to his knee and thumbed open the

loading gate. The *segundo* hadn't plucked a single shell from his cartridge belt before a bullet tore into his forehead. Quirt flew up off his heels, bounced off the stable wall, and piled up at the wall's base, dead.

Cuno slid his Winchester toward the Indian galloping past the corrals on the far side of the yard, fifty yards away and racking a fresh shell into his Spencer's breech. The brave's dark gaze was cast toward Cuno, lower jaw rising and falling as he shrieked.

Before the brave could raise his carbine to his shoulder once more, Cuno blew him off his horse and slammed him up against the corral gate with a crunching and cracking of strained wooden slats and breaking bones. The brave's horse whinnied and buck-kicked, turned sharply, collided with another brave's horse, unseating the surprised brave, and galloped back toward the creek.

Cuno quickly thumbed fresh shells through his Winchester's loading gate and peered through the dust wafting amidst the gradually receding shadows. Most of the horses around him now were riderless and shaken. Guns continued to pop.

Serenity's high-pitched shout cut through the din. "Cuno!"

The young freighter turned sharply left. A horseback warrior galloped toward him, aiming an old Colt pistol tied to his wrist by a horsehair thong. The Indian's face was a lip-stretched mask of wide-eyed fury as his head bobbed above that of his speckle-rumped black mustang.

Pop!

A bullet kissed the nap on Cuno's tunic and plowed into the stable wall. Cuno snapped the Winchester to his shoulder and fired once, twice, three times. The brave continued toward him, screaming, *"Aiyyeeeee-yawwwwww!"*

Pop! Pop!

The brave's bullets sizzled passed Cuno and into the stable wall. Knowing he'd fired the three fresh rounds he'd managed to slip into his receiver, Cuno flipped the rifle around, grabbing it by its barrel, and stepped up in the Indian's path. As the horse approached, wide eyes ringed with white, the brave aimed the pistol at Cuno once more.

The hammer pinged benignly onto the firing pin, and Cuno felt an icy nip in his bowels, knowing he'd come to within one misfired cartridge of his final resting place.

He smashed his Winchester's butt across the Indian's face—a solid, cracking hit that Cuno could feel up into his shoulders. The war cries died on the Ute's lips as he careened off his galloping black's right hip, turning two complete somersaults before hitting the ground, rolling in the churning dust, and coming to rest on his belly.

The black continued on past Cuno, smelling gamey with bear grease and sweat, and galloped back toward the creek, its rope reins trailing along the ground behind him. Cuno looked around for another Indian to shoot, but there was only wafting dust and scattered dead warriors and dead drovers.

Several braves galloped back across the creek, still yelling.

"Shit almighty!" one of the ranch hands cried, grabbing his right leg and rolling around in the dirt between the bunkhouse and one of the headquarters' two barns. "Someone pull this fuckin' arrow outta my knee!"

Just then a girl's scream rose from the direction of the main house. Cuno had dropped to a knee to thumb more cartridges into his Winchester.

"Christ, that's Trent's daughter!" rasped Henry Kuttner, rising from behind one of the two stock troughs fronting the bunkhouse. He took a couple of steps and dropped to his knee, his lower right leg bloody.

The girl screamed again. It was more like a wail this time. It sent a whipcord of electricity snapping up Cuno's back.

He bolted off his heels and sprinted toward the house.

10

CUNO RAN AROUND the stable in which the mules were braying raucously and thumping their stalls. He sprinted up the gentle grade toward the house at the base of the mountain wall.

The sprawling lodge was purple-black in the dawn shadows, but Cuno could see pale gray smoke wisping from the open front door. Arrows bristled from the log walls and porch posts and from a few of the closed shutters on the first floor. Dust sifted through the gradually lightening air in front of the house, and the ground was freshly churned with the prints of unshod ponies.

Cuno was twenty yards from the porch when hoof thuds rose to his left. He turned to see a horseback brave galloping out from around the lodge's west side. The brave turned his feather-adorned head toward Cuno, then crouched low and squeezed his knees against the horse's sides, urging more speed. He howled wildly, victoriously, as horse and rider whipped past Cuno and headed south toward the creek.

Cuno didn't waste time with a shot at the fleeing Indian. The girl had screamed again from inside the house—a horrific exclamation of bald terror—and Cuno took the porch steps two at a time . . . and stopped suddenly, whipping his Winchester up with a startled grunt.

But it was no Indian standing there in the open doorway. It was Jedediah Gallantly, clad only in white silk longhandles. The man was barefoot. His hair was mussed, and his dark eyes were sunk deep in their pale sockets.

He leaned against the open door, on the other side of the threshold, pressing one hand back against the door behind him while wrapping his other hand against the Ute-fletched arrow protruding from his belly. Blood shone darkly just up from his crotch, and dribbled down both thighs of his longhandles.

Gallantly cleared his throat and regarded Cuno miserably. His voice was so soft that Cuno could barely hear him. "Can . . . can . . . you . . . help . . . me?"

He looked down at the arrow, as if to indicate the problem.

Cuno began to reach for the arrow, but stopped. If he tried to pull the shaft out of Gallantly's belly, he'd pull half of the man's insides out, as well. He was a goner.

"I don't think so," Cuno said regretfully, stepping gingerly past the dying man.

Michelle screamed again from deep inside the bowels of the house, and Cuno lunged ahead down the dim, smoky hall, following her screams into the large dining room. He stopped just inside the door and squinted his stinging eyes against the smoke.

The drapes on the other side of the table were burning. The smell of kerosene was sharp. In the middle of the room, a figure was down and crawling awkwardly. It was Trent.

He wore a red-plaid robe over a nightgown, and elkskin slippers. He was trying to crawl across the room, toward the kitchen door, using a long-barreled, double-bore shotgun as an oar. He looked like a landed fish trying to make it back to the stream.

As Cuno ran up to him, Trent turned suddenly, bellowing savagely and swinging the shotgun around.

"It's Cuno, Trent! Where's Michelle!"

Trent turned his enraged gaze toward the door on the far side of the room, and, with an enraged grunt, threw the shotgun, which landed just short of the door with a clattering thump. *"Kitchen!"*

Cuno had heard the girl's sobs and pleas and the guttural exclamations of the Indians and was already striding toward the kitchen door. His heart hammering and his ears ringing, eyes stinging, he bunched his lips and kicked the door wide, stepping quickly inside and raising his Winchester.

Three Indians had the girl down on a long wooden table against the far wall, in front of a low, sashed window. She was naked, her nightclothes strewn about the floor amidst spilled flour and broken jars and bottles. Two Indians held her arms down on the table above her head. One had his deerskins breeches down around his knees.

The third brave, who'd also dropped his breeches, crouched between her legs, holding her slender, cream thighs in his brown hands while he thrust his hips savagely against her. He wore a crisp black beaver hat that he'd obviously found inside the house, when he was hauling the girl out of her room, no doubt. It looked ridiculous on the brave's savage head.

Spittle stringed from his lips as he leaned forward to shout mockingly into Michelle's pain-racked face, his tightly wound braids jostling down the back of his wolf-skin tunic, the banded tips brushing the oak-colored lobes of his naked ass.

One of the braves at the head of the table cried out suddenly, snapping his head toward Cuno. His grotesquely painted face shown in the growing light pushing through the window, and the beads studding his headband glistened dully. The wild smell of the Indians filled the kitchen with the smell of a bear den.

Cuno drew a bead on the headband and squeezed the Winchester's trigger. The boom filled the room, causing another jar to shatter on the wooden floor.

As the first Indian was punched against the brave to his right, the one raping Michelle jerked his dusky, eagle-featured face toward Cuno, his mixed breed's hazel eyes flashing with exasperation beneath the beaver hat's narrow curled brim, his lower jaw dropping. Cuno drilled a round through his chest, levered a fresh one, and shot the third brave, who'd turned to run toward the open back door.

The .44-40 round took him through his right shoulder blade. He yelped and stumbled forward, twisted around and falling.

The brave who'd been raping Michelle now stood facing Cuno, his back to the window, head turned to one side, stretching his lips back from his teeth as the hole in his chest gushed blood onto his wolf-skin tunic liberally decorated with bone talismans.

Cuno stepped forward, ejecting a spent round, which bounced off his chest and clattered onto the floor around a massive black cook range. Gritting his teeth, he seated a fresh cartridge and shot the half-naked brave once more in his chest and then pumped one more into his left cheek.

The rapist's head slammed back, cracking the window. The beaver hat tumbled off his head. His body spasmed wildly before he sagged forward, knees buckling, and fell face down beneath Michelle's bare feet dangling down the end of the table.

Scuffs and grunts sounded at the right end of the kitchen. Cuno moved around the table to the open timbered door. The shoulder-shot brave was half crawling, half running toward the three Indian ponies tied in the cottonwoods near a large, L-shaped pile of split firewood.

Cuno thumbed fresh rounds into the Winchester's loading gate. Standing just outside the open door, he coolly raised the rifle to his shoulder and drilled three more quick slugs into the fleeing Indian's back, on either side of his arrow-filled quiver—slamming him forward into a long, loose run. The brave hit the ground and rolled, groaning and causing the tied ponies to whinny and skitter-hop sideways.

"Son of a bitch." Cuno ejected the smoking cartridge casing.

There was a thump behind him, and Michelle groaned. He wheeled and ran back into the kitchen. The girl was on the floor, crawling on her hands and knees toward the door to the dining room. She was sort of mewling and sobbing. Gooseflesh stood out on the milk-colored skin of her curved, slender back and rounded hips.

Before Cuno got to her, she fell onto her side, silently sobbing, tears streaking her bruised cheeks. Her split, bloody lips were drawn wide, quivering. She drew her knees up toward her chafed breasts, and pressed her long, pale, bare feet together.

"Easy now, easy," Cuno said, looking around. He could hear running feet behind him and men shouting and the whumps of someone trying to put out the fire in the dining room.

A large denim jacket hung on a nearby wall hook. He rushed over, grabbed it, and threw it over the girl, then set his rifle on the table. Kneeling, he snaked his arms under Michelle's neck and beneath her knees and rose with her slowly.

"Easy now, easy, I got you—you're gonna be okay." Cuno pushed through the door into the dining room. Henry Kuttner was helping Trent to his feet while two other men from the bunkhouse were ripping the burning drapes down and stomping on them, one beating the flames with chair cushions.

Cuno realized he'd been in the house probably no more than two minutes. Time had slowed down. That and the smoke and the horror of what he'd witnessed in the kitchen disoriented him. He felt as though he'd taken a war club to the solar plexus.

Stumbling, he crossed the dining room. Trent wobbled toward him, blood from a nasty gash in his forehead dribbling down his weathered, brick-red face.

"Oh, Christ—what'd they do to my girl?"

"Where's her bed?" Cuno choked.

Kuttner jerked his head toward the dining room door. "Upstairs!"

"Oh, no!" Trent wailed, stretching an arthritic hand toward Michelle's blond head. "What'd they do to her?"

"What the hell do you think they did to her?" Cuno said with exasperation.

He had to get the girl to a bed so that someone who knew what they were doing could help her. He could tell from her dimming eyes and her silent, choking sobs that she was probably in shock. The cuts and bruises on her face didn't look too bad, but she might have taken one hell of a clubbing on top of everything else they'd done to her.

Cuno started down the hall with Kuttner and Trent trailing him, Trent limping and cursing.

"Through the parlor!" Trent yelled. "There's a stairway—closer!"

One hell of an oddly designed house. The house of a man with a whimsical, independent mind. Cuno turned into the sitting room adorned with a giant bear rug, leather couches, and heavy wooden tables. There was a half-open stairway against the west wall, and Cuno took the steps two at a time.

Behind him, he heard Trent order Kuttner outside to see to his men and organize a posse to trail the savages to their lair—*"and bring back every one of their fucking heads on a stick!"*

At the top of the stairs, Cuno moved down the broad hall, the walls on both sides constructed of square-hewn pine timbers chinked with cement and trimmed with occasional tintypes and oil paintings. Three doors stood ajar, two on either side of the hall and one at the end.

Likely the one appointed with the pink lamps, a dressing table strewn with perfume bottles and combs, and a frilly canopied bed was Michelle's. He laid her gently on the bed. She gave a start and clung to him for a second, then, turning her head and seeing the bed beneath her, removed her hands from his neck. She had a dim, faraway look in her glassy eyes.

"It's okay," Cuno said. "You're all right now. There, easy . . ."

As he drew the cotton sheets and heavy quilts and a panther hide up over her trim, frail, heartbreakingly fragile-looking body, she turned away from him slowly, buried her head in her feather pillow, and drew her knees up to her chest, shivering.

"It's okay," Cuno whispered again.

He turned as Trent came in, clad in only his nightgown, his silver, curly hair mussed about his head. Blood continued to run down from the nasty gash in the side of his head. As he moved toward the bed, he said hoarsely, feebly, "Ming. Please . . . fetch Ming. He'll know what to do for my daughter . . ."

Cuno hadn't been formally introduced to the Chinese cook and bathhouse captain, but Ming was no doubt him. He backed toward the door as Trent leaned over the bed, half lying on it and patting the head of his daughter, who lay staring silently at the far wall, unmoving.

"Oh, my dear girl," the rancher sobbed. "Oh, Jesus, what'd they do to you?"

Cuno left the room feeling as though he had a large rock in his gut. He retraced his steps to the dining room, trying to remember where he'd left his rifle. When he got to the kitchen, the two men who'd been stomping out the flames in the dining room were now dragging one of the two dead Indians out of the kitchen.

The Sioux cook, Runs-with-the-Ponies, sat at the table, stiff-backed and puffy-faced, his eyes red and rheumy from drink. Cuno had forgotten about him. He must have been passed out in the room off the kitchen when the Indians had attacked. He was clad in suspenders, a ragged undershirt, and baggy buckskin trousers. His stocking feet were set flat on the floor beneath the table, one hideously twisted and swollen.

He sat with a bottle and a half-filled glass of whiskey in front of him, a cornhusk cigarette clamped between two callused fingers. His was singing softly, almost under his breath, his lips barely moving. Some Sioux dirge, no doubt. Or a prayer. It sounded like a morning breeze over a weed-sheathed pond.

Now he prays, Cuno thought with a vague spurt of anger, reaching for his rifle.

"Verr bad."

Cuno looked at the Indian. Run's red eyes were fixed on Cuno now, or somewhere just over Cuno's right shoulder. Run tilted his head at the Indian whom the two half-clad drovers were now dragging around the table, toward the open door.

"Verr bad," the Indian repeated, blowing smoke out his broad, dark nostrils. "Him a son of Leaping Wolf."

Cuno looked at the dead Indian who'd been wearing the hat and savaging Michelle when Cuno had entered the kitchen. The two drovers looked at Cuno, faintly incredulous, and then they hauled the bloody carcass out the door and into the yard, leaving a long, broad smear of blood, flour, and cornmeal on the wooden floor behind them.

"Ahh-eeeee!" The Sioux sighed, lifting his chin toward the rafters. "Verr, verr bad."

11

CUNO LEFT THE kitchen and headed down the smoky hall of the Trent house to the front door. Dawn had broken and the birds were chirping as though it were a morning like any other. Magpies wheeled, their long, iridescent blue wings and tails flashing against the sky.

Cuno stopped ten feet from the front door and stared straight ahead. Jedediah Gallantly sat with his back to the hall's right side, leaning his head back against the wall. His hands rested on his thighs, and one leg was curled beneath the other. His other bare, pink foot was extended over the threshold onto the porch.

Cuno moved closer. Gallantly's head was tilted toward his shoulder, and his cheeks were already ashen. Blood still gushed out around the arrow to pool on the porch between his legs. His half-open eyes seemed to study something in vague fascination on the opposite side of the door frame.

Cuno considered dragging the body out of the doorway and onto the porch, but he decided to leave the job to Trent or one of Trent's men.

He stepped over the dead man's legs. Boot thumps and

spur chings rose from the yard, and he looked out to see Henry Kuttner approaching—fully dressed now, with a .45 thonged on his thigh. Gloves were wedged behind his shell belt. He limped slightly on his grazed right leg, blood spotting his denim trousers just below the knee.

Cuno stood at the top of the steps as Kuttner moved up past him, his face a bitter mask, and looked down at Gallantly's corpse. "Poor son of a bitch." He looked at Cuno. "I reckon you're feelin' pretty smug. Them Injuns did a real nice job of proving the point you made over supper last night."

"I didn't need their help."

"Yep, feelin' pretty smug."

Cuno's chest heaved and his jaws hardened. "What do I have to feel smug about, Kuttner? Because two of your cork-headed line riders raped an Indian girl, I have a man dead, a burned wagon, and six dead mules. I just watched a pretty girl get mauled on her own kitchen table, and I'm pinned down here with Utes swarming like bees in a clover field."

Cuno shook his head tightly and squared his shoulders at the foreman. "Don't give me any of your copper-plated grief, Kuttner. I got a burr under my tail and one hell of an itchy trigger finger."

Kuttner's eyes dropped to Cuno's bone-gripped .45 jutting from the holster on the freighter's stout, right thigh. They flicked up again to Cuno's face. The foreman said nothing. His features maintained that grave, masklike expression.

Cuno swung around and dropped down the steps. He was striding down the hill when Kuttner said, "Massey?"

Cuno turned.

Kuttner was still standing on the porch. "You got another man down." The foreman jerked his head toward the outbuildings and said softly, "In the bunkhouse."

"Which one?"

"Snowberger."

"How bad?"

"Bad enough." Kuttner reached down to pull Gallantly's corpse out of the doorway.

Cuno cursed under his breath and continued down the hill, moving quickly, his expression grim beneath his hat brim. He slowed, his expression softening, when the clatter of a wagon rose in the west. He directed his gaze that way, through the shadows the rising sun was spreading across the road and the rolling, sage-and-cedar-stippled tableland of the valley beyond the creek and the ranch portal.

A wagon was rattling along the curving trail, the bay in the traces galloping full out, its jostling mane glistening as the sun peeked over the high eastern ridge. The wagon behind it was a simple farm wagon, painted dark red, with a woman in a long gray dress in the traces, her hair piled atop her head.

There were two more people on the seat beside her. Two girls—one a little towhead wrapped in blankets and wearing a pink knit cap with earflaps. The other girl was older, maybe seventeen or eighteen, with long dark hair and Mexican features. She wore a man's denim jacket over a worn, green wool dress, and her felt hat was tied to her head with a spruce green scarf. The morning breeze whipped her hair and her red neckerchief out behind her in the wind.

The driver hoorahed the horse like a seasoned mule skinner, flicking the reins wildly across the charging animal's back. No one drove a wagon at that speed unless they were trying to outrun trouble. Indeed, trouble shone in the face of the woman and the two girls, Cuno saw, as the horse and the wagon bounded over the bridge and under the portal, then angled across the yard and headed up the grade toward the house.

"Mr. Trent!" the woman yelled as the wagon approached the house. Her plain-featured face—Cuno figured she was in her early or mid-forties—was gaunt and pale, the eyes bright with anxiety and exasperation. *"Trent!"*

The woman hauled the horse to a stop near Cuno and,

ramming the brake home with a wince, glanced at the freighter. "Is your boss here?"

Cuno hesitated, realizing the woman naturally assumed he worked here. Hooking his thumb at the lodge, he said, "In the house."

He moved toward the wagon as the woman reached to her left and lifted the blond girl onto her lap. The blonde, between ten and twelve, owned the same blank, shocked look as Cuno had seen in Michelle Trent's face only a few minutes ago.

The woman rose in her seat slightly and held the girl down to Cuno, who took the expressionless, blue-eyed child in his arms and eased her onto the ground. She set her feet beneath her and looked around as though lost, fear now showing in her face, and tears beginning to squeeze out from her eyes to roll down her smooth, plump cheeks streaked with dust and soot.

Cuno reached up for the woman and set her down beside the girl. As the woman scrambled around to the back of the wagon, Cuno looked up at the other girl on the driver's seat. Her long, raven hair framed a pretty oval face with a straight nose and broad, high, flat cheeks.

Tentatively, she moved toward the edge of the wagon. Cuno held up his hand to her. Ignoring his offered help, she steadied herself on the wagon seat, dropped her left foot to the front wheel, and leapt fleetly from there to the ground, giving a little grunt.

She smelled smoky, and her olive features were streaked with soot and dust. There was a slight cut on the nub of her left cheek, and a long, pale scar traced her right jawline. Her eyes grave, she said nothing as she moved up behind the little blonde and set her mittened hands on the girl's shoulders.

"You all right?" Cuno said, kneeling beside the little blonde and placing a hand on her shoulder.

She wouldn't look at him, but only continued to stare across the yard. Cuno followed her frightened, tearful gaze south toward the rolling hills turning copper and lime green under the sun's first, soft rays. The girl raised her right hand beneath the blanket wrapped around her, and he saw that it held a stuffed, slightly fire-charred bear.

Cuno straightened and looked at the Mexican girl standing in grim silence behind the blonde. "What happened?"

The girl parted her lips to speak, but stopped when the woman behind Cuno said, "All right, boys, go to the house, now. Hurry!"

Cuno turned. He hadn't seen the boys when the wagon had first pulled up. They'd been hidden by the sideboards and the robes piled in the box. There were two of them—one seven or eight, the other thirteen or fourteen, both dressed in homespun shirts and patched denim coveralls. They moved out in front of the woman, sullen-faced, eyes downcast, the older one with his hands in his pockets, and began scuffling toward the house.

"Come, come," the harried woman said to the girls, wrapping an arm around the little blonde's shoulders. "Go, now!"

Boots thumped on the porch, and Trent and Kuttner came out. Trent, dressed now, but hatless, his hair uncombed, negotiated the steps and limped down the grade to the woman and the children. "Louise, for chrissakes!" Trent said. "What're you doing here?"

"Indians burned us out, Logan," the woman sobbed, ushering the little blonde along ahead of her, her gray skirts swishing about her legs and heavy, black shoes. "They killed Harry and the hired man . . . and they burned everything!"

"Ah, for chrissakes!" Trent said, throwing up his hands.

"Can you send men out after them, Logan?"

Trent glanced at Kuttner flanking him, feet spread wide, his thumbs hooked behind his cartridge belts. "Henry's sending men out now, Louise. As many as I can spare."

Trent wrapped an arm around the woman's shoulders, and they all continued toward the house, their backs to Cuno, the Mexican girl tagging along behind the woman and the boys as though she didn't quite belong.

They were drifting beyond Cuno now, mounting the porch, but the freighter heard the rancher say, "We, too, were hit about a half hour ago. Henry says I lost five men, with three more wounded. Children, turn away. Henry, get something and *cover* Jedediah, for *chrissakes*!"

Trent's shrill voice faded as the group headed on into the house, the tall, rangy Kuttner bringing up the rear, behind the Mexican girl.

Cuno hiked his cartridge belt higher on his hips and glanced southward as he continued across the yard, where several drovers, fully clothed now, some wearing bandages or arm slings, were dragging off the dead Indians. Arrows bristled from the log buildings and even a couple of the adobe-brick hovels and corral slats. The corralled horses were running in several circles, tails arched and eyes fearful.

Cuno was glad to see Renegade among them, looking unharmed but nervous.

Blood smeared the dust and manure of the yard. One Indian, wearing the blue, gold-buttoned tunic of a cavalry sergeant and the checked trousers of a whiskey drummer, had piled up against a stock tank fronting the blacksmith shop. His liver-colored innards were piled up in front of his badly torn belly. Half his face was gone. Doubtless the work of the cowboy with the barn blaster.

Cuno heard the mules braying inside the stables. One of the wounded ranch hands, on the ground in front of a hay barn, was sobbing and shouting curses while two others tried to lift him to his feet. One arrow protruded from his left knee while another bristled from his crotch.

He was screaming like a woman in labor as Cuno mounted the bunkhouse porch, the floor of which owned several pools of fresh, glistening blood. Serenity was squatting near a water barrel, staring out across the yard, smoking a quirley.

"You hit?" Cuno asked the wizened old freighter.

"Takin' a break. Damn near threw my back out helpin' Dallas inside."

"How bad's he hit?"

"Bad."

"Will he make it?"

"I've seen folks make it after worse, but he don't look good." Serenity rolled his pale blue eyes up to Cuno. "I've seen mad Injuns before, but never ones as mad as these."

Cuno moved toward the bunkhouse's open door.

"How's it up to the house?" Serenity asked.

"Bad," Cuno said, moving into the bunkhouse and squinting around through the wafting powder smoke.

One of the drovers—a middle-aged gent with close-cropped gray hair and a goatee—and the Chinaman, Ming, were tending two wounded men on bunks to Cuno's left. On a bottom bunk to his right, Dallas Snowberger lay on his side, facing the center of the room and stretching his lips back from his teeth.

Dallas's face was pale and sweat-streaked. A blanket was pulled up to his neck, but he was shivering like it was forty below zero.

"Ming, I'm gonna need help over here with Timmy," the gray-haired drover, apparently the ranch's medico, said as Cuno moved over to his mule skinner. "This arrow's buried deep in his shin bone!"

Cuno dragged a chair up beside Snowberger's bunk and sank into it. "How you doin', Dallas? How bad you hit?"

"Those sons o' bitches," the freighter rasped, using his left hand to slide the blanket back off his left hip. The fletched end of one arrow protruded from his upper right chest, while the fletched end of a second arrow protruded from his left butt cheek.

The corn-stuffed pad beneath him was soaked with so much blood it was seeping through the bottom of the bunk to the floor.

Snowberger laughed through his teeth, spittle bubbling behind his lips. "Seen one trying to sneak around behind the bunkhouse, and I shot him. Didn't see the other one by the privy. Scrawny little savage drilled one arrow through my chest and, when it turned me around and threw me against the bunkhouse, the bastard shot another arrow through my *ass*!"

"All right," Cuno said, setting the palm of his hand over the end of the arrow sticking out of the freighter's chest. "We gotta get this out before you bleed to death."

"No, no, no," Snowberger said quickly, shaking his head. "The hombre over yonder—Riker's his name—used to be an army surgeon. He'll be over here just as soon as he gets that arrow outta the shin of the fella I fleeced last night at cards."

The freighter was rambling, his eyes dancing in their sockets. He was in shock, and, mercifully, his inner lights were dimming.

"Poor bastard," he continued hoarsely. "They scalped him, too. Dragged him off into the brush behind the hay barn and scalped him. I won fifty dollars off ole Schotzy last night and then, first thing this morning, some Comanche shoots him in the *shin* and then him and another'n drag him off and *scalp* him. *Damn!* That's gotta hurt so fuckin' *bad*!"

There was a screeching yell, and Cuno turned to see the two men carrying the man with the arrow in his crotch through the bunkhouse door. They carried the man between them, each with an arm around his back and another under his thighs. The poor man's face was even more a picture of raging agony than was Snowberger's.

"Dub took one to the oysters!" one of the other men said.

The surgeon, Riker, looked up from Schotzy's leg. His rawboned, blood-splattered face crumpled, and he cursed. "Put him on the table . . . gentle." Returning his attention to the arrow jutting from Schotzy's shin, the medico grumbled, "Never had to pull one out of a man's balls before. What I wouldn't give to dig those two raping bastards up and spit in what's left of their eyeballs!"

"Can I get you anything while you're waitin'?" Cuno asked Snowberger. "A shot of whiskey . . . ?"

The freighter shook his head. “You . . . you know what I’d really like . . . more than anything?”

“Tell me.”

“A cup of hot coffee. Got up so damn fast, never even had a cup of belly wash yet this mornin’.” The freighter shook violently, gritting his teeth so hard they made slight cracking sounds. “Cravin’ a cup real bad, Cuno.”

Cuno walked over to the stove and placed a hand on it. Cold. No one had had time to build a fire, much less brew coffee.

When he’d gotten a fire going, he found the big, black percolator on a shelf, along with a half sack of Arbuckles. He went out to the porch, filled the percolator from the water barrel, tossed in a few handfuls of coffee, and set the pot on the stove.

Adding more wood to the firebox, he moved back over to Snowberger, who was still shivering and gritting his teeth and staring at the floor. “It’s coming, Dallas. Hold on.”

Snowberger nodded slightly.

“I’m gonna go outside and see if anyone else needs help.” Truth was, he couldn’t stand watching the man suffer any longer, especially since there was nothing, aside from making coffee, that Cuno could do for him.

Snowberger nodded again, and Cuno headed back toward the door. Five men had gathered around the table on the other side of the range. They were passing a bottle and loading their six-shooters and carbines, red-faced with fury and arguing over ammunition.

Cuno swerved away from the door and strode over to the table. “You fellas headin’ after the Injuns?”

“That’s right,” said one of the men. “Wanna ride along, mule skinner?”

“How do you know it’s not a trap?”

“Well, now, I reckon we don’t know that, do we?” said one of the others, puffing a half-smoked cheroot while filling his cartridge belt from an open box. The man’s long face was etched with anger, and he batted his lids against the smoke. "But we sure as shit up a cow's ass are gonna find out."

"They're hoping you'll do just what you're doing—leave the ranch and fog their trail. Meanwhile, one faction's likely to circle back and hit us from another direction. Hit us while we're short-handed."

The man with the cheroot chuckled as he glanced at one of his partners. "The mule skinner sounds yaller to me, boys!"

"You go off half-cocked," Cuno warned, "and you're gonna get yourselves coldcocked out there, without help and damn little cover. Looks to me like there's a hell of a lot more braves out there than Trent first counted."

"What makes you such an expert on Injuns?" asked the first man who'd spoken.

Before Cuno could reply that he'd been hauling freight through Indian country since he was ten years old, a short, grizzled man with a two-day beard rammed a fresh load into his shiny new Winchester and said, "Look, son, those orders came down from the main house. It ain't our job to question 'em, just follow 'em. Savvy? Besides, Luke here lost his best friend a few minutes ago, so you can't really expect him or any of the rest of us to sit back on our spurs, now, can you?"

Luke blew smoke through his sunburned nostrils and gave Cuno a mocking, sidelong look. "Savvy, mule skinner?"

"Besides," the older man said, "those Injuns have about one firestick for every ten braves. Now, thanks to your freight run, we have these purty new Winchester repeaters."

"They're no guarantee," Cuno growled as, knowing the men were being led by passion and not reason, he swung back to the stove. He tossed two more logs into the firebox and headed outside.

Serenity was sitting on the top porch step now, smoking a loosely rolled quirley and taking apart a short-barreled Bisley, setting each part including bullets on the red neckerchief spread out beside him. He had his regular two pistols—a Colt Trapper model and an old, rusty Paterson, large as a smithy's hammer—resting on the splintered step between his knee-high, lace-up boots.

The graybeard glanced over his shoulder at Cuno, squinting one pale blue eye. "Heard ya in there. You're pissin' into a prairie cyclone."

"You ain't just choppin' tobacky."

"Best clean your guns and sharpen your knives. I took this here spare off the man who dropped dead beside me. He ain't gonna need it where he's goin', but when old Dancin' Wolf returns, I sure am!"

"Leapin' Wolf."

"Leapin', Dancin'—he'll be back just as soon as those five big chunks of wolf bait behind you ride out the southern trail. Take my advice and save a bullet for yourself. As mad as that old war chief is over the killin' of his little girl—and I can't say as I blame him one damn bit—he's fixin' to roast us all over low fires while his squaws cut little bitty chunks out of our hides just to hear how loud we can scream."

"I just love talkin' to you when I'm in a tight spot," Cuno grunted. "You always make me feel better."

When he heard the percolator coughing and sputtering, he went into the bunkhouse, filled a tin cup, and took it over to Snowberger's bunk. Crouching, he said, "Here you go, Dallas. Good and strong, just like—"

The wounded freighter lay as before, on his side. Only now he wasn't moving. The skin of his face hung slack, and his liquid brown eyes were death-glazed.

12

"THOSE SONS O' bitches didn't need to kill Dallas," Serenity said as he and Cuno stood over the grave that Cuno had dug while the older freighter had fashioned a crude wooden cross from cedar branches and rawhide. "He didn't have nothin' to do with rapin' and killin' ole Dancing Wolf's daughter."

Cuno stared grimly down at the blanket-wrapped bundle that was Dallas Snowberger lying at the bottom of the black hole. "I told you, Serenity, it's Leapin' Wolf."

"Leapin', Dancin' . . ."

"You wanna say a few words?"

"Wouldn't wanna embarrass him. Dallas was a man of few words. Too much talkin' made him antsy."

"All right, then."

Cuno picked up his shovel and, sweaty from the half hour he'd spent digging the grave in the sunshine atop a low knoll just east of the Trent ranchstead, began shoveling the orange dirt and gravel back into the grave. The first few shovelfuls thumped dully atop the mounded, zigzag-striped trade blanket Dallas had used for a bedroll.

The breeze brushed the grass around him, and a couple

of magpies were skulking and mewling in a wind-gnarled cedar.

"He have a family?" Cuno asked while he tossed another load into the hole and Serenity adjusted the cross with a bunch-lipped grunt. "The man never talked to me about anything but mules and wagons. Most I ever heard him say at one time was in the bunkhouse, just before he died, grievin' over Schotzy."

"He told me one night, when whiskey made him downright chatty, that he had a ma in Chugwater. Said she raised chickens, and that's about all I ever knowed about Dallas . . . 'cept he liked that pretty little mulatto whore, Lillyanna, in Crow Feather." Serenity chuckled and straightened, his knees creaking.

"If we get outta this, I'll get his pay to her."

"If we get outta this—shit!"

Breathing hard, his old 1862 Colt Trapper model hanging off his hip in its soft, clay-colored holster, and his Colt Paterson wedged behind his cartridge belt, pressed against his belly, Serenity looked around cautiously. He nibbled the ends of his ragged gray mustache.

"I got me a feelin' that before the sun rises again—hell, maybe before the moon comes up tonight—there ain't gonna be one white man within a hundred square miles of this boil on the devil's ass. It's apparent to this yellow-toothed squaw dog that ole Dancin' Wolf sent for a whole heap more Utes and maybe even smoked the peace pipe with a few colicky Crows."

It was sunny and clear, and a good thermometer would probably register the low fifties. The valley rolled out to the west, incredibly clear in the cool saffron light, to a steep-walled mesa still pushing out a slight shadow now at ten o'clock in the morning. In the north and south, many distant peaks loomed blue in the far distance, like summer rain clouds.

In the east, the high mountain wall, Old Stone Face, stood tall and vast, almost too much to take in from a half mile out from its base. The ridge was high enough to tickle low cloud bellies. It was bald except for tough, light green shrubs and cedars curling up from the rock-strewn troughs. The talus slides that Cuno could see from this angle appeared thumbnail-sized but were likely several acres square.

He sleeved sweat from his forehead and looked west again, at the ranchstead sitting a hundred yards away, resembling a child's collection of toy buildings nestled at the base of the mountain, with the gold-leafed aspens and cottonwoods following the curve of the creek at the yard's west edge. Smoke rose from the lodge's several chimneys, and Cuno wondered how Michelle was faring.

He no longer harbored any animosity toward the girl. He felt deeply, genuinely sorry for her. He'd have given anything if she'd been able to live out her life holding to the convictions she'd espoused over last night's supper—in spite of how they'd piss-burned him at the time—than to have them so abruptly, savagely disproved.

"You got better eyes than me," Cuno said as he resumed tossing dirt into Snowberger's grave. "You see anything out there?"

Serenity stood, slowly turning his head from right to left and back again, his jaws moving as he nibbled his mustache. "Nah. I don't see shit, and I don't expect to. We won't see shit till Dancin' Wolf is good and ready for us to see shit. Then it's gonna *storm* shit!"

Cuno sunk the shovel blade into the mound of freshly turned dirt once more. "You're a dark son of a bitch, old-timer. Remind me to fire you when we get back to Crow Feather and hire a freighter with a sunnier disposition."

The graybeard chuckled caustically and shook his head as he continued scanning the distance. "When we get back to Crow Feather—!"

"I know, I know—*shit*!"

When he'd finished filling in Snowberger's grave and mounding it with rocks, he and Serenity picked up their rifles leaning against a nearby boulder, cast a parting glance at their partner's resting place, and started back toward the ranch yard. Cuno set his rifle on one shoulder, the shovel on the other shoulder, and spat dust from his lips.

"The way I see it," he said, "you and me are on our own. Trent's men are madder'n old wet hens, and they're used to bein' the cock of the walk out here. They're long on rage and short on sense."

"That's how I see it, too," Serenity said. "And if any of 'em have ever fought Injuns before, they done forgot it ain't like fightin' white men. It's more like fightin' a pack of hungry wolves on open ground."

"In other words, we watch each other's backs."

"I've got yours if you got mine." The oldster snorted with an air of manufactured optimism. "I reckon I got lucky there, since yours is a whole lot bigger than mi—!"

He and Cuno jerked their heads up with a start as a gopher rose up from its hole, wringing its ratlike paws and scolding the two intruders raucously.

"Ah, shut up, ya little snipe," Serenity barked, kicking dirt. "As if my nerves ain't shot enough!"

He shook his head, sucked a deep breath into his spindly chest, adjusted the Colt Paterson over his belly, and continued walking as well as talking. "We best make every shot count. Even with all that ammo we brought in, we're liable to run out if them red devils play cat and mouse with us. They'll likely try to draw our fire the way the Sioux did to my freight outfit in the Big Horns six years ago last October. When we're close to shot-out, and our nerves are so fried that we're shootin' at every breeze and bird chirp, they'll close like a friggin' twister. And that little dustup earlier'll look like a Fourth of July rodeo parade!"

Cuno adjusted the shovel on his shoulder and gave his old partner a wry, sidelong glance. "So you're sayin' our odds are a mite long?"

"Long?" Serenity chuckled as they strode between two haystacks, approaching the eerily quiet yard. "Long as the teeth on a fifty-year-old whore, amigo!"

Cuno stopped abruptly and stared west through the cottonwoods.

"What is it?"

"Look there."

A long mare's tail of dust rose beyond the trees, from a hundred yards out across the tumbling hills of the valley. Faintly, the dull, muffled rumble of distant hooves sounded, and a horse whinnied.

"Hellkatoot!" Serenity rasped.

A horse appeared, and then another, galloping out from behind a low hill and following a long curve in the trail toward the ranch yard. Three more horses followed the first two in a shaggy line—a couple of duns, a paint, a bay, and a short, bucket-headed buckskin. Cuno recognized all five horses from the corral in which Trent kept his working remuda.

He squinted at the five mounts curving off toward his right, heading for the portal and the bridge. The horses were riderless, but long packs appeared to be strapped over their saddles. "What the hell are they . . . ?"

He and Serenity figured out what the horses were carrying at the same time, and both men lurched into jogs, cleaving the gap between the bunkhouse and the cook shack where a couple of drovers sat on upended logs, smoking and drinking coffee, one dabbing at a wound on his cheek with a handkerchief.

"Hey," the wounded man snarled, turning his head toward the freighters with an angry start. "Where're you two goin' in such a damn . . . ?"

"I do believe your friends are back," Serenity said through ragged breaths as he and Cuno passed the two loafers and headed into the hard-packed ranch yard.

"*Company!*" someone yelled from a corral behind the blacksmith shop.

Two hands leapt down from the corral west of the shop, where they'd apparently been posted to keep watch with new rifles, jumped into the yard suddenly, and sprinted west. A couple of other men filtered out of the stables and the bunkhouse as the horses thundered into the yard, sweat-lathered and wide-eyed, the buckskin and one dun buck-kicking savagely and crow-hopping as if to rid themselves of the bundles on their backs.

"Grab 'em!" roared the big, bearded blacksmith, Hahnsbach, reaching for the dun's reins. He wore a black leather apron over his buckskin breeches, and the sleeves of his linsey tunic were rolled up to his bulging biceps.

The men were shouting now, and the horses were whinnying and the mules were braying inside the stables. Cuno had set his rifle and shovel down against the bunkhouse. He rushed the buckskin suddenly and grabbed its reins up close to its bit. The end of the reins had been tied around its saddle horn.

"Ay-yi," Serenity said, crumpling his face as he moved up to the buckskin's right side.

A body dangled across the saddle, gloved fingertips nearly brushing the ground. A three-inch, hide-wrapped braid curled up over the back of the dead man's head. Two arrows protruded from his back. What had caught the brunt of Cuno's attention was the top of the man's head, which was as red as freshly butchered beef where the scalp had been hastily sliced and ripped away.

"Son of a bitch!" Hahnsbach cried when he, too, saw the grisly cargoes strapped to the back of each of the five horses. Just loudly enough to be heard above the hoof stomps and chuffs and frightened knickers, he added, "Murderin' *savages*!"

Cuno knelt down beside the buckskin and lifted the chin of the man draped across its back. The blood-smeared face and half-closed eyes and slack-jawed mouth of Henry Kuttner stared back at him, salt-and-pepper hair curling along the sides of his hacked-up head.

Feeling as though he'd been punched in the gut, Cuno released the foreman's chin, letting it slap back down against the buckskin's latigo strap, and straightened. He looked around at the other horses, all carrying arrow-pierced dead men surrounded by ten or so drovers and the Chinese cook, all regarding the grisly cargoes with looks ranging from disbelief to rage.

No one said anything.

The men, some holding the reins taut, moved slowly around the horses. The horses stomped and blew and fidgeted nervously. Flies had found the blood, the coppery stench of which filled the mild late-morning air. They swarmed loudly over the bodies and the bristling arrows.

A half dozen magpies swooped over the horses, cawing hungrily.

There was a gagging sound. Cuno turned to see the big blacksmith, Hahnsbach, bent at the waist and upchucking his breakfast into the freshly churned dirt. No one else said anything; they just sidestepped around the horses or stood dumbfounded beside the dead men, scratching their heads and trying to wrap their minds around what their eyes were telling their brains.

Distant shuffling footsteps sounded.

Cuno raked his gaze from the body of Henry Kuttner hanging slack down the buckskin's side to the big lodge sitting bathed in clear golden sunshine at the mountain's base, smoke still unspooling from its big stone chimneys.

Logan Trent was making his way down from the house, limping and dragging one boot heel. He was dressed as he'd been dressed last night, in baggy denims with a clawhammer coat over a doeskin tunic embroidered in red and blue thread. From his broad hips hung a Colt Long Cylinder conversion with pearl grips and a big bowie knife in an elaborately beaded buckskin sheath. On his curly, silver head he wore a black stovepipe hat boasting a red-tailed hawk feather.

He came on grimly, the lump on the side of his nose looking larger today than it had yesterday. His eyes were pinched and dark. He raked his gaze across the horses, and his men sort of shuffled back away from him slightly, looking somehow guilty and dread-filled.

The rancher stopped at the edge of the grouped horses, his back to the hulking, sun-blasted lodge, brown hands on his hips. His flat chest rose and fell heavily, and his mouth was a long knife slash beneath his silver mustache.

The horses blew and stomped, and the flies buzzed.

Behind Trent, a young boy ran out on the lodge's front porch. The woman who'd driven the wagon into the yard earlier gave a shriek, bounded out after the boy, and dragged him back inside, slamming the door loudly behind them, the wooden bang not reaching the lower ranch yard till a full second later.

Trent didn't look back. He continued to rake his brooding, angry gaze across the frightened horses.

Finally, his gaze holding on the buckskin that Cuno stood beside, he moved up to the horse, bent low, and lifted Kuttner's head by the fringe of rawhide-wrapped braid at the back.

Trent worked his jaws from side to side, and his eyes glinted angrily. "Henry, damn you. How could you let this happen, you son of a bitch?"

"Easy, Trent," Cuno said, barely able to contain his own rage.

If the scalpings and killings were anyone's fault, it was Trent's. He'd lived in this country long enough to know better than to send men after the raiding Indians. He should have known they'd ride into a massacre.

The old rancher was off his nut. Too many long winters. Too much time alone out here.

"Goddamn you, Henry!" Trent raged, glowering down at Kuttner's scalped head. The rancher removed his hat and swiped it hard across the foreman's head and shoulders. *"How could you do this to me?"*

Cuno stepped forward. "Trent."

The rancher continued to pummel his foreman's bloody head.

"Trent!" Cuno grabbed the man by his coat lapels and shoved him straight back. "If you wanna blame someone for this, blame yourself."

Trent's face swelled with rage. "Unhand me, young firebrand, or I'll—"

Trent tripped over his own feet and he would have fallen if Cuno hadn't held him upright. When he saw that the rancher had regained his balance, Cuno let him go but he stood there, only two feet away from him, staring up into the taller man's gray eyes with challenge.

Trent's eyes sparked with untrammeled fury, and he started to raise a fist when one of the other men shouted, *"Boss!"*

Cuno and Trent whipped their heads around to see the man pointing across the corral of milling ranch horses. Cuno's throat tied itself in a knot when he saw five braves sitting five short-legged, broad-barreled Indian ponies side by side across the main trail, on the near side of the ranch's wooden portal—close enough so that Cuno could see the sun reflecting off their heavily painted faces as well as the new Winchester repeaters in their hands.

13

INSTANTLY, CUNO AND the other men clawed their pistols from their hips and looked around wildly, expecting to find a horde of the red devils swarming onto them from all directions.

But there were only the five, sitting their war-painted ponies at the south edge of the ranch yard, staring with silent menace toward Cuno, Trent, Serenity, and the shuffling, exclaiming waddies.

As Cuno sidestepped toward the west edge of the yard, continuing to swing his cautious gaze in all directions, he got a better look at the five braves. All five were painted for war, with feathers braided into their long obsidian hair, which framed the brick-red ovals of their faces. They wore wolf or bear or coyote skins from head to their furry moccasins, though one brave wore patched denims.

Quivers bristling with feathered arrows jutted up from behind their necks, bows were slung over their shoulders, and war clubs dangled down their thighs. But in their hands, resting butt down against their hips, were the Winchester rifles they'd taken off Kuttner and the other men they'd recently killed. The smooth, freshly varnished stocks and oiled receivers glistened in the cool, high-country sun.

"Oh, for chrissakes," Trent groaned.

Instantly, Cuno saw what the rancher saw. From the barrels of the new Winchesters dangled five scalps, four in various shades of brown. The fifth one, of wavy pewter, had belonged to the foreman.

When the breeze jostled the grisly trophies, Cuno could see their bright red undersides.

His gut clenched, and he squeezed the ivory grips of his Colt in his right hand. The five were just out of pistol range, and Cuno and the ranch hands had all rushed into the yard with only their six-shooters.

Trent had edged up toward Cuno, making scuffing sounds in the dirt as he dragged his right boot, and, his big, pearl-gripped pistol cocked and extended in his right fist, he yelled at the Indians, "Where's Leaping Wolf?"

The Indians said nothing. They just stared brashly toward the ranch yard, their molasses-colored eyes unreadable within the bizarre rings of war paint. One of their ponies shook its head and blew. The wolf snout resting atop its rider's head jostled from side to side, dead jaws set in a perpetual snarl.

"I said, where's Leaping Wolf, you cow-eyed savages?" Trent quickly translated the question into Ute, or what Cuno took to be Ute, but repeated the trailing insult in English.

Trent's face and chest swelled. He adjusted his grip on the big conversion pistol in frustration as the five Indians merely stared back at him as though he weren't there.

Finally, one of the braves—a stocky Ute with high, ridged cheeks and wearing a bearskin tunic and Levis, with the cuffs stuffed down into high, brightly beaded doeskin moccasins trimmed with rabbit fur at the top—gave a grim smile. A couple of teeth appeared between his leathery lips. Then, in unison, all five swung their horses around, touched heels to flanks, and galloped west, heading back the way they'd come.

No doubt riding off to join the rest of their band hunkered down behind the near ridges, trapping the ranch hands and Trent and Cuno and Serenity at the base of Old Stone Face. With nowhere to run or hide even if they were inclined to.

The Utes' hoof clomps dwindled gradually. They rounded a second curve, about a hundred yards across the valley, and disappeared, their dust sifting behind them.

"Want we should go after them, Mr. Trent?"

It was one of the hands who, holding the reins of a dead rider's horse in one hand, his Smith & Wesson .44 in the other, narrowed a sharp eye at his employer, unshaven cheeks lifting with an oily smile.

"There's only five," the waddie added. "We could catch 'em before they rejoin their group."

Trent said nothing. He continued staring after the braves for a long time. Then, as though awakening from a trance, he cast his faintly chagrined, coyote-like glance at the hands staring at him expectantly.

Trent didn't look at the man who'd spoken, however. He raised his voice to the group. "Grab your rifles and spread out. Make a complete circle around the ranch yard, anywhere there's cover. Use two quick shots to signal an attack."

"What about the dead men, Mr. Trent?" asked the ex-army surgeon, Riker. "Shouldn't we bury 'em?"

"We'll bury 'em tomorrow," Trent growled as he wheeled awkwardly on his bad leg and started up the grade toward the lodge. He stopped so suddenly that he almost tripped over his bad leg and drilled that owly gaze at Cuno. "Massey." He jerked his head toward the house. "We got an important matter that needs discussin'."

He turned again and continued limping on up the grade.

Cuno glanced at Serenity, frowning.

"Now, what'd you do?" the graybeard asked.

Cuno hiked a shoulder. "Maybe he doesn't like the rifles, 'specially when they end up in the hands of the Injuns."

As the others, including Serenity, began cutting the dead men out of their saddles, Cuno tramped to the bunkhouse for his rifle. He brushed dust and hay flecks from the '73's scratched stock and octagonal barrel, then set the rifle across his shoulder and headed back into the yard.

The magpies were winging over the dead men whom the living men were dragging into the stables as they looked edgily around for more Indians, muttering amongst themselves, snarling like coyotes starting to turn on themselves.

There would be a bloodbath soon. The Utes had gathered their cards and were waiting around, probably just out of sight in the valley, to play their final hand. No point in hurrying. Why not let the white eyes sweat a good, long time before they gave up their topknots?

Cuno walked slowly up to the house, looking around and listening, seeing nothing but sunlight and sage and occasional dust devils when the cool breeze stirred. When he got close to the house, he could hear a woman's voice upstairs—probably that of the woman who'd brought the kids in earlier.

"That's Mrs. Lassiter. She's upstairs with Michelle."

Cuno stopped in his tracks and dropped his eyes from one of the upstairs windows to the porch. Trent sat in a deep wicker chair, skinny legs crossed, smoking a briar pipe.

He had a stone mug of coffee and a small uncorked bottle of rye whiskey on an overturned barrel beside him. Also on the barrel was his old conversion pistol. An 1860s-model single-shot buffalo rifle leaned against his chair—a long, heavy gun that probably fired a thumb-sized bullet of around seventy grains of gunpowder. Good at long range but overkill up close, and the breechloader was slow to reload.

"How is your daughter, Mr. Trent?" Cuno said, continuing onto the porch and climbing the steps.

Trent shook his head slightly, frowning and puffing his pipe. "I'm leaving her to Mrs. Lassiter. Can't bear to go up there now myself. Poor girl's never experienced such horror. Have a chair. Would you like a cup of coffee? Run done made some fresh. I like it with a jigger of rye these days. Takes the sting out of my hip, no thanks to a green-broke stallion I, at my age, never should have been trying to finish off in the first place."

"No, thanks." Cuno crossed in front of Trent and moved to the far west edge of the porch, from where, through some scattered cottonwoods and cedars, he could see past a hayfield to the open valley beyond. "My stomach's feeding on itself the way it is."

Trent chuckled—a low, slow rumbling.

Cuno glanced over his shoulder at the man. "Isn't yours?"

"Of course." Trent frowned angrily now, that knot alongside his nose swelling. "A man'd be a fool not to be afraid with them Injuns on the lurk. They're out they're waitin'. I can smell 'em. Leapin' Wolf's band and several other bands he probably called in from Wyoming. Gonna give us white eyes our just deserts."

Trent chuffed a laugh again and he lowered his eyes bemusedly. What the hell was he laughing at? Cuno wondered. Cuno saw little to laugh at. In fact, since watching Trent's daughter mauled on Trent's own kitchen table, he'd found nothing to laugh about this morning at all.

Cuno turned his head back westward. His eyes saw Indians in every rock shadow and breeze-jostled twig. His palms were perpetually sweaty. "You said you wanted to talk to me, Trent."

Behind him, only silence. Cuno turned to see the rancher staring solemnly west. Not like he was seeing anything except maybe a memory or two. Maybe memories of when he first came to this country and beat this ranch out of the brush.

Cuno said, "Trent?"

The rancher turned to him slowly, his gray eyes glassy. Suddenly, he blinked, and recognition returned to his gaze. He removed his pipe from his teeth, knocked the dottle onto the wide-boarded floor, and lifted the coffee mug from the table.

"What would you say to hitchin' up one of your wagons and getting my daughter and the Lassiter kids the hell out of here?"

"Out of here?" Cuno almost laughed. The man really was crazier than a tree full of owls. "You're hemmed in by Indians on three sides, might even be some behind the house. Even if you aren't totally surrounded, in case you haven't checked recently, you've got one hell of a high granite ridge behind you. The only way outta here is to fly, and my wagons haven't sprouted any wings."

Trent sipped his coffee, then sucked the moisture off his mustache. "There's a way through the ridge about one mile north. About six years ago, an earthquake widened a natural cleft. Slid the mountain apart like Moses partin' the Red Sea. Just wide enough for a wagon and a team of mules. Once you're through the cleft, you still got a piece o' work ahead of you, climbing and windin' through the Rawhides, but you can make it with the wagons. I'll draw you a map."

"Where might we be heading?"

"I want you to get my daughter and the Lassiter kids over to Fort Jessup on the eastern slopes of the mountains. It ain't much of a fort, just what's left of a tradin' post, but the army usually keeps about fifty men and a Gatling gun there over the winter, to monitor the gold camps as well as the Injuns in this area."

Cuno studied the rancher. Trent stared back at him, and there was little of the folly that had been in his eyes a few moments ago. He looked clear, and he looked serious.

"I'll pay you," the old rancher added with a faint air of desperation. "A thousand dollars in addition to that draft I already wrote you. Cash."

"You don't think you have a chance here?"

Trent shook his head. "I know Leapin' Wolf. Made a truce with him 'bout fifteen years ago, after ten years of skirmishing with his cow-stealin' braves. He's a hard man. What my men did to his daughter . . ." Trent shook his head again, and his eyes turned dark as he cast his look westward again, across the valley toward the mesa. ". . . He hasn't even started to get even for that.

"You see," Trent added, stifling a belch, "his son was supposed to take Michelle out of here, so Leapin' Wolf could kill her in his own creative fashion and then send the parts back to me. One at a time, most like. If he'd done that, I might have been able to hold on to the ranch. But Leapin' Wolf failed, and that means he'll be back with every man he has—maybe tonight, maybe at first light tomorrow. And he won't leave a single log unburned or a brick uncharred."

Trent belched loudly and winced, pressing a fist to his chest.

"What he'd do to her if he got ahold of her, I don't even want to think about, young Massey. A bit ago, I almost went upstairs and put a bullet through her head to spare her the grief of what she's already been through and that which is comin'. But then, when I was talkin' with Runs-with-the-Ponies earlier, I remembered the fault in the mountain wall."

He turned his hard, sad, desperate eyes on Cuno. "It's a long shot. But here you got no shot at all."

14

CUNO WAS MORE than a little taken aback by the casualness with which Logan Trent spoke of putting his daughter out of her misery.

He studied the daffy old rancher as Trent splashed more whiskey into his coffee and chuckled. "Damn, if Run didn't overcook it again! This oughta thin it out." He chuckled again and set the bottle down beside the coffee mug.

Cuno swung around and planted his hands on the porch, gazing east along the side of the house, toward the weeds, cottonwoods, and brush slowly rising to the base of Old Stone Face.

"I don't know," he said, returning to the conversation at hand. "Trying to light out in those wagons seems mighty risky. We could get run down before we even make the cleft." He lifted his gaze up the steep side of the mountain strewn with rocks and boulders and spindly shrubs and pines. "Even if we make the high country, it's no doubt nearly winter up there. The wagons could get bogged down in deep snow, and we'd all freeze . . . or starve. I'd say those kids and your daughter have better odds here in the lodge."

"I disagree." Trent stared at Cuno gravely, holding his steaming mug on one slender thigh clad in worn, baggy denims. "You don't know Leaping Wolf. I do. He'll attack, and when he does, we're all going to think hell split wide and spit out a thousand howling demons."

Trent raised the mug at Cuno. "The Lassiter kids and Michelle have a better chance with you. As far as snow in the high country, it don't usually get socked in up there until late next month. You should be able to make the run in a week, if all goes well. If not, there's plenty of caves and abandoned trappers' cabins. You could hole up in those if you needed to wait out a squall or while you fixed a wagon wheel."

"Both wagons?"

"You'll need both in case you lose one, and to haul supplies, foodstuffs, and ammunition."

"Might have it easier on horseback."

"Michelle can't ride in her condition, and neither can the Lassister girl, Margaret." Trent shook his head. "A good mule skinner, and one who's also good with a forty-five, has a fair-to-middlin' chance of getting them through."

Cuno had already made up his mind that Trent was probably right, but something still held him back. "Look, Mr. Trent, I've never run from a fight. You're gonna need all the help you can get here . . ."

Trent shook his head and, with a long, fateful sigh, heaved himself to his feet and stood staring off toward the western ranch yard and the peeled pine corrals and cottonwoods beyond. "No, you don't owe me your life, Cuno. I appreciate the sentiment. Damn little of it in the house of late, as you saw last night. But if you stay here—any man who stays here—is going to die here.

"My men have no choice. They signed up to ride for the Double-Horseshoe brand. You're the best of all the men here with a team of mules and a gun, and I'm begging you to at least *try* to get my daughter and the Lassiter children to safety." Trent shook his head, and his voice suddenly sounded raspy. "Be a damn shame if they all burned up here on account of something my men did."

"You're sure it's not over, then?"

"I'm sure. He'll attack once more. Only once more. Probably make us wait the rest of the day, hit us tonight, after sundown. Really make us soil our drawers, waiting and imagining what his braves have in store for us."

Trent turned toward Cuno. He lifted the mug to his lips. His hand shook slightly as he sipped. "If you're of a mind, I'd like you to pull out at dusk. There'll be a moon, so you shouldn't have trouble finding the route. I'll map it out for you. Leaping Wolf will be watching the main trail out of here, and all routes through the western valley. He won't cover the cleft."

"What if you're wrong?"

Trent snorted, but he stared at Cuno with watery gray eyes that were pink around the rims, and his Adam's apple wriggled around in his leathery neck with barely restrained emotion. "Won't really make that much difference, will it?" A single tear rolled out from the rancher's right eye, curved along the growth on his nose, and dribbled down his ragged cheek. "But if it looks like you won't make it, I'd like you to promise me you'll end it quickly for Michelle."

"What if he hits before dusk?"

"You be ready to pull out at the drop of the hat, young firebrand. I'll have Mrs. Lassiter prepare the children."

"She won't be joining us?"

Trent shook his head and tapped his chest. "A fever a while back did something to her ticker. She'd never make it. Couldn't take the strain or the cold in the back of that wagon." Trent sipped his coffee and sagged back down in his chair, looking down again with that bewildered gaze he'd showed before. "I owe her this, poor woman. Saw 'em only 'bout three, four times a year, but her and her husband and me were friends. Damn few friends out here . . ."

It was a question that Cuno knew he shouldn't ask, but his curiosity got the better of him. "What happened to your wife, Mr. Trent? Where're the sons you mentioned last night?"

Trent looked up at him, blinked first one eye and then the other quickly, as though the question had taken him off guard. "Dead. One boy, Phillip, rolled his horse into a ravine. The other one fancied him a pistoleer. Logan Jr. Got liquored up, and a gambler shot him down deader'n a week-old side of bad beef in Ute. My wife had thinner blood than I, Cuno. She couldn't withstand such grief in addition to the general hardships of living out here with a singular old reprobate like myself. She walked out into a blizzard nigh on three years ago now. Didn't find her till spring—frozen rock hard as she sat against a tree, staring east at Old Stone Face."

Trent looked down at his empty cup, tilting it this way and that as though surprised to find it empty. "Strange the way things happen, after you've tried so damn hard for so damn long to carve a good life for yourself."

Cuno knew how the man felt. He often felt the same way. Now he felt a sudden, unexpected pang of sympathy for Logan Trent. He sensed the man's desperation. It was a catching feeling.

He glanced into the distance. The shadows were growing, and in every one he saw a flicker of movement—the Indians slowly closing in for their final act of vengeance.

Starting down the porch steps, Cuno said, "Serenity and I'll prepare the teams and wagons."

"Cuno?"

He turned back. Trent stood a little unsteadily before his chair. "You haven't yet promised me about that bullet for my daughter?"

Cuno sighed and ran a sleeve across his chin. He nodded. "All right."

He turned and continued down the hill toward the stables.

Cuno relayed the plan to Serenity. Incredulous and skeptical, the oldster said he'd rather take an arrow to the front than the back, but since loco old Trent figured on trying to save the shavetails and the girl, he'd throw in.

"Always did think it better for a man to die for a noble cause than how I figured I'd go," he added as he and Cuno walked toward the wagons.

"How'd you think you'd go?"

"I figured I'd die of a heartstroke in the ole mattress sack with a half-breed whore in Sonora somewheres." Serenity shrugged as he crouched down to inspect the tongue of one of the two surviving Conestogas. "I reckon this way is better. Not near as much fun, but better . . ."

Cuno leapt onto the side of one of the wagons, toeing the inch-wide ledge running along the edge of the bed. "We'll only take eight of the mules. Have to leave the other four behind."

"Why?"

"You know why. Lighter load. We won't need 'em. And it'll be a hell of a lot easier to run eight up those mountains than twelve."

"Ah, shit!" Serenity barked as he dragged a jack down from the swagger bed. "Grace is the best leader I got. I ain't leavin' her behind!"

"She's the only one who'll sleep with ya, too. Take any four you want, but we gotta leave four behind and you might as well get used to it."

Cuno didn't like the idea of leaving the mules, either. He'd paid thirty dollars apiece for them. Besides, any mule skinner worth his salt felt an affinity for his pullers. He got to know each one personally, knew their quirks and pulling habits and how much grain or grass each one needed. Knew what scared or thrilled them.

"Ah, hell," Serenity grouched. He dropped the jack and rolled up the sleeves of his buckskin tunic, eyeing the rim of the off-rear wheel, which needed reshaping and setting. "We're all wolf bait, anyways. Don't matter if we get it here or up in the mountains somewhere. And we got old Trent to thank for that."

Using a crowbar to loosen the cleats, Cuno removed the

top half of the wagon's side panel. Since they weren't hauling a thousand pounds of freight, but only the kids and trail supplies, they wouldn't need the top panels. They'd cut the wagons down to the size of army ambulances—lighter and easier to maneuver.

As Serenity continued yammering like an old coyote, Cuno looked down at him. "Shut up and get to work, old-timer."

Serenity looked up at him, slack-jawed. "What the hell's the matter with you?"

Cuno remembered the desperation and utter befuddlement in Trent's eyes, and it made him owly and sick to his gut. "I'm trying to work, but I can't even hear myself think with all your jawin'."

When he'd removed the top right side panel, he removed the left, and then went to work on the other wagon, removing those panels, as well. They probably wouldn't need both wagons, but they'd take both, anyway, in case they lost one in the mountains. Also, if push came to shove, they might need the spare one for parts . . . or mules.

When he and Serenity had made sure all the wheels, felloes, rims, axles, and brakes were sound, they attached heavy log chains from the front axles to the doubletrees on both wagons for sharp cornering. Then they hauled all the tack including hames and collars outside, into the shade of the stables, and sat on a long wooden bench, soaping and repairing all the harness leather.

Meanwhile, an eerie silence had settled over the ranch compound. All the able men except Riker, who remained in the bunkhouse with the wounded, were hunkered down in a long semicircle around the western perimeter of the ranchstead, from north to south, bundled against the air's crisp autumn edge in their mackinaws and blanket coats, some in coonskin or rabbit hats with earflaps, keeping watch with their new Winchester repeaters.

Some had turned over hay wagons or were crouched behind boulders, rock piles, and trees. Several were holed up in the creek bottom. Occasionally, Cuno caught a whiff of cigarette or cigar smoke wafting toward him from the cottonwoods, or he heard the low, brief rumble of an argument caused by strained nerves.

Except for the breeze stirring dust in the sunlit yard, there was very little movement. Two or three times every hour, one of the men, clad in a heavy coat and carrying his Winchester, would slog grimly back to the bunkhouse for a fresh cup of coffee or a sandwich.

But mostly the ranch was as quiet as a cemetery in a long-abandoned churchyard.

The only sign of the waiting Indians, who were probably holed up a couple of hundred yards out from the ranch, were three smoke puffs rising in the northwest, about a half mile away. It was a signal of some kind, and Cuno, watching it, felt the blood spurt in his veins and the hair stand up beneath his coat collar.

"What's that mean, you s'pose?" Cuno said, running a heavy, greased needle through a bridle seam.

"I look Injun to you?"

"I thought you knew everything."

"I'm tryin' to work here," the graybeard grouched edgily, oiling a harness strap. "Can't even hear myself think with all your jawin'!"

Later, one of the men, hearing a rustle in some wild mahogany, mistook a young mule deer buck for an Indian and shot it three times before he realized what he was shooting at. The man took some ribbing by the other men, and Trent ordered him to carve the badly chopped up deer, and load it into the wagons to supplement the wagon party's food provisions.

An hour before dusk, Cuno and Serenity had the wagons ready. The mules were leathered up and hitched to the doubletrees. Renegade was saddled and tied to the back of Cuno's outfit. The skewbald paint would be used, as Cuno always used him, for scouting.

The freighters had outfitted the wagon with a month's

worth of food and trail supplies and plenty of skins, robes, and quilts to ward off the high-country cold. They also packed one extra Winchester and several boxes of ammo.

At dusk, Trent came out from the house carrying his old buffalo rifle over his shoulder. He reeked of booze but he looked no drunker than before. Cuno and Serenity were eating jerky and drinking coffee on the open tailgate of one of the wagons.

"You fellas ready?"

Cuno nodded. Trent had brought down a hand-drawn map earlier, and he, Cuno, and Serenity had gone over it thoroughly.

"Drive around to the back of the house. I'll have the young'uns waiting by the back door. In a half hour, the hands're gonna start a fire on the other side of the creek, give the Injuns somethin' to ponder while you're headin' northeast along the mountain toward the canyon that'll take you to the gap."

With that, Trent looked around warily, squinting his rheumy eyes beneath the brim of his shabby, feather-trimmed opera hat. Then he limped back up the hill to the house sitting dark and silent, its chimneys spewing gray smoke against the near-dark sky.

It was full dark when Cuno and Serenity swung their wagons up the slope behind the Trent lodge, Renegade tied to the rear of Cuno's Conestoga. The house was dark and the ghostly figures of Trent, the Lassiter woman, the two boys, the young blond girl, Margaret, the Mexican whose name Cuno hadn't learned, and Michelle Trent stood huddled in blankets near a large cottonwood.

The cold wind blew and Cuno could hear the blond girl and the smallest boy sobbing. Trent stood with an arm wrapped around his daughter.

Michelle held a buffalo robe around her shoulders and for a moment Cuno remembered the first time he'd seen her, soaking wet on the stairs and wrapped in a similar garment. She'd been worried that Cuno wouldn't return to the lodge to entertain her father.

So much had happened in the past twenty-four hours that last night seemed months ago. She'd been brutalized by Leaping Wolf's braves, and her well-heeled beau, Jedediah Gallantly, had died miserably in his silk longhandles with an arrow through his gut.

"Momma, I don't want to leave you," the young blonde sobbed as Cuno drew the first wagon up beside the group and pulled the brake handle back.

"Margaret, you hush. We had this talk."

Mrs. Lassiter's voice was stern, but there was a brittleness to it that betrayed the woman's terror as well as her own reluctance to part with her children whom she likely would never see again. But she was strong, and she knew what they had to do. If her last words to her children were coldly commanding, so be it.

Cuno climbed down out of the driver's box and grabbed a couple of the carpetbags standing around the base of the cottonwood. He looked at Michelle Trent as her father led her to the back of the wagon.

She moved as though in a dream, not saying anything as her father whispered into her ear, then suddenly stooped, picked her up his arms, and with a wince against the pain in his bum leg, lifted her up into the back of the wagon box.

Michelle said nothing. She unwrapped her arms from around her father's neck, turned, and sat quickly down amongst the robes and blankets padding the floor and the sides of the box. She drew her knees up to her chest, hugging them, and held her head forward, staring out from beneath the flat brim of a man's bullet-crowned hat.

The hat was tied to her head with a thick, red scarf. She wore a heavy blanket coat over a simple traveling dress and low-topped, lace-up black boots. Beneath the hem of the dress several layers of underwear showed.

The Mexican girl, oddly silent and grimly purposeful, climbed into the box and sat down beside Michelle, arranging a couple of buffalo robes over them both as well as the sobbing Margaret. The Mexican girl was dressed as before in layers with a long, denim coat and several wool skirts, a red neckerchief, and her floppy-brimmed hat tied to her head with a green scarf. On her feet were fur-trimmed knee-high moccasins.

As Cuno loaded the bags into the wagon—they'd reserved Serenity's wagon for the trail supplies, allowing plenty of room in Cuno's for the passengers—he saw Trent standing at the Conestoga's open tailgate, staring along the box at his daughter.

He seemed to want to say something but couldn't come up with the words. Finally, as Mrs. Lassiter's boys climbed reluctantly into the box, the rancher backed away from the tailgate in a shuffling, halting gait and ran a handkerchief across his nose.

When all the children were aboard the wagon and Mrs. Lassiter was issuing her last orders over the side panel, Trent grabbed Cuno's arm. In his other hand he held up a burlap pouch.

"This is all the cash I have here at the ranch. Fifty-five hundred dollars. There's a thousand for yourself and Mr. Parker, upon your arrival at Fort Jessup. The rest is for my daughter. Also in the pouch is a letter to my sister in Cleveland, explaining the situation in case Michelle is still unable to explain it herself. Mildred will take Michelle in and give her a home. Please see that she gets the letter and the money."

Cuno took the pouch. "She'll get both, Mr. Trent." Cuno glanced at Michelle still sitting and staring as before beside the dark-haired girl. "I take it she's . . ."

"She won't say a thing. Just stares off as though seeing those savages that ravaged her. I don't know if she even knows what's going on. Mrs. Lassiter's hired girl has promised to look after her."

"What's the hired girl's name?"

Trent shook his head quickly. "I forget. Some orphaned half-breed out of Mexico. Dime a dozen around here. She'll help with Michelle. It might be best if she doesn't wake up from this nightmare until you arrive at Fort Jessup."

"Don't worry, Trent. She'll be all right." Cuno heard the lack of conviction in his own voice, but it seemed the appropriate thing to say.

The rancher drew a deep breath, the air rattling in his chest as though several ribs had cracked from sheer emotional strain. "Good luck, Cuno. Farewell. If you get them through, I'll be smilin' down on you . . . bald-headed as I may very well be!"

As Mrs. Lassiter hugged her sons and daughter once more, and the hired girl and Michelle sat placidly against the wagon box, Cuno climbed up onto the Conestoga's driver's seat. The little girl, Margaret, was still crying, and Mrs. Lassiter and the boys were crying now, too.

Behind them all, Serenity sat in his own driver's box, keeping a taut hold on his team's reins and staring around the house toward the open valley.

Cuno followed the graybeard's gaze. A bright glow shone south of the ranch yard, just beyond the creek and partially obscured by the breeze-jostled brush and trees. The ranch hands had lit the bonfire. It sent sparks and bayonet-shaped flames high in the air.

Renegade, standing a ways out from the rear of Cuno's wagon, stared at the flames and nickered worriedly.

"There's your signal," Trent said. He raised a small uncorked bottle in his hand. "Hurry on, gentlemen. Keep an eye out for the cleft. If we make it, I'll send a rider for you."

"Luck, Trent," Cuno said, releasing the brake and flicking the reins across the mules' backs.

The mules brayed.

Behind Cuno, the Lassiter children sobbed and called for their mother, who stood beside Trent, her shoulders jerking. The wagon lurched forward with a thundering rattle, and they were off.

15

CUNO ANGLED THE team toward the vast mountain wall looming on his right, following a shallow ravine that he hoped would muffle the rattle of the wagon and the clomps of the mules' hooves.

Occasionally he looked back over the wagon bed and the trailing skewbald paint to see Serenity pulling the second Conestoga along behind him, about twenty yards back of Renegade, starlight glistening off the oiled tack and metal fittings and off the graybeard's bristled cheeks.

It was good to have Serenity here. He'd hate to have to rely on only himself to get these kids safely across the Rawhides to Fort Jessup. Serenity knew the mountains and the Indians as well as he knew wagons and mules, and Cuno had more than a few times relied on the oldster's wily wisdom.

And he was a comforting, if cantankerous, companion. He and Cuno had been through a lot together.

Cuno kept his Winchester close beside him on the wagon's high seat. The slight knocks it made against the wood were as reassuring as the sound of Serenity's nickering mules and the occasional thud of a wagon wheel nudging a rock. Occasionally, the old man would cough, spit chaw into the brush, or rasp a soft command to his mules. The night was clear, and sound carried crisply on the cold, dry air.

The ravine walls dropped back behind Cuno, and the mountain wall angled toward him, the creased and crenelated slope rising about twenty yards to his right, strewn with boulders and troughs and brush snags.

As Trent had shown him on the map residing in Cuno's right tunic pocket, there was a wagon trail here—two pale lines cleaved by a swatch of spindly buckbrush and sage. It had been carved by Trent's men during roundups and woodcutting expeditions into the Rawhides, and it would lead them to the cleft that would, in turn, grant them passage into the greater range.

Cuno pulled the wagon onto the trail. As the Conestoga began moving straight north along the uneven line of the mountain's base, Cuno glanced to his left and then back toward the ranch headquarters.

Nothing but darkness interrupted by the sparse, starlight-limned shapes of cottonwoods, cedars, or boulders.

So far, so good.

Maybe the Indians wouldn't attack, after all. Maybe they'd done all the damage Leaping Wolf had intended and had headed on back to their lodges. In that case, this would be a short trip, and what a relief it would be to see one of Trent's riders coming for them in a day or two with news that the war was over.

Suddenly, there was a stirring in the box behind Cuno.

"Margaret, no!" one of the boys yelled.

"I want Momma!" A figure bounded up from the side of the wagon. It was the little blond Lassiter girl. As she scrambled toward the rear of the wagon, one of the boys reached for her.

"Margaret!" the hired Mexican girl called suddenly, bolting forward and throwing out one of her hands.

But Margaret, shedding blankets and a doll she'd been carrying, threw herself atop the tailgate, and before Cuno could begin to haul back on the mules' reins, she'd disappeared over the other side with a terrified, defiant wail followed by a thud as she hit the ground in front of Renegade, who shied away and nickered.

"Hold up, there, little miss!" Serenity yowled, planting his boots against the dashboard and hauling back on his ribbons.

Cuno cursed as he stopped his own team, quickly set the brake, and leapt over the left front wheel. He hit the ground flat-flooted and ran toward the back of the wagon while the boys scrambled toward the tailgate and continued calling for their sister.

Before he'd reached the rear wheel, a figure leapt over the tailgate and hit the ground in front of him. The Mexican girl turned to him sharply, her black hair flying out beneath her hat, and her brown eyes glistened sharply in the starlight.

"I will see to her," she said curtly, in a heavy Spanish accent.

Cuno watched her stride out to where little Margaret sat in the brush along the trail, one leg straight out in front of her, the other curled beneath her hip. She'd fallen when she'd tried to run back the way they'd come. The girl's mouth was thrown wide in a sob so shrill and filled with such inconsolable misery that it was nearly silent.

The Mexican picked Margaret up in her arms. "There, there, Margaret," the girl said. "Your mother will be along soon. But she won't come if you're going to act like a baby!"

"She's not coming!" Margaret nearly screamed, causing Cuno to wince and peer off into the eerily silent night, half expecting to see Utes, drawn by the scream, bearing down on him.

The Mexican girl moved back toward the wagon, hugging Margaret tightly. "No, she's not going to come if you act like a baby. Now, you hush and get back in the wagon. You don't want Leaping Wolf to catch us, now, do you?"

Cuno tripped the latch and dropped the tailgate.

"But she's *not* coming, Camilla!" Margaret retorted. "You *know* she's not!"

Camilla lifted Margaret onto the tailgate, then climbed up beside her. Her tone was at once reassuring and stern. "Now we must be very quiet. Come, let's get back under the robes and play a game."

Camilla drew Margaret back into the wagon box, the boys watching anxiously over their knees. Michelle stared indifferently into the night. Cuno closed the tailgate and latched it.

"Let's see how many stars we can count above the mountain, Margaret. Can you count with me in Spanish?" The girl called Camilla arranged the robes and blankets over Margaret's skinny legs. "I bet I can count more than you can, and even more than Jack and Karl."

"Hogwash, Camilla!" Margaret would have none of it as she lifted the edge of a robe up beneath her chin, shivering and staring back toward the still-dark ranch. "She's not coming. She's back there, and Leaping Wolf is going to get her, and we're never going to see her or Papa ever again!"

But the girl seemed resigned to sit in the wagon box between Camilla and her brothers. The hired girl wrapped an arm around the little blonde's spindly shoulders. When the boys, too, had settled back under the robes, Cuno glanced at Serenity waiting behind him.

He shook his head gravely at his old partner, then jogged back to the front of the wagon, scrambled up into the box, and they were off once more. Cuno slid the rifle onto his lap and balanced it there as he swung his gaze back and forth between the trail and the western darkness, expecting to see the silhouettes of rampaging Indians storming toward him at any moment, arrows whistling.

The uneven mountain wall moved forward and back on the right, and Cuno kept watching for the large cracked boulder and the lightning-topped pine that, according to Trent, marked the entrance to the gap that led to the mouth of the cleft.

To his left, he watched and listened for the Indians, resisting the urge to whip the mules into a run that would speed his approach to the gap but would also raise a din the Utes might hear.

Anxiety nipped at him. If the Indians came now, he and Serenity wouldn't have a chance against them.

Finally, the cracked boulder appeared. Just beyond, the lightning-topped pine. Between lay a gap as wide as two wagons.

Relieved that he hadn't somehow passed it, Cuno turned the mules into the canyon mouth and whipped the reins across their backs. One of the mules brayed. They all were skittish, not liking the uncertainty of the steep walls on either side and the inky darkness closing around them, relieved only by vagrant starlight.

"Pick it up there, El Paso!" Cuno called softly to the leader.

Removing his blacksnake from its holder, he cracked the whip over the team, the pop resounding like a rifle report in the close confines. In the box behind Cuno, Margaret gave a frightened sob. Camilla cooed to her, shushing her. The boys shifted around, thumping the wagon's floor and muttering to themselves.

Cuno glanced over his shoulder. Serenity's team was trailing close behind Renegade, who followed Cuno's wagon with his head and tail arched, no doubt sensing the humans' desperation.

The canyon angled back into the mountain, at times barely wide enough for one wagon, then opening again to a width of fifty or sixty yards. The floor was scalloped sand and gravel with occasional boulders fallen from above. The smell of minerals and bat guano clung to the cool air, and from one narrow, off-shooting cleft—too narrow to be the defile Cuno was looking for—he thought he heard a brief, distant mewl.

"Panther," muttered the eldest boy in the box.

"How do you know?" asked the other, his voice low but audible in the canyon's hushed silence.

"Heard one before when I was out with Pa . . ."

"Did not."

"Did, too!"

The Mexican girl hushed them both with a shrill *"Silencio!"*

Trent said the off-shooting gap they were looking for lay about two hundred yards within the box canyon, and that they couldn't miss it on the darkest night. Not necessarily a good thing, because it meant the Indians would find it, too. Cuno didn't want to get trapped in there with a horde of screaming Utes on his tail.

The thought had barely brushed across his brain when a shrill yip rose from the night behind him. Keeping the team moving at a brisk trot, occasionally cracking the whip, he turned his head and pricked his ears.

More yips rose, faint with distance. At first Cuno thought the muffled but raucous cries were the sounds of a hunting coyote pack, but as they grew louder and were joined by several sets of thudding hooves, he knew better.

A bayonet of dread poked at his gut. He looked behind. Serenity had heard the cries, as well, and was turned to gaze along their back trail. Cuno could see the tension in the old man's back and shoulders.

He turned toward Cuno, who could see only the man's gray sombrero and gray beard in the darkness. "Got me a suspicion they're onto us," he said in a flip tone that lifted gooseflesh across Cuno's back.

The young freighter swung his head forward. At the same time, a gap shone in the wall to his left—just wide enough for one wagon at a time. It was the gap they were looking for.

Cuno glanced at Serenity once more. "Found the crack," he said, his voice sounding louder than he'd intended, reverberating off the high, stone walls.

Cuno swung the team into the fault, having to use his blacksnake a few times until the lead mules had the wheelers inside the narrow gap, pulling. The air in the gap felt a good ten degrees colder than the air in the larger canyon.

The mules' shod hooves clomped loudly, echoing. The

wheels and the boards of the wagon bed clattered beneath the blankets and robes. Tools rattled in the box hanging beneath the swagger bed.

Cuno could still hear the eerie yips and yowls in the distance, and the thuds of galloping horses.

When Serenity had swung his own Conestoga in behind Cuno, Cuno's wagon approached a broad section of the cleft. The young freighter turned to look into the wagon bed behind him. "Which one of you boys wants to take the reins for me?"

Both boys sat against the right side of the wagon bed, the younger, blond kid's head only coming up to the older boy's ear. "I will," the young one said quickly.

The older boy, who had longish brown hair curling over his ears, beneath a heavy brown scarf securing his felt hat down tight on his head, chuffed and scrambled to his feet.

"I wanna do it, Karl!"

"I'm gonna let Karl drive first," Cuno said, his taut voice betraying his nerves. "I'll let you drive next time—okay, Jack? It is Jack, isn't it?"

Jack only frowned as his older brother climbed over the front of the box and into the driver's seat. The older boy was probably about five-four, and all arms, legs, hands, and feet, with his big ears protruding from the hand-knit scarf on his head.

"Drive a team before?" Cuno asked him, handing the boy the reins.

"Some," Karl said, looking at the leather ribbons in his mittened hands as though at a book he was having trouble deciphering.

Cuno grabbed his Winchester and sidled to the edge of the wagon. "Just keep 'em moving at an even pace. They're scared as hell in this pit, so the trick'll be to keep 'em moving. Shouldn't have to worry about them running away on you. Don't drop the reins, though, or you'll be in trouble."

Karl nodded as he wriggled around in the seat and stared straight out over the mules' jostling backs, his back straight and tense.

Cuno dropped to the floor of the defile and quickly untied Renegade's reins from the back of the Conestoga.

"What're you cipherin'?" Serenity said behind him. His voice was low and dark now. "Sounds to me like there's quite a damn few ridin' purty damn fast."

"I'm gonna ride back and give 'em somethin' to study on." Cuno led Renegade to the cleft's wall and swung into the saddle as Serenity drew up beside him. "Whatever you do, you keep the wagons moving."

"Yeah, it's way too early to stop fer a picnic," Serenity growled, shaking his ribbons across his mules' backs and continuing on down the defile.

16

CUNO HUNKERED LOW in the saddle as Renegade raced back the way they'd come down the narrow, gently winding defile. When they arrived at the main canyon, Cuno jerked the horse sharply right, and the skewbald paint dug its hooves into the scalloped sand and lunged down the canyon toward the mouth.

He could hear the Indians galloping toward him, hear the yips and yowls and the thuds of their racing horses—probably seventy yards away and closing fast. Cuno remembered a ledge protruding from the canyon's north wall. He raced toward it now—it looked like part of the sheer ridge had bulged outward, nearly separating from the rest, and on its crest sat a flat-topped boulder with a scrub cedar growing from a crack in its center.

Cuno swung Renegade toward the knob, then hauled back on the reins. He tossed the reins to the ground, slid his Winchester from the saddle boot, and rose out of the stirrups, placing his feet atop the saddle. He flung his rifle up onto the ledge, the crest of which was about six feet above his head.

"Stay, boy!"

The war cries of the approaching savages were growing louder. One of the Indians shouted a guttural command, and Renegade shook his head warily.

Cuno leapt straight up from the saddle, grabbed a stone knob protruding from the ridge wall, and pulled himself up. He dug a boot into a crack, thrust the other into another crack, and seconds later he was hoisting himself over the top of the knob and scooping up his Winchester.

He dropped to a knee and, quietly racking a shell into the rifle's breech, stared up canyon. The chasm was a light cream swath of sand between velvet black ridge walls vaguely defined here and there by starlight.

Down the middle of the swath, the Indians galloped, four or five jostling silhouettes of horses and long-haired riders clad in animal hides and skins. Starlight winked off rifle barrels and knives and spear blades. Their shadows slid along the pale canyon floor beside them. The Indians sounded like a pack of hungry wolves determined to chill the blood of their prey before they made the final, killing lunge.

Cuno hadn't known how many Utes were trailing him. Half of Leaping Wolf's lighthorsemen might have been back here.

He stayed low until the two lead riders were thirty yards away and closing fast, their horses chuffing, the Indians' yowls echoing eerily around the canyon. Then, remaining on one knee, Cuno raised the rifle to his shoulder, lined up the sights on one of the two lead riders, and squeezed the trigger.

The rifle cracked sharply, loudly, echoing.

One Indian's yowling died abruptly, replaced by a strangled sound. He flew back off his pony's right hip to hit the canyon floor with a thud, his bow clattering against the rocks at the base of the ridge wall behind him.

Cuno's Winchester roared again, leaping and bucking against his shoulder, flames stabbing from the octagonal barrel. The second lead rider screamed shrilly as he tumbled straight back off his lunging pony's butt. One of the three pursuing riders chopped the wounded brave up beneath his horse's hammering hooves. Then, he, too, was blown off his mount's back.

Cuno stood as the trampled brave screamed and groaned and, ejecting the spent brass while seating a fresh one, fired four more quick rounds from his right hip, cocking and firing, cocking and firing, the cartridge casings clinking off the rocks around him.

When all five Indian ponies had galloped up canyon, whinnying and nickering and buck-kicking angrily, and the five braves lay in rumpled, dark heaps, unmoving on the canyon floor, sheathed in wafting powder smoke, Cuno turned and scrambled back down the escarpment.

Renegade had shifted position, sidestepping skittishly at the racket. Cuno whistled. The horse stepped toward the scarp, turning slightly. Cuno dropped down the wall and into the saddle with a grunt of expelled air. Sliding his Winchester into the saddle boot, he leaned forward, grabbed up the reins, and turned Renegade up canyon.

He caught up to the wagons a minute later as they cleaved the narrow chasm, rattling and rocking, hooves clomping like cracked bells on the uneven stone floor.

"Jumpin' Jehoshaphat!" Serenity bellowed as Cuno put Renegade up beside the graybeard's driver's seat. "You're like to give me a heartstroke, comin' up on me like that. I thought you was one o' them Injuns!"

"There were five. I got the jump on 'em."

"I heard the shootin'. Figured someone got the jump on someone." Serenity shook his head wearily and sleeved sweat from his brow. "Only five, you say?"

"They must have heard us outside the canyon and savvied our plan. There'll likely be more, but our back trail's clear for now."

"Any shootin' from back toward the ranch?" Serenity called as Cuno gigged Renegade up along the other wagon, heading for the driver's box.

"Not yet."

Cuno knew the old graybeard wanted to shout, "That

don't mean there won't be some soon!" but he held his tongue in deference to the children and the two older girls.

Cuno dallied his reins around his saddle horn, then stepped fluidly out of his stirrups and, grabbing the side of the driver's seat, onto the wagon. Renegade would keep pace with the freighters not only because Cuno had trained him well but because of the trouble the horse knew was behind them.

"How you doing, Karl?" he asked the older Lassiter boy, tensely sitting the driver's box. He held the reins loosely, though, not all balled up like a greenhorn would do, jerking them this way and that.

"All right, I reckon," the boy said. "Heard shootin'."

Cuno saw no reason to mince words. He was close enough to Karl's age to remember how much he'd hated being lied to for his own good.

"Five Injuns caught our scent." Cuno took the reins from the boy. "They're not on it anymore."

"That's Margaret's fault, I 'spect," Karl said, keeping his voice low, the hoof clomps and the clatter of the wagons echoing off the walls around them. "The girl never could keep her mouth shut, mister . . ."

"Cuno. Cuno Massey. Don't cotton to bein' called mister. It sounds like folks are addressing my old man, and he's been dead now nearly four years."

Karl swallowed as he stared out over the mules' dark, bobbing heads. "Them bastard Injuns killed my old man. Hit him with a war club, then stuck him with a lance."

"It ain't easy, losing your pa. Especially when you seen it happen right out in front of you."

Karl glanced at Cuno, and the boy's rawboned features with blunt nose and close-set eyes were drawn taut as a drumhead. He had a thumb-shaped birthmark on the nub of his right cheek and several red pimples spread across his forehead. "That how yours died?"

Cuno nodded.

"Injuns?"

Cuno shook his head. "One was a white man but more

vicious than all those sons o' bitches behind us put together. The other was a half-breed named Sammy Spoon."

"Did the law track 'em?"

Just then rocks tumbled down the wall just ahead and left and shattered on the cleft floor. "Whoa!" Cuno said, drawing back on the reins and standing up in the driver's box, hand on his pistol grips.

As the wagon rocked to a halt, a faint keening whine rose from the sloping ridge. Another rock dropped and broke on the ground before the mules. The team jostled around in their traces, and one brayed, but Cuno held taut to the reins.

He released his pistol's grips. "Bobcat, sounds like."

"Sounds that way to me," Karl said.

"Sounded like a panther," the younger Lassiter boy said behind them, his voice hushed and conspiratorial.

"Shut up, Jack," Karl said.

"You shut up!"

There was a smacking sound, and Cuno chuckled ruefully. The Mexican girl, Camilla, had rendered the argument stillborn with a quick, resolute slap to the side of Jack's head. There was a soft, plaintive "Ouch!" and then silence.

Cuno looked behind his own wagon at Serenity. The graybeard sat his driver's seat tensely, staring up the ridge.

"Cat," Cuno said just loudly enough for his partner to hear.

Then he shook the reins across the mules' backs, and the wagon rolled forward once more.

The cleft opened and closed around the wagons. In several places, Cuno saw rock and boulder snags blasted to bits by Trent's men, who'd kept the passage open for wood-hauling expeditions into the mountains. In a couple of places over the next couple of hours, he and Serenity had to lever with jacks and crowbars three recently fallen boulders out of the passage.

About three hours after they'd started into it, the cleft opened on a wide, boulder-and-cottonwood-stippled wash bathed in the light of the recently risen moon. In the milky light, steam snaked up from the mules' backs, and their breath jetted from their nostrils and around their heads.

Cuno and Serenity pushed the teams across the wash, negotiating boulders and fallen cottonwoods and scrub cedars. When they'd reached the other side and found a passage—a broad, intersecting wash—that rose gradually into the mountains, they halted the wagons and unhitched the mules for water and rest.

They picketed the mules amongst a few leafless cottonwoods growing around a spring-fed pool furred with ice. Leaving Serenity to tend the animals, Cuno walked back to the bivouac. He'd put Karl and Jack to work gathering wood and digging a small fire pit, but the girls had stayed inside the wagon, half buried beneath the quilts and hides.

When he'd checked on the boys' progress with the fire, he strode over to the wagons parked in the shadow of a giant boulder, tongues hanging. Inside, Margaret sat on Camilla's lap, her blond head resting against the Mexican girl's shoulder. A couple of feet to Camilla's left, Michelle lay on her side beneath the covers. Cuno couldn't tell if she was asleep.

"We'll have a fire built soon," he told Camilla. "Best climb out and warm yourselves for a spell. There'll be coffee, and I'll open a can of peaches."

Camilla glanced at Michelle. "I will carry Margaret. Can you help her?"

"I'll try."

Camilla flipped the covers aside and shifted the sound-asleep Margaret this way and that as she gained her feet. Cradling Margaret in her arms, she moved to the back of the wagon. She handed Margaret down to Cuno, who held the blonde until Camilla had dropped down from the tailgate. Camilla took Margaret back in her own arms and strode wordlessly off to the fire.

Cuno climbed into the back of the wagon and hunkered down in front of Michelle. She had the covers pulled up so high that he could only see the upper half of her face beneath her hat. Her eyes appeared to be open, staring vacantly at the padded bed of the wagon.

Haltingly, he said, "Miss Trent?"

She offered no response or gave any indication that she'd heard him.

"Miss Trent, boys're building a fire," Cuno said. "Might do you good to come on over and get yourself warm."

He didn't think she was going to respond to him this time, either. But then she folded her upper lip down, stuck her tongue out slightly, and said so softly that Cuno could barely hear, "I'd like to stay here, please."

"Can I bring you some coffee?"

"No, thanks."

"All right." Cuno looked down at her. She was pressing her body so snug against the wagon bed that she seemed to be trying to disappear. "Let me know if I can bring you anything."

Cuno started to rise.

"Mr. Massey?"

He dropped back to his haunches.

"Is Jedediah dead?" Michelle's voice was louder than before, but she did not move, just continued staring down at the wagon box as though an enormous weight were holding her down. She licked her lips. "My father wouldn't tell me."

Cuno filled his lungs. "Yes, ma'am. He's dead."

She squeezed her eyes closed and tightened her jaws but otherwise did not move. She said nothing more.

Cuno straightened and leapt down out of the wagon, leaving the tailgate open as he turned away and headed for the leaping flames of the coffee fire. He'd been intending to start the coffee, but Camilla was already down on both knees beside the fire ring, filling the percolator he'd set out with handfuls of ground beans from an open coffee sack.

The boys sat around, staring glumly into the flames.

Margaret sat between the older boy's legs, resting her head against his knee, her eyes closed, mouth open slightly as she breathed. Camilla had wrapped her in a striped trade blanket, and it sagged down from the girl's spindly right shoulder.

Camilla looked up at Cuno from beneath her dark brows. The long scar along her jaw shone dully in the flickering firelight. "How much?"

"Make it strong," Cuno said. He picked up his rifle and racked a fresh shell into the chamber. "Good and strong."

He walked back across the wash they'd crossed when they'd left the cleft, holding the off-cocked rifle high across his chest. On the other side of the rock-strewn wash, which the moon silvered so magnificently that it would have been worth admiring in another situation, he concealed himself in the scrub beside a cottonwood.

He pricked his ears, listening. There was nothing except the occasional tooth-gnashing screech of a hunting owl, the ticking of the frost in the tree's bare branches, and the tinny murmur of a distant spring bubbling out of rocks.

He waited there beside the tree, watching and listening, for a good fifteen minutes. When he figured the coffee was ready, he started back to the fire. He'd throw down a quick cup before hitching the mules again to the wagons.

He stopped abruptly and swung back around.

Faintly, the cracks of distant gunfire rose on the idle, quiet darkness. They were almost too faint to be heard unless you were listening for them, as they were carrying several miles up the mountain from the valley where the Trent ranch nestled.

17

SMOKE ROSE ON the bright mid-morning air.

It was as thin as a hair ribbon from this distance of eight or nine miles as the crow flies, across several ridges and just beyond the right, sloping shoulder of the high, granite peak keeping watch at the western edge of the Rawhides—Old Stone Face. At the opposite base of the hulking ridge, the Trent ranch nestled.

The ribbon was dark enough to distinguish itself from dust or a trick of the high-altitude light, and it rose from where the ranch would be. Or used to be.

Smoke, all right.

Cuno wrapped his reins around his saddle horn, then leaned back to reach into his left saddlebag. When he snagged his field glasses, he slipped them out of their case and, balancing the case on the saddle pommel, raised the glasses to his eyes, adjusting the focus.

The granite ridge slid up close, its fissures and faults revealed, the sun reflecting harshly off its gray surface. To the right of the peak, the smoke appeared not so much like a ribbon now but like a wafting, black curtain, thinning and thickening with the vagaries of the southwestern breeze and the guttering flames feeding it.

It was the smoke of a large, dying fire.

Wheezing, rasping breath sounded behind Cuno. "What do you see?"

Cuno continued staring through the glasses. "Smoke in the valley."

"The ranch?"

"It's not a grass fire."

Cuno turned as Serenity came huffing and puffing along the ridge to stand on the left side of the paint, staring toward the ridge. The wind whooshed over the ridges rippling all around them—a hollow sound like a strong breeze through a tunnel. It nibbled at the brim of the graybeard's weather-stained sombrero and lifted the tails of his yellow neckerchief that, while dusty and sweat-stained, almost looked new in contrast to his thin, saddle-leather neck.

Smoke dribbled out around the cornhusk quirley clamped between the old man's lips. "Let me see."

When Serenity had raised the glasses and adjusted the focus, he shook his head slowly, then handed them back to Cuno. His gray-blue, washed-out eyes were bright in the ten o'clock sun. "My restless liver is flarin' up."

"Chew it finer, hoss."

"Them Injuns don't have much else to think about now, with the ranch gone. And we gotta assume it's gone. They'll be trailin' us."

Cuno stared grimly down at the glasses as he slipped them back into their case. "You don't think Leaping Wolf will satisfy himself with burning the ranch?"

"'Pears to me he wants to mop every trace of the white eyes from the area. Now, *maybe* he'll satisfy himself with the valley and leave us, in the Rawhides, alone . . ."

"But you doubt it," Cuno said with a grunt, reaching back to return the glasses to the saddlebags.

"I pure-dee-damn do." Serenity drew deep on the quirley, lifting his knobby, brown chin as he sucked the smoke deep into his lungs, lifting his scrawny chest. "Especially with the girl up here. He might even be keepin' ole Trent alive just so the man can watch what ole Dancin' Wolf does to his daughter."

Cuno hipped around in his saddle to stare back down the sloping ridge at the wagons halted in a rock-lined hollow sheltered by firs and pines. They'd pulled hard all night, following troughs and dry water courses, and it had been too rough a ride for anyone to sleep except in fits and dozes.

When they'd stopped an hour ago to rest themselves as well as the mules, the three girls and the two boys were too exhausted to step down from the wagon. They all appeared asleep now, slumped amongst the blankets and robes in the back of Cuno's Conestoga—too worn out to even pine for all that they had left behind them.

The mules nibbled oats from grain sacks hooked over their ears, the sun silvering the sweat on their backs and withers, the breeze brushing their thick tails. The well-muscled, deep-bottomed beasts had made the climb from the valley floor relatively easily, but they still had a tough climb ahead, up one watershed and down the other.

Cuno, scouting ahead and following Trent's sketchy map, had been picking the easiest routes. But it was rough country, and they were still climbing, the air thinning as the valley dropped farther away beneath and behind them.

Cuno could feel the altitude himself—a faint light-headedness and the need to draw extra hard to gain strength from his breaths. The mules, working harder, likely felt it even more than he did.

"I haven't seen sign of us being followed all morning," Cuno said, adding, "but I know, I know . . . that don't mean they're not behind us."

The oldster chuckled as he field-stripped his quirley between gnarled, brick-red fingers. "Son, you might learn somethin' from me yet!"

"What do you say we quit jawin' and get movin'?" Cuno growled, neck-reining Renegade around and booting him down the slope toward the wagons as he called over his shoulder, "I'm gonna scout ahead!"

"Don't forget to scout behind us, too, dagnabbit!" the graybeard bellowed above the sighing wind.

Cuno put Renegade up beside the driver's box of his Conestoga. The older Lassiter boy, Karl, slumped in the seat, the reins wrapped around the brake handle.

"Ready to roll, boy?" Cuno said.

He had to repeat the question once more before the boy's head jerked up with a start, and he reached for the big horse pistol on the seat beside him—his father's old gun, which the boy had packed to protect his sister and younger brother. When he saw it was Cuno beside him, he stayed his hand and blinked sleepily, hacking phlegm from his throat and nodding. His face was red from the sun and wind, his brows bleached and his broad nose peeling.

Karl spat over the wagon wheel and nodded again.

"Follow me," Cuno said. "You see any Injun sign, fire that big iron of yours into the air."

He glanced into the box. The others were awake now, too, blinking sleepily. Michelle lay back with her robes pulled up to her chin, staring dreamily up at the low, puffy clouds as though trying to read something there.

The Mexican, Camilla, was staring over her shoulder at Cuno, her large brown eyes hooded with annoyance. "We must stop soon to sleep. Michelle and Margaret are tired. The boys are tired. *I* am tired."

Cuno glanced up the long ridge angling up to a grassy, pine-carpeted peak. "It'll be a while."

As Cuno rode off, he heard the girl growl behind him in Spanish, something about her wondering if the bull-chested, mule-skinning gringo even knew where he was going . . .

They pulled hard up and down the ridges for another twenty-four hours, stopping to rest for only a couple of hours at a time and to eat chunks of roasted venison, biscuits, and canned peaches washed down with coffee.

Cuno saw plenty of deer on the high, short-grass slopes,

and he spotted a brown bear lumbering along a beaver meadow, scrounging for the year's last berries. But he resisted the temptation to take the fresh meat; the deer they were carrying was nearly gone, but the shot might give away their position to the Utes.

On their fourth day out from the ranch, they mounted a high, windy divide—a long stretch of camelbacks rolling off to the eastern horizon. Cuno had scouted their back trail and side trails thoroughly enough that he decided it was time to take a break. He led the wagons, driven by Serenity and Karl Lassiter, down through aspens and scattered birch into a deep crease in the ridge.

He estimated from the thinness of the air and the sharpness of the light that they were nearly ten thousand feet above sea level. It would get damn cold up here at night. Hell, it was cold now at three o'clock in the afternoon. But according to Trent's map, they'd be in the high country another day or so before starting the slow, winding descent to Fort Jessup, which wasn't so low itself at around seven thousand feet.

As he put Renegade down the slope through the scattered deciduous forest, squirrels and jays chittering around him, Cuno was glad that he'd seen no menacing clouds. A storm up this high at this time of year would likely prove deadly.

He picked out a relatively sheltered spot to bivouac at the bottom of the gully, between two steep banks with a stream chuckling over ice-crusted stones. There were plenty of scrub trees to help break the wind that would funnel down the gorge. Here, though early, a strange twilight had already settled, with lemon-salmon light burnishing the far ridge about fifty yards up from the stream.

As he put up his hand, Karl and Serenity halted their teams, and the wagons clattered to a slow, grinding halt amongst the creaking, scratching aspens and birches. The passengers in Cuno's wagon didn't so much climb out as crawl, so heavily bundled in blankets and robes that they were almost indistinguishable from each other.

They were all sunburned, windburned, exhausted, and chilled to the bone. Stiffly, the Mexican girl reached up to lift Margaret down from the back of the wagon. When she'd set the little girl down, Camilla helped Michelle down, taking her hand to steady her. The two older girls exchanged a few words, and Cuno was glad to see that Michelle had come at least partially out of her dolor.

To a certain extent, they each needed to be able to fend for themselves.

Cuno set the two boys to gathering firewood while he quickly built a lean-to for the girls. He erected the shelter in the trees against the steep northern bank, using canvas wagon sheeting for the three walls and angling the roof so it would shed moisture.

He dug a fire pit in front of the lean-to, far enough away that the canvas wasn't likely to catch fire but close enough that the heat would reflect off the shelter's back wall. As Camilla began moving the bedding from the back of the wagon to the lean-to, leaving Margaret perched sullenly on a log, a blanket wrapped around her shoulders, Michelle moved over to the wagon to help.

Trent's daughter moved stiffly, haltingly, unsure what to do, as if her thoughts weren't completely connecting yet, but it was a good sign. Maybe she'd come out of it.

When the shelter was filled with bedding, Michelle and Camilla each took one of Margaret's hands and led the girl downstream. Cuno, building up the fire and preparing coffee, was about to yell to them to stay close, but he stopped when he realized they were probably just stepping away to tend nature. They hadn't taken a break in a couple of hours.

Cuno looked around, making sure they were still alone down here. The tension, the hunted feeling, was a constant tightness in the back of his neck. It made him jumpy, starting at the slightest unexpected sound and at even subtle changes in the wind.

He'd been through a lot in his young life. But he'd never undertaken such an enormous responsibility as transporting a passel of young'uns to safety across a rugged stretch of mountains, in late fall, with kill-crazy Indians on his tail. Recently, he'd found himself driving a jail wagon loaded with four deadly brigands, including one snarling beast known as Colorado Bob King, across the Mexico Mountains up Wyoming way.

He'd thought he'd had his hands full then.

The husky young freighter chuckled ruefully at the memory as he set a knotted aspen branch on the licking, popping flames. When he made sure the fire and coffee were both going good, he got up to help Serenity with the mules. It was nearly dark in the canyon when they had all the mules staked out on a long picket line near the stream and in deep grass, eating parched corn from feed bags.

Cuno hadn't yet unsaddled Renegade, for he wanted to take one more swing around the camp before good dark. The horse, tied in the trees just beyond the fire, lifted his head suddenly and loosed a whinny.

Cuno was down on one knee, pouring himself a cup of the smoking, black coffee. As the whinny echoed around the canyon, he set both cup and pot down abruptly and laid his gloved right hand on his holstered .45's ivory grips.

Renegade was staring warily upstream.

As Cuno swung his gaze in the same direction, beyond the parked wagons resting single file in the brush, an answering whinny rose on the cold breeze. Three horseback riders materialized amongst the dark tree trunks, coming on slowly along the stream.

They rode side by side, roughly ten feet apart—three bearded men in heavy fur coats, fur hats, and wooly chaps strapped over buckskin breeches. Two wore pistols and cartridge belts over their coats while another had his bearskin coat pulled up over the walnut butt of a revolver positioned for the cross draw on his right hip.

All three had rifles snugged in saddle boots, the stocks of the guns jutting up near their right knees.

Serenity was sitting on a rock near the fire. He had one boot off, intending to dry his socks and warm his bare feet in front of the flames.

"What have we here?" the oldster breathed, dropping the boot, slowly reaching for his Winchester, and resting it nonchalantly across his skinny thighs.

"Hello the camp!" one of the strangers called as all three angled their horses away from the stream and came on toward the fire.

Cuno lifted his coat above his .45's handle and released the keeper thong from the hammer.

18

THE HOOF THUDS sounded dully above the fire's crackling flames as the three riders rode past the mules and the wagons and approached the fire. Serenity had left his boot off, and he sat ten yards to Cuno's right, on the other side of the leaping flames, keeping one hand on his rifle's receiver.

In the periphery of his vision, Cuno saw the old man curling his white, yellow-nailed toes beneath his feet, and he could sense the oldster's tension.

"No call for that, now," said the man plodding slowly forward on a blood bay gelding, on the group's far left side.

He glanced at the ivory grips of Cuno's low-slung .45 exposed by the raised coat flap.

"We're territorial marshals," the man added, canting his head toward the other two men—a hawk-nosed gent with a three-day growth of salt-and-pepper whiskers and a fair-skinned man with bulbous blue eyes and a thick, cinnamon beard. Hair of the same color dropped low across his fore-head, beneath his black, heavy wool hat. He wore a half grin on his face as he moved his jaws slowly from side to side, tobacco juice dribbling down the right corner of his mouth and into his beard.

"That's Bone there on the far side," the first man said, canting his head to indicate the hawk-nosed man. "And this is Hayes. I'm Lipton. Pius Lipton. We're out of Ute on official business."

"Marshals, huh?" Serenity growled, skepticism pitching his voice low.

"We can show you our badges if you like," the man called Bone said, trying a mild grin that looked as at home on his face as a pair of women's hoop rings would look on his ears. "But we ain't here on business. We just seen your fire, that's all."

His eyes flicked toward the lean-to behind Cuno, in which the girls and the youngest Lassiter boy sat huddled together to stay warm. A slight, weird light shone in the man's eyes for about half a second, before he returned his gaze to Cuno and lifted the corner of his mouth once more in that taut, counterfeit smile.

The flickering firelight made his pitted cheeks above his beard look oily. "Noticed you had a good one goin'. Hayes shot a deer a couple ridges back. It's too much for us, and don't care to haul it. We'd be more than happy to share if we can cook it over that nice fire you got goin'."

"How 'bout it, ladies?" the red-bearded man called Hayes drawled in a thick Missouri accent. "You up to roasted venison this evenin'?" He dropped his chin and pinched his cap brim, peeling it out away from his forehead.

"We had a long haul," Cuno said. "Injun trouble. Not sure we're up to entertaining this evening."

Lipton was a tall gent with a thick gray-brown mustache drooping down around his thin mouth and badly pocked, windburned cheeks. He wore a red muffler snugged up under his hard, straight jaws, beneath a jutting, dimpled chin. His eyes were like brown marbles set deep in bony sockets. His voice was higher pitched than you'd expect from such a severely featured hombre. "Injun trouble?"

Cuno didn't want to mention in front of Michelle that

the Trent ranch had been burned. He merely nodded and said, "You seen any westward? That's the direction we're from, headed east to Fort Jessup."

"Not only *seen* three," Lipton said. "We pinked three. Shot 'em all three down like cans on fence posts. Just chance we were upwind from 'em, or those savages woulda smelled or heard us for sure."

In the periphery of his vision, Cuno saw Serenity glance at him. Cuno kept his eyes on the strangers.

"There's safety in numbers," Bone said. "And no point in lettin' good deer meat go to—"

He stopped when the Mexican girl, Camilla, said in a taut, even voice brimming with hatred, "Send them on their way." She whipped an arm out suddenly. *"Vamos!"*

He glanced back at her quickly, startled by the girl's sudden passion when she'd been so silent that Cuno had often forgotten she was here. She sat beside Margaret, who had her arms wrapped around one of the older girl's upraised knees and was regarding the newcomers with the same wary, angry expression as Camilla. Michelle, sitting right of Margaret, sat with her own knees drawn up, and she had a similarly fearful expression in her lake-blue eyes, which kept darting between Camilla and the newcomers.

Cuno turned back to the three hard-faced men sitting their mounts side by side, staring with various degrees of annoyance at Camilla. On the far side of the fire from Cuno, Karl Lassiter stood with the same armful of firewood he'd brought up when the three riders had approached from the creek.

He cut his eyes between Cuno and the three strangers, the boy's own expression more puzzled than frightened, as though he were waiting to see how Cuno would handle it. His nose was running onto his upper lip, and he sniffed it back softly.

"You know how it is," Cuno said, shrugging. "A woman's opinion trumps a man's every time."

The strangers stared owlishly at Cuno, curling their noses or chewing their mustaches, all three incredulous.

"You ain't no man," Bone growled, spitting the words out like prune pits, his anger building. "Why, you're just a wet-behind-the-ears kid, only a little older than that snot-nosed brat with the firewood. The only man here's that old, stove-up graybeard, and he can't even get his sock on."

Serenity rose slowly, his jaws hard. "I weren't trying to get it on. I was tryin' to get it off, so's I could dry it . . . if it's any of your business, which it ain't. Now, you heard the girl. Pull your picket pins an' *hoof*!"

Behind Cuno, Margaret gave a muffled screech against Camilla's knee. Across the dwindling fire, Karl sniffed sharply, his load of wood rising and falling as he breathed.

The strangers scowled down at the group before them. Finally, Lipton said, not taking his eyes off Camilla, "Come on, boys. Let's go build us a fire and roast us up some supper."

He reined out around the fire and spurred his horse into a trot. The other two lingered, glaring down at the campers. Cuno kept his hand near his Colt, and his heart thudded dully.

Finally, Hayes reined his red gelding around the fire, grunting, "Good luck if them Injuns come callin'!"

He tipped his hat to the girl, snarling. Then he and Bone, riding single file, trotted down canyon after Lipton, and Renegade stood lifting his hooves in place and nickering amongst the trees behind them.

Cuno turned to watch them disappear into the darkening woods, following a slow bend in the stream-cleaved canyon.

"Trouble," Serenity said, holding his rifle down low by his side. One foot still bare, he spat into the fire to hear it sizzle. "Copper-riveted scalawags, with the boots on!"

"You think they were lawmen?"

Serenity shook his head. "Maybe, but it's my guess they ain't nothin' but owlhoots on the dodge. They just said they was badge toters so we'd let 'em light here with us and the girls . . . and help us against the redskins . . . if there are any redskins, which I doubt. We woulda heard the shots."

Cuno glanced at the older Lassiter boy as he grabbed his rifle. "Keep the fire built up, Karl. I'm gonna take a ride."

"Where you goin'?" Serenity said, squatting to lay his sock near the fire to which Karl was adding the dry, crackling wood.

Cuno grabbed Renegade's dangling reins and stepped into the saddle. "I'm gonna see where they camp. Go ahead and start supper. I'll be back."

Cuno slid the Winchester into his saddle boot and urged Renegade down canyon. He stopped when he saw Camilla standing just outside the lean-to, staring into the gathering darkness in which the three strangers had disappeared.

"Be careful," Camilla said quietly, holding a buffalo robe around her shoulders. Her long hair danced out in the breeze like long, slender fingers.

"I will."

Camilla reached up with one hand to slide her hair away from her eyes, then turned slowly and knelt beside the food sack to begin preparing supper.

Cuno rode slowly through the trees along the murmuring stream, the cold breeze pressing against his back. Weaving around the aspens, he followed the canyon's first slow curve and started tracing another.

Voices sounded from downwind—muffled and ghostly. There was the snap of a stout twig beneath a heavy foot.

Cuno held his reins taut and stared straight out over Renegade's head. Three shadows moved amongst the gnarled, black trees, just beyond a deadfall that had gotten hung up against a tree still standing.

Cuno reined the paint sharply left and held up behind a flame-shaped, cabin-sized boulder, then swung Renegade around until he was facing the stream winking dully in the fading gray light.

The hoof thuds grew gradually louder. The voices grew, as well.

One of the men—Cuno recognized Bone's voice—said,

"That little Mex is sure gonna feel good in *my* blanket roll tonight! *Damn*, it's cold!"

There was a light thump, as though one of the men had softly punched another man's shoulder. "I told ya—since I seen her first, she's *mine*. You know I'm partial to—"

The red-bearded Hayes cut himself off when Cuno gigged Renegade out from behind the boulder, turned the horse down canyon, and stopped, facing the three riders. The three hard cases, silhouettes in the darkness of the windy canyon, all jerked with starts and hauled back on their reins, stopping their horses suddenly.

One of the horses snorted angrily. Another whinnied.

Renegade shook his head fatefully, as though he knew from experience what was coming.

Bone cursed and pulled his head up high. "Where the hell you come from, *boy*?"

"You followin' us?" Lipton said in his oddly feminine voice.

Cuno raised his coat flap above his holstered .45, so that the grips were clear. He kept his voice hard but even. "We asked you boys to ride on. Since you didn't, I reckon I've got no choice but to kill you."

The boldness of Cuno's statement took all three men aback for about three seconds. Bone chuckled with exasperation, glancing at a partner on either side of him. "You *think* so, *do* ya, boy?"

Lipton was the first to reach for the big, pearl-gripped Colt Navy holstered just right of his saddle horn. Cuno palmed his Colt without thinking about it but only staring at the place where he intended the bullet to go.

Automatically, he sent the slug punching through the dead center of Lipton's bear coat. The mustached gent, whose Colt Navy hadn't even finished clearing leather, screamed and bounded straight back in his saddle, showing his white teeth between stretched lips in the thickening darkness.

As the two other men jerked their hands toward their weapons, Cuno's pistol bucked and roared twice more.

Bone lurched back just as Lipton's bucking horse rammed Bone's horse, and he and Lipton both whipped sideways out of their saddles.

Meanwhile, Hayes crouched forward over his own saddle horn, holding the reins taut in one hand and firing his long-barreled Peacemaker over his horse's left wither.

The bullets sizzled past Cuno's right hip and plunked into a tree behind him. Cuno quickly cocked his Colt and fired another round into Hayes's chest. The red-bearded man lurched back and fired his Peacemaker once more, this time shooting his horse in the neck.

Cuno reined Renegade quickly to the left as Hayes's red gelding screamed and, whipping its head up and around, staggered sideways. The deer tied behind Hayes's saddle flopped around wildly.

As Renegade, nickering nervously, wheeled in a tight circle, Cuno watched the other two horses run off buck-kicking down canyon while the red rolled atop the groaning Hayes in the high grass between two cottonwoods. The horse's tooth-gnashing screams echoed shrilly around the canyon.

Holding Renegade's reins taut in one hand, Cuno extended his cocked Colt, angling it down and aiming carefully this time, and drilled a round through the gelding's head. The horse sagged as it died, hooves thrashing automatically, pummeling the groaning, sobbing Hayes into a veritable pulp in the grass.

Cuno looked around at the other two men. Lipton lay belly down ahead and left, about thirty yards away. Bone lay on his back, neck twisted oddly, one leg curled beneath the other, arms thrown out to both sides as though in supplication. His unblinking eyes glistened in the light of the night's first stars.

Cuno swung down from his saddle and, dropping the paint's reins, stood looking around and listening like a hunter. He flipped the Colt's loading gate open, extracted the spent shells, and replaced them with fresh from his cartridge belt.

When he was sure that no one had been attracted by the gunfire—at least not yet—he holstered the Colt and walked over to where Hayes now lay unmoving, his torso protruding from under the dead horse's left shoulder, the snout of the dead buck snugged up against the man's neck.

The man's eyes were half open and staring down his nose, with his mouth stretched wide as though the horse was still grinding Hayes's pelvis into a fine powder. Curious about the men's identities, Cuno began to open Hayes's bloody, bullet-torn coat. He glanced across the horse to see a rifle lying in the brush where the dying beast's spasms had apparently tossed it from the dead man's saddle sheath.

Cuno removed his hands from the coat buttons, rose, and reached across the horse for the rifle. Holding it up to the vagrant light, he ran a hand down the smooth forestock and inspected the receiver still glistening with factory oil.

A new gun. Undoubtedly one of those that Cuno had hauled to the Trent ranch.

He lowered the rifle and looked down at Hayes again. Leaning the rifle against the dead horse, Cuno dropped back to a crouch and undid the man's coat buttons.

He opened the coat's flaps and froze. Winking up at him from the man's left breast, just over his heart, was a blood-drenched copper moon-and-star badge.

Engraved in the copper badge were the words WYOMING TERRITORY and MARSHAL.

19

CUNO'S HEARTBEAT QUICKENED.

He jerked back with a start, as though he'd discovered that the red-bearded Hayes had been booby-trapped with a live rattlesnake. Staring down at the blood-drenched badge, he straightened slowly.

Hand hooked over his holstered Colt, he stepped over Hayes and the legs of the dead horse and strode back to where Bone lay staring up at the sky. Cuno quickly opened the man's coat, and the same heart-leaping feeling came over him again when he saw the badge.

He walked over to Lipton and opened the man's bloody coat. Lipton's badge had been half embedded in Lipton's chest by one of Cuno's bullets.

Cuno looked around for Lipton's and Bone's rifles. He got up and kicked around through the grass but found nothing. Both rifles must still be in their saddle boots.

Cuno wanted a look at those rifles badly enough that, even in the chill darkness, he swung up onto Renegade's back and urged the horse down the steeply falling canyon, the silver stream gurgling and bubbling off to his right.

As he'd figured, the horses hadn't run far. One gave an angry whinny as Cuno approached, and he saw both their silhouettes standing near the stream, their eyes flashing like tarnished copper amongst the black trunks of the trees. He dismounted about twenty yards away and approached the horses slowly, holding his hands out as though with sugar or grain, clucking.

The saddle on one horse had slid down its side, and the boot was dangling beneath its belly. Grabbing the horse's drooping reins, Cuno crouched down, jerked the rifle from its sheath, and held it up to inspect it.

A shiny new Winchester, just like the one Hayes had been carrying.

His blood quickening, Cuno walked around to the other horse, who had now turned his head to the stream as though indignant that Cuno's offer of food had been a ruse. Its saddle was still on its back though sitting askew. Cuno could tell by the glistening walnut stock that the rifle in the boot was another new Winchester.

He pulled it out, and instantly on the cold air he smelled the oil and varnish and the coal-oil smell of new iron. He ran his hand across a blood splotch up near the forestock. Strands of brown hair were stuck to the blood . . . as though a scalp had hung there.

Quickly, he unleathered both mounts and, leaving them to find their own way or to be picked up by other travelers, he gathered the two rifles and both men's cartridge belts, including the spares he found in their saddlebags. Mounting his own horse, he rode back to where he'd left Hayes and the dead red gelding.

After collecting Hayes's rifle and cartridge belt, and taking two spare boxes of .44 shells from the lawman's saddlebags, he cut the deer free of the dead horse. He lashed the field-dressed buck behind his own saddle, mounted up once more, and put Renegade into a careful walk up the deadfall-littered canyon.

He brought the fire of his own camp up a half hour later. Serenity, sitting on a rock a few yards in front of the dancing flames and hunkered deep in his quilted hide, fleece-lined coat, stood abruptly, raising his rifle.

Cuno called out above the rushing wind and popping flames and swung down from the saddle.

"Where you been?" Serenity said. "You been gone longer'n I reckoned on."

The old man's voice dropped suddenly when he saw the three spare rifles bristling from Cuno's cradled arms.

"Where in the lady's crapper'd you find those?"

"The lawmen."

"Lawmen?"

"All three were wearing territorial marshal badges, just like they said."

"Were?"

"They were headin' back this way." Cuno set the rifles down against a boulder and glanced at the humped figures of the girls in the lean-to.

Serenity picked up one of the Winchesters, raising it slowly in both hands and frowning down at it. "I'll be jiggered. Where you suppose they got their hands on these?"

"Looks like they mighta been telling the truth."

Serenity raised his eyes to Cuno. Firelight danced in their corners. He turned to slide a wary glance across the ravine.

Again, Cuno glanced toward the lean-to on the other side of the fire. It was too dark to see much except a few humped figures as the firelight played shadows across the blankets and robes. "They all in there?"

"Been sound asleep since about five minutes after you left."

"Christ, I could use some shut-eye myself."

"Go ahead. I'll keep the first watch."

Cuno shook his head and, setting his Winchester '73 on his shoulder, turned to stare up canyon, which was now almost completely concealed in darkness. The firelight played off the sides of the wagons and showed red in the eyes of the picketed mules, a couple of whom had lain down to sleep, stretched out on their sides.

"Can't take a chance that Leaping Wolf hasn't sent his entire band after us. No, I ain't gonna sleep much tonight. Maybe just doze a little." Cuno dropped to a knee and poured himself a cup of coffee. Setting the pot back on a rock to one side of the leaping flames, he picked up his rifle again and started walking up canyon, blowing on his coffee. "I'll scout around a little. You stay with the young'uns."

"I'll go ahead and carve up the deer," Serenity said, regarding the carcass lashed to Renegade's back. "We'll have venison for breakfast. Got the lawmen to thank for the fresh meat, anyways . . ."

Cuno sipped his coffee and muttered to himself, "That wasn't the only fresh meat they were after."

Remembering those badges pinned to the men's shirts made him extra jumpy. He'd never shot a lawman before. Now he'd shot three. They were obviously rogues in need of killing, but killing a lawman was a hard thing to defend, and it was a hanging offense, to boot.

He was glad no one had been around to see.

Cuno dozed only once all night.

He combated sleep with coffee and anxiety and kept his ears tuned to the wind, listening for any unnatural sounds and watching his horse and the mules, as well. They'd sense danger long before he and Serenity would.

Renegade and the horses seemed relatively peaceful all night, and when false dawn pushed a wan gray light up from the eastern horizon, silhouetting the distant ridges against it, the animals were far better rested than the men were. They shook and blew and pulled at the long, tawny grass with abandon.

Cuno, Serenity, and their five charges all had a breakfast of corn cakes, roasted venison, and coffee and, while it was a task getting the two younger children back into the dreaded wagon bed—Margaret especially put up a fuss as Camilla wrapped her in a thick quilt and lifted her over the tailgate—they were off and rolling before sunrise.

They followed the path laid out by Trent's map, Serenity leading the way, with Karl Lassiter driving Cuno's wagon behind him. Cuno scouted their back trail, sweeping right and left of it, inspecting the canyons, gorges, ravines, and stony escarpments jutting above the pines.

It was a sprawling, humping heap of backbone they were on, heading east through the easiest route possible, between grassy, conifer-carpeted ridges. There were plenty of places for shadowing warriors to hide. But Cuno saw no sign that they were being followed, and this made him feel better about stopping the wagons at two o'clock in the afternoon, to let Michelle, Camilla, and the children climb out of the wagon to tend nature and to eat more of the roasted venison that Serenity had wrapped in burlap.

Cuno put the boys to the task of building a fire while the girls headed off to a nearby aspen stand. He and Serenity watered and fed the mules and inspected their harnesses and hooves.

Soon they all sat down to a lunch of coffee and venison, which they consumed in moody silence, huddled around the small fire in the crisp mountain sunshine, Camilla cajoling Margaret to take a few bites and Margaret shaking her head, refusing. Later, after two cups of coffee and a half pound of deer haunch, Cuno walked up a low hill to glass the terrain around them.

When he'd had a thorough inspection and still saw no sign of pursuing Indians, he cast his naked gaze back down to the wagons. They stood single file, most of the mules still eating grain from the feed sacks. The low-sided wagons looked bleached out and dusty. On this side of them and between them, the motley-looking party knelt or sat on rocks around the fire.

Serenity knelt on one knee beside Margaret. He was gnawing on a deer shoulder and making exaggerated motions, trying to show the little blonde how good it was. Margaret merely sat on her stone, one elbow resting on her knee, her chin in her hand, shaking her head from side to side.

Michelle sat on the ground, knees drawn up and staring

into the flames that looked almost opaque in the brassy sunlight. Camilla knelt behind her on both knees, combing out her long blond hair, not saying anything, her dark features expressionless.

What a strange, hard-eyed girl—Camilla. Cuno wondered what her story was. Of course, he'd had plenty of opportunity to inquire, but it wouldn't have been an appropriate question. Besides, she seemed somehow separate, isolated from the group despite her physical presence. She spoke little even to the other two girls, and it wasn't Cuno's place to try to break into her private world.

He had no idea what she was protecting or hiding . . . what wound she was tending . . . and he had no right to know.

The younger Lassiter boy, Jack, had wandered off a ways behind the wagons, tapping at the ground with a crooked branch. He was likely distracting himself from his own worries with an imaginary game. The older boy, Karl, had broken off from the group, as well, and now he was striding slowly up the hill toward Cuno.

The older boy's blunt features looked pensive, his eyes pinched against the sun. His mint-green, hand-knit scarf blew out behind him in the wind, and he had his gloved hands shoved down in the pockets of his heavy, deerhide mackinaw. His cap—a wool, leather-billed watch cap with pull-down earflaps—must have belonged to his father, because it was too big for him, the flaps sitting too low on his ears.

"Cuno, you want I should grease the axles?" the boy said in his characteristically uninflected tone.

"You greased 'em this mornin', didn't ya?"

"Yeah."

"They'll be all right till tonight."

Karl stood a ways off, one foot up higher on the slope than the other, one hand on his thigh, looking back westward. Toward the home he'd left behind.

The wind blew the ends of his scarf and nipped at the bill of his cap. He licked at his chapped lips.

"I reckon," he said matter-of-factly, "the Injuns done burned the Trent ranch."

Again, Cuno saw no reason to mince words. He cast his own gaze westward, and nodded. "I saw the smoke."

"Ma's likely dead, then."

"Trent would have sent riders if they'd made it."

Karl hardened his jaws as he continued staring westward. "Ma, Pa—they didn't do nothin' to Leapin' Wolf. He had no cause to do what he done."

Cuno dropped to his haunches, pulled a weed stem, and fingered it absently as he looked up at the kid's implacable profile. "It ain't right, but there's nothin' you can do about it. Let it go. You and your brother and your little sis—you gotta dig deep and hold on tight. Even after we're out of this, things aren't gonna be easy. Just remember what your parents taught you. Remind yourself all the time, and don't let yourselves stray. Always do what you need to do to do what's right."

Karl's chest rose and fell heavily as he stared into the wind. Finally, he glanced at Cuno, and there was just the slightest hint of understanding in his eyes.

"Let's mosey." Cuno straightened, tossed the weed stem away, and started down the hill toward the wagons. "We still got a long pull ahead."

As he approached the bottom of the hill, Serenity was kicking dirt on the fire. Camilla was helping the sullen Margaret back into the wagon. The little girl clutched a doll to her chest, the legs protruding from her trade blanket.

Michelle was tying her scarf over her head as she put her face to the strong sunlight, a faint celestial smile turning up the corners of her delicate mouth. Her brushed hair glistened like ripe wheat in the mountain light and blew around in the wind.

"Where we headed?" Serenity said, eating the last of his venison haunch with his greasy hands, his gloves stuffed into his coat pockets. "Give me a landmark to reckon on."

"We keep pullin' west with a little dogleg to the north." Cuno was staring west over a broad valley of varied formations while shading his eyes with his field glasses. "Key on that white chunk of rock that looks like a horse's tooth jutting up from that red ridge yonder. Don't look like it from here, but according to Trent's map, there's a saddle in there somewheres that'll see us onto our last pull out of the Rawhides."

"There is a shorter way."

Cuno and Serenity turned to see Camilla standing in the back of the passenger wagon, her body facing southeast, her head turned to peer at them over her left shoulder. She pointed. "There's a long canyon sloping down to an abandoned mining camp. Just beyond is the fort."

"It's not on Trent's map," Cuno said.

"Maybe he did not know about it," Camilla said. "But it is there—a shorter way to the fort. There is no need to swing north and then return south."

Serenity frowned and wiped grease from his beard with his coat sleeve. "How do you know, senorita?"

"I worked at the camp before the silver disappeared." Camilla turned her gaze straight west. "At the bottom of this ridge is a stream, and a horse trail follows the stream southeast through a canyon and then up and over the ridge."

Cuno turned his own gaze to the southeast. He thought he could see, in the far distance and obscured by sunlight, a gap through that devil's backbone of red sandstone that ran the entire length of the Rawhides and which, in fact, looking so much like a long strip of bald, dry, weather-gnawed leather, gave the Rawhides their name.

Cuno walked over to Renegade and dropped his field glasses into his saddlebags. "I'll scout it, make sure we can get the wagons through."

"Head straight south from here," Camilla instructed. "It will save you time. You can meet the wagons at the stream."

Cuno swung up into the saddle as Serenity closed the tailgate and latched it, and Karl Lassiter crawled up into the driver's box of the passenger wagon.

"You better show me," Cuno said, putting Renegade up beside the wagon and extending his hand to Camilla, who stood amongst the hides. Not knowing the country, he was liable to get lost down there and never find his way back to the wagons, much less the gap that the Mexican girl spoke of.

Camilla looked down into the wagon uncertainly, apparently expecting Margaret to object to her leaving. But the girl had already fallen asleep beside her younger brother, her doll peeking out from between the folds of her blankets. Jack Lassiter squinted against the sunlight as he shuttled his gaze uncertainly between Cuno and Camilla.

Her back to the front of the wagon, Michelle was staring at Cuno as though she could see right through him. For a moment, he wondered what she was thinking, and then Camilla stepped to the side of the wagon, extending her hand. Cuno took it, and the girl hiked a leg over the panel and sat down behind Cuno's blanket roll on Renegade's back.

Serenity was climbing into his own wagon as Cuno kneed the paint up beside him, Camilla's hands wrapped around his waist. "I'll meet you at the stream. If I'm not there first, come on south and we'll meet up with you somewhere before the gap."

"Fine as frog hair," Serenity said, casting a wary glance along their back trail. "Good luck."

Cuno gigged Renegade into a trot south of the wagons, heading down the rounded shoulder of the grassy ridge and dropping toward the wild canyon country beyond.

"You two mind your topknots." The old man's raspy voice tore on the wind behind them. "Dancin' Wolf might be on the lurk behind any rock or cactus!"

"It's Leapin' Wolf, ya ole mossy horn," Cuno muttered.

20

"CRISTO!" CAMILLA SAID over Cuno's right shoulder. *"De que es una oso grande!"*

Cuno studied the trunk of the pine tree ahead of him. It was scarred with the long, deep slashes of a bear's claws—some a half inch deep and nearly eight feet up from the ground. Some of the bark around the tree's base looked damp.

Cuno swung his right leg over the saddle horn, dropped straight down to the ground, and hitched his deerskin breeches up his thighs as he crouched. He picked up a chunk of the damp bark, and made a face as the vinegar and raw-alcohol scent of the bear piss, mixed with the tang of pine sap, assaulted his senses.

"Not only a big bear," he said, looking around warily as he straightened and dropped the fetid bark, "but a recent one. This marking is only about a half hour old."

"What are you waiting for?" the girl said, turning her head this way and that, her large brown eyes fearful. She grabbed the saddle's cantle and leaned forward as though to launch the paint into a run. "Let's go! *Vamos!*"

Cuno had already grabbed the apple and was hauling

himself back into the saddle. He didn't care to tangle with any grizzly, especially the size of the one who'd marked the pine, any more than the girl did.

As he settled into the saddle and loosened his Winchester in the sheath under his knee, the girl wrapped her arms tightly around his waist. Nudging Renegade with his heels and starting forward, he studied the pine-studded canyon floor around him, hoping the bear had headed in a different direction than the one he and the girl were heading.

However, after having ridden an hour away from the wagons, angling southeast, he was no longer sure he was following the course he'd intended.

As Renegade clomped forward, toward a slight clearing in the canyon where the sunlight splashed down unimpeded on scalloped sand and boulder snags, he said, unable to keep the irritation from his voice, "Are you sure this is the right way? When we were higher, you said it was the next canyon south."

Camilla said, "No, I am no longer certain. I told you to go back and we would try the other one."

"I thought this one would *lead* to the other one, and it still might. I'd just like a little assurance that we're even still headed toward the gap."

"It looked simpler when we were higher up."

"It usually does," Cuno grunted.

"Go here," Camilla said as a lightning-topped cedar slipped past them on their right.

"Where?"

"Here." Camilla pointed her mittened hand to the left, rocking back and forth impatiently once again. "Down that passage, see? That should take us to the passage we are looking for. I remember that one now."

"Sure you do," Cuno grunted, his unease about the bear and his fear of getting lost raking his tender nerves.

He heard the girl mutter something behind him in Spanish. She'd spoken too softly and quickly for him to be sure but he thought she'd called him a bullheaded gringo who lies down with mules or somesuch. He snorted and watched the walls of the canyon drop down around him, purple shade angling out from the ridge to his right.

He didn't see any more bear sign here, but in the gravel and sand of the wash's floor he spied the tracks of two horses. Not Indian ponies; Indians didn't shoe their mounts, and both these horses were shod.

Camilla saw the tracks as well, and she said, "We are not the first ones through here today."

"They might be soldiers scouting out from the fort." Cuno looked around at the canyon's steep walls, which, a hundred yards up, leaned back away from the canyon, strewn with large boulders pushing out velvet shade wedges contrasting sharply with the sun-blasted rock around them. "Or market hunters."

"They might be desperadoes," Camilla said dully. "Like the lawmen you killed last night. These mountains are honeycombed with *all* kinds."

Cuno glanced over his shoulder. "How did you know I killed the lawmen?"

"I heard you speaking to Senor Parker."

Cuno turned forward. "I figured you were asleep."

"Who can sleep out here, with men like that lurking, and Indians chasing us?"

"Well, you read the lawmen right," Cuno said, moving with the horse's sway. "They weren't all that law-abiding."

"It takes a woman to read a man."

"I reckon."

Camilla was right—the narrow canyon led into the one she'd been looking for. The floor of this canyon rose steeply as it curved to the south, and in the mid-afternoon Cuno stopped Renegade on a high, cold saddle showing the deep ruts of many wagons over the years, but few recent ones.

To the left of the saddle was a higher ridge with scattered pines growing out of a sandstone dike. To the right was a deep river canyon in which a violet stream slid, glistening around large boulders and naked pines that had fallen from the slopes during rock slides.

Cuno glanced at the gap between the slope on his left and the canyon on his right.

"Just enough room for the wagons," he said, as he dropped down from Renegade's back.

"Watch your step."

Cuno turned to the girl. She nodded at a large plop of bear scat pebbled with bright red berries and bristling with deer fur. Glancing around the plop, he found a paw print as large as the ones that had marked the pine.

"Our friend gets around."

"And he probably doesn't want anyone else around," Camilla said.

Cuno stared back the way they'd come, then up toward the ridge crest. Hoping the bear was somewhere up there now, looking for a place to hole up for the winter, he turned to peer down the eastern side of the saddle.

Low ridges—some rocky dikes, others carpeted with fur or the short, tough grass that grows at high altitudes—tumbled away in the purple distance. There was a slight tan gap marking a broad valley at the edge of the Rawhides before more ridges rose, shouldering against each other and defining another, separate range—either the Mummies or the Never Summers.

He knew he wouldn't see it from here even with his binoculars, but the army outpost lay in the valley at the edge of the Rawhides. Still a good two- or three-day pull with the wagons, but at least he could see their destination from here.

Relief swelled in him, and he glanced back at Camilla. "You were right. This pass should take us down to the fort."

The girl just stared at him, her dark brown face and almond-shaped brown eyes expressionless as her hair whipped around in the cold breeze.

"Right," Cuno growled, grabbing Renegade's reins. "We ain't there yet . . ."

The horse dropped down the gradually sloping ridge

with his head hanging and his knees starting to get that flop that meant he was tired.

When they gained the narrow valley bottom, Cuno gigged the horse down through pines to a stream in a deep, rocky bed and dismounted. The wind whooshed in the tops of the pines and firs. Squirrels chattered angrily. Occasional branches broke and fell with a muffled crash.

"We'll rest here." Cuno reached up and placed his hands around Camilla's waist. "Gotta give Renegade a breather and a few oats before we head back to the wagons."

He pulled the girl out of the saddle. He smelled her earthy fragrance—an odd mix of cherry, wood, and salt—and felt her long, coarse hair blowing against his windburned cheeks as he set her down.

He kept his hands around her waist for a moment, staring down at her. He hadn't been this close to her before, and he hadn't realized how pretty she was. Aside from the scar along her jaw, her cheeks were incredibly smooth, her hair the color of dark chocolate. Her lips, too wide to be called delicate, were alluring just the same.

Her brown eyes were guarded and grave, as though she were withholding a terrible secret. With hands laid flat against his chest, she looked up at him, frowning, a vaguely puzzled, faintly annoyed expression in her gaze. She held her lips in a straight line.

Blood warmed Cuno's ears as he felt a primordial pull in his loins. What bliss it would be to ignore the peril they were all in and pull this girl to him and kiss her and make love to her for the rest of the day, here in the crisp sunlight with his bedroll wrapped around them. His heart thudded as he realized his hand was moving up to slide a lock of hair from her right eye. At once chagrined and incredulous, he dropped his gaze and stayed his hand and turned toward Renegade.

"We'll take about twenty minutes," he grunted, loosening the latigo cinch with a single, hard pull. "Best tend to business, if you got any. I'll build a fire, brew some coffee."

In the periphery of his vision, he saw her standing behind him, flanking him, not moving or saying anything. He tightened his jaws and took his time with the buckle and then untying his blanket roll from the saddle. When he turned, she was striding off through the wind-tossed trees, ducking under pine boughs, her heavy wool skirts blowing out around the tops of her beaded moccasins.

When she returned, he had a small fire going and the coffeepot was chugging on a flat stone. He'd fed Renegade a couple handfuls of oats, and now the horse stood droopy-eyed in the golden sunlight shafting through the trees, latigo and reins hanging free.

Cuno sat on a fallen log from the end of which a chipmunk kept appearing to read him the riot act before ducking back inside the log, which apparently was nearly hollow. The warmth of the fire felt good, for even at midday the temperature hadn't risen much above thirty degrees.

Eyes down, Camilla strode up to a tree kitty-corner to Cuno and slumped down on the ground, in a broad patch of sunlight, drawing her knees up and wrapping her arms around them. She leaned her head back, still not looking at Cuno, but gazing off through the trees and lifting a hand to slide her blowing hair away from her eyes.

Cuno tossed his bedroll toward her. It hit the ground and rolled to her right. "Cover up with that, if you like."

She looked at the bedroll almost angrily, then lifted her face again to the golden light shafting through the trees. "The sun is enough."

Cuno shrugged, then dropped to a knee by the fire to fill the two tin cups he'd set out. He'd filled one of the cups when the girl rose suddenly and strode out toward the stream murmuring in its narrow, rocky bed.

He lowered the pot to watch her, frowning. A few yards from the water she stopped and raised a hand to shield the light from her eyes. She was staring up the opposite slope sparsely studded with pines, cedars, and firs, with here and there a lumpy boulder sheathed in dead brush.

Suddenly, a bugling scream sounded behind Cuno. Heart hammering and ears ringing, he whipped around.

At first, he thought Renegade had been bit by a rattlesnake, as the horse, screaming, leapt nearly straight up in the air so that all four hooves left the ground at the same time. When the paint hit the ground again, he skitter-hopped sideways and, turning his head with white-ringed eyes toward Cuno, gave another drum-rattling whinny.

Cuno's eyes dropped to look around for a snake, forgetting for a half second that snakes wouldn't be up this high nor out this late in the season. Then he whipped around again as Renegade lifted another bugling cry and, following the horse's terrified gaze across the rocky streambed beyond Camilla, saw the grizzly moving down the far slope in a shamble-footed gait, its haunches rippling, its shaggy cinnamon coat blowing in the wind.

The bear was a big male with powerful shoulders and hips and with paws the size of dinner plates. Moving swiftly down through the sunlight-dappled slope, meandering around trees and boulders and dislodging sliderock around him, he swung his head from side to side and loosed an enraged bellow that joined Renegade's terrified screams in an otherworldly din that echoed off the ridges like a warlock's cry.

Adding to the din was Camilla's scream. She wheeled toward Cuno, tripped in the rocks, and fell.

Hearing Renegade's hooves thudding away behind him, Cuno bolted through the trees and over the rocks to the girl. She was just gaining her feet when he reached her, and, on the other side of the streambed, the roaring, rambling bruin was just making the base of the hill.

Cuno grabbed Camilla's mittened hand. "Come on!"

He pulled her back across the rocks and through the branches, hoping like hell that Renegade hadn't run far. As they approached the edge of the trees, just beyond the fire, he shouted, "Renegade . . . *goddamnit*!"

The horse galloped up canyon, sixty yards away and growing smaller as the reins bounced along the ground behind him and the saddle hung down his side—not only the saddle, but the saddle sheath with the Winchester '73, as well.

Cuno cursed again. There was no point calling for the horse. Horses had an instinctual, primordial terror of bears and bobcats, and the paint wasn't coming back till the bruin was gone.

Cuno swung back around to see the bear lumbering at an angle across the streambed, heading toward him and Camilla. His thoughts raced, and he looked around wildly. They couldn't climb any of the surrounding trees, because the lowest branches were too high, and the bear would merely shake them out of the pines like ripe apples.

Peering north across the canyon, he saw a clay-colored shelf of sandstone jutting out of the bank and surrounded by shrubs and stunt confiers. It looked like a giant, sun-dried cow pie. There were several slot caves between the layers—a good hundred yards away, but one of those caves was their only hope of escape.

If the slots were deep enough.

"Run!" Cuno said, pushing Camilla toward the humping sandstone. "Head for those rocks yonder. I'm right behind you!"

Camilla stood, bald terror in her eyes. The bear was mewling and kicking stones as he crossed the stream. "Why don't you shoot him?"

"Only got my forty-five. It'll just rile him." Cuno grabbed his saddlebags and shouted without turning around. *"Run!"*

He draped his saddlebags over his shoulder and grabbed his blanket roll. As he headed back away from the smoking fire, he glanced over his shoulder.

The bruin had stopped in the middle of the streambed to stand on his hind legs, lift his snout, and beat his chest like an enraged ape as he loosed a tooth-splintering roar. Cuno stopped and turned back toward the stream, palming his .45. The bullets would only nip the bear like annoying blackflies, but the reports might scare him off.

Cuno hammered two rounds into a tree at the edge of the streambed, blowing out gouts of bark and pine slivers.

The bear lifted his snout again and roared even louder. Then he dropped down to all fours and bolted off his back feet, driving forward like a large, furry locomotive on a downhill run, making a beeline for Cuno.

"Bad idea," the freighter muttered, wheeling, holstering his .45, and snapping the keeper thong over the hammer as he broke into a sprint across the canyon.

Behind him, the bear's running footsteps thudded loudly as the bear bolted through the trees, breaking branches and mewling like a Brahma bull in a cholla patch.

"Oh, Christ," Cuno muttered, breath raking in and out of his lungs. "If it ain't one damn thing, it's another!"

21

CUNO BOUNDED FORWARD, running hard, the saddlebags flapping down his chest and back, as he clutched his blanket roll in his right hand. He'd instinctively grabbed the gear, knowing he and Camilla would need it if they survived the bear.

Ahead, Camilla was running through another streambed branching off from the one behind, lifting her skirts above her ankles and snatching terrified looks over her shoulder.

Cuno shouted, "Keep going!"

The girl hissed something in Spanish, and Cuno wasn't sure if she was berating him or the bear.

The water of this intersecting stream wasn't as deep as the first—probably just a feeder creek—but it splashed up above Cuno's knees as he lunged forward, nearly slipping on the ice-rimed stones. As Camilla approached the stream's opposite side, she slipped on one of the icy rocks and fell to a knee but pushed herself back up quickly and scrambled, half crawling, up the grassy bank beyond.

As Cuno made the stream's opposite side, he turned to look behind. The bear was running full out, charging like a bull buffalo with his head down, razor-edge fangs bared.

As the bruin plunged into the shallow stream, Cuno lunged up the bank.

"Hurry!" He slipped the bedroll into his left hand and reached down to grab Camilla's arm with his right, then hoisted her up the slope behind him. In the corner of his vision, the bear was gaining on them, the harsh sunlight reflecting off the beast's thick, silvery-cinnamon coat and off the water droplets flying up around him.

"Santa Maria!" Camilla screamed as Cuno pulled her up off her right knee and she glanced behind to see the bear barreling across the rocky streambed. "I won't make it!"

Cuno gave her arm another tug and she screamed as he pulled her onto both feet, half dragging the girl along behind him. The largest slot cave was now fifty yards away, the gap widening with agonizing slowness, the bear trudging up the hill behind them, so close that Cuno could hear the bruin's ragged breaths.

There were several gaps between layers of the crenellated sandstone. Cuno headed for the largest one, about as long as he was tall and about two feet high. Impossible to tell how deep it was, but they were about to find out.

Cuno glanced behind once more. The bear was so close he could see the whites in the animal's eyes. There were several hairless patches along his neck and shoulders—likely old battle scars—and his smell was nearly as eye-watering strong as a skunk's.

Cuno pushed Camilla down in front of him with more force than he'd intended. "Go on!"

The girl gave a yowl as she hit the ground, then scrambled on hands and knees into the gap, gravel flying out around her. Cuno dropped to his knees as the shadow of the charging bear passed over him and brushed across the face of the scarp. He threw down the saddlebags, blanket roll, and himself when the bear was about ten feet behind him. Diving into the gap, he felt a sharp scrape across his boot as the bear swept a claw-tined paw at him, bellowing raucously.

"Hurry!" Camilla shrieked as, grabbing Cuno's right shoulder, she pulled him back into the dark, musty gap.

Cuno lunged back toward the long, narrow opening, grabbing a saddlebag pouch with one hand and pulling it in behind him. He did the same with the blanket roll. Then, as the bear swatted at the opening with both paws, slashing with those sickle-like, razor-edged claws and mewling and bellowing so loudly that Cuno thought his eardrums would shatter, the young freighter kicked himself as far into the cave as he could.

He was glad to find that he could slide back a good ten feet before the back of his head and his shoulder smacked a solid stone wall. The bear's shadow slid this way and that across the gap and across a small, cup-sized hole a couple of feet above it, and in that hole Cuno saw a flash of white, snarling teeth and blazing red eyes.

A shudder racked him.

"Go 'way!" Camilla cried, heeling sand and gravel toward the gap.

One of the bear's flailing paws almost caught her right moccasin, and Cuno grabbed her arm and pulled her taut against him, his voice nearly drowned by the bear's bellowing tirade as he yelled, "Keep your legs in, girl, or he'll rip 'em off!"

"Son of a bitch!" the girl cried again, closing her hands over her ears. "*El oso loco*, go away!"

Raising her knees to her chest, she pressed the side of her face against Cuno's shoulder, clutching his left arm with both her hands, digging her fingers painfully into his bicep as she drew him taut against her. Cuno kept his own knees raised and angled toward the girl, and he laid a shielding hand across her head, feeling her starts and shudders beneath it. He gritted his teeth against the din, against the smell of the bear pushing through the gap and the sand he was throwing up into their faces.

He planted his right hand over his .45's ivory grips, and he considered taking another shot as he watched the bear scoop sand out away from the gap now and occasionally lower his head to peer with those blazing eyes into the cave. The bear sniffed loudly, then opened his mouth, unfolding that broad, pink tongue and revealing those long, savage fangs.

Camilla pushed even harder against Cuno, driving her knees up against his side and cowering against his shoulder as she yelled incoherently amidst the bear's mad roar. The griz closed his mouth, pulled back slightly, and for a moment hope welled in Cuno like an elixir.

Had the beast given up?

But then the broad shadow closed like a savage fetid night of hell over the gap once more, and the broad, shaggy paws with those horrific claws appeared, swiping at the orange sand and gravel at the bottom of the opening.

"He's trying to work his way in," Cuno muttered, hearing the awe in his own voice as the bear grunted and snorted and made snicking and scratching sounds as he dug a hole at the bottom of the gap.

Cuno flicked the keeper thong from over his .45's hammer with his index finger and pulled the iron from its holster. He held the six-shooter out halfheartedly, staring at the gap in which the paws worked and the broad snout with contracting and expanding nostrils appeared fleetingly from time to time.

If Cuno could shoot the bear through one of its eyes, he might kill it.

Cuno waited.

The bear dug, grunting and groaning with savage eagerness, no doubt anticipating the taste of the human flesh on his tongue.

Camilla sobbed and pulled at Cuno's arm. He could feel the wetness of her tears through the sleeve of his buckskin tunic.

He rocked the Colt's hammer back. At almost the same time, the bear loosed another bellowing, echoing roar as he lay flat on his side and threw one front paw deep into the hole. The claw slashed the sand only a few feet in front of Cuno's boots. One eye at the bottom of the gap flashed.

Cuno aimed the Colt at the bear's eye and began taking the slack from his trigger finger. Suddenly, the bear lifted his head, and the eye was gone. The paw snaked back out of the hole. Cuno muttered a curse and let the Colt sag in his hand. The bear went to work wildly again on the hole at the bottom of the gap's entrance, roaring and raging, sand flying in all directions.

Then he stopped. Dust sifted. The bear grunted, and Cuno could hear him out there, crunching sand and kicking gravel, breathing hard and sort of groaning as though with defeat. The bulky shadow slid back away from the gap, and the grunts and groans and the crunch of sand and gravel and grass dwindled gradually.

The silence inside the cave was like a heavy physical presence. It was so quiet that Cuno thought he could hear the quiet ticking of the dust settling back down on the floor. Camilla sniffed and turned her head quickly, startled by the sudden silence.

They both listened for a time, saying nothing.

Camilla turned to Cuno and whispered, "He is gone?"

The bear was still grunting and groaning angrily, but the sounds seemed to emanate from the bottom of the canyon. There was the distant snap of a twig under a heavy foot.

Cuno drew his legs under him and crawled over to the cave's opening and, crouching, peered out. The bear was on the canyon floor, ambling slowly back across the stream, his heavy shoulders and haunches rippling with each step, his big head swinging under the large hump between his shoulders.

Cuno glanced back at Camilla still hunched up against the cave's rear wall, her hair mussed, her brown eyes glistening in the light from the entrance. "Stay put."

He crawled out and knelt in front of the opening, hands

on his thighs, staring down the slope toward where the bear was now ambling across the rocks on the far side of the stream. He was heading back toward the trees between this lesser stream and the main one snaking along the base of the opposite canyon wall.

Cuno started to rise but stopped when the bear wheeled suddenly. He dropped back down to his knees and lowered his head as the massive bruin rose up on his rear legs and, throwing his head back on his shoulders and clawing at the air with his raised front paws, loosed another bellow that echoed around the canyon like near thunder.

He kept the bellow up a good, long time, shambling back toward Cuno and the cave.

Cuno turned and crawled back into the notch cave.

Camilla regarded him sidelong and skeptically, sliding her mussed hair back from one side of her face.

"I'm not all that familiar with bears," Cuno said, sagging back down against the wall beside the girl. "But I have a suspicion he's trying to lure us out. We best settle in here for a time, see if he moseys along." He snapped a curse, biting his lower lip and resting an arm on his upraised knee. "I wish I had my Winchester!"

"You shouldn't have left it on your horse," Camilla whispered.

Cuno gave her a wry glance, then swept his gaze back toward the low, oval opening letting in just enough gray daylight to fill the cave with shadows.

"We never should have stopped here," Camilla continued in her admonishing whisper. "It was foolish with a bear around!"

"I thought he was up on the rim, holing up with all the other bears holing up this time of the year," Cuno grunted, the tips of his ears warming with chagrin. "Besides, damnit, the horse needed a blow. He's not used to having two people on his back, and you're not exactly a little wisp, you know."

The girl only snorted and raked her angry gaze from him

to the cave entry. She extended her right leg and sucked a sharp breath through gritted teeth.

Cuno looked at her. "What's the matter?"

"Nothing," she said, in a snit.

"Come on—what'd you do to your leg?"

"It's not my leg. It's my ankle. It's all right."

Cuno slid out from the wall and lifted the hems of the girl's skirts above her ankle-high moccasin, then rolled up a cuff of the men's red longhandles she wore, as well. Camilla sucked a breath but made no move to stop him.

Cuno leaned down to inspect her ankle. It seemed to be swelling around the top of the beaded moccasin and turning the color of rifle bluing under her natural tan. "What'd you do?"

"What did *you* do? It twisted when you jerked my arm."

"Oh, so this is my fault, too, huh?" Cuno chuckled without humor as he continued inspecting her ankle.

He moved her foot from side to side, and Camilla lunged forward from the cave wall. "*Mierda!* It hurts, damnit!"

"Shit. Now we're really fixed. You can't walk and we got no horse."

Cuno jerked her longhandle cuff down, and then the hems of her skirts. He sagged back against the cave wall, running his hands up his face in frustration and dislodging his hat. It tumbled off his shoulder and landed crown down on the cave floor.

It wasn't just him and Camilla he was concerned about. This fix was Serenity and the children's fix, as well. Valuable time was ticking away and, meanwhile, Leaping Wolf's braves might be closing in on the wagons.

Cuno thought it over for a time.

"I reckon we wait till the bear leaves. Then I'll try to run down Renegade and bring him back here."

Camilla leaned forward and down, turning her head up slightly to glance at the sky. "It is getting late. Only a few hours before the sun sets."

"I know that," Cuno said, unable to keep the frustration from his voice.

"I was just saying it," the girl said sharply, leaning back against the wall and crossing her arms on her chest in disgust.

The bear went on bellowing and stomping around the canyon bottom. Cuno and Camilla settled into an uneasy wait, staring at the cave mouth and watching the sunlight angle steadily to the right as the afternoon drew toward early evening.

With his mind, Cuno tried to hold the light. He wanted to find Renegade—if the horse was anywhere within ten miles of here—and get back to the wagons before good night closed down over the mountains. Serenity was probably waiting for him at the stream at the base of the high saddle, or he might have come on south, expecting to run into Cuno and Camilla along the way.

He wouldn't make it this far before nightfall, however. He'd have to hole up somewhere north of here. If the bruin didn't find him, the Indians might. Serenity was tough as wang leather, but he wasn't as handy as he claimed he was with a rifle. He and the kids would be easy prey.

Christ!

Cuno wished he hadn't listened to Camilla's idea about the shortcut. It wasn't her fault they'd run into the bear—they might have run into one the other way, as well—but sitting quietly like this, horseless and rifleless—the mind tended to imagine all the possibilities and chew on all the should/shouldn't haves.

About an hour before sunset, the grizzly fell silent, and Cuno decided to scout around and see if the beast was still nearby. If not, he'd head out after Renegade and hope to find the horse before good dark. He was halfway across the stream, however, when the bear—a dark, lumbering shape in the grass and black tree columns—came lumbering and rumbling up out of the pines.

Cuno cursed, scrambled back up the slope and into the cave.

"What happened?" Camilla asked.

Cuno winced at the cold stream water freshly soaking his deerhide breeches. "Best get comfortable. Looks like we're gonna be spending the night right here."

22

"WHAT HAS MADE Leaping Wolf so killing angry?" Camilla asked later than night, when the mountain night had filled the cave with black ink.

She and Cuno had found a passageway to a wider cavern with a gap at the top for a smoke hole. The cavern was only about the size of a large wagon bed, but it was well protected from the outside. Cuno had gathered wood along the outside slope and built a fire in the middle of the cavern floor.

Now the umber flames sparkled in the girl's dark eyes as she regarded Cuno curiously, a strip of jerky in one hand, a cup of smoking coffee in the other.

Cuno set a small chunk of wood on the fire. Out of shame, Trent had probably never confessed the reason for the Indian attack to Mrs. Lassiter, who had lost her husband because of it, and then, probably, her own life. Of course, no one would have told the children or Camilla. Michelle still didn't know the reason, and there was no point in her knowing.

Camilla had a right to know, however. Cuno told her as he stared at the light of the flames dancing on the cracked stone wall on the other side of the fire.

The girl only nodded knowingly, fatefully, and ripped a chunk of jerky from the strip in her hands and chewed. She sat Indian style, her elbows on her knees, as she stared into the dancing flames.

After a time, Cuno dug another strip of jerky out of the pouch lying between them, and leaned back against the wall. "How long you worked for the Lassiters?"

"Almost a year." She frowned as she studied the flames. "No, a year now."

Since she offered nothing more, he threw politeness to the wind. "Where you from?"

She continued chewing as she stared into the fire as though mesmerized. She spoke softly, dreamily. "All over. I was born in the Arizona Territory." She glanced at Cuno. "You?"

"Nebraska Territory. My parents were killed a few years back. My old man was a freighter, so I took up the trade. Didn't know what else to do." Cuno chuckled around a mouthful of jerky. "Pays the bill if you can hold on to your wagons and your mules. And you don't get all your drivers shot."

"It is better here," Camilla said. "In Arizona, the Apaches make Leaping Wolf look tame."

"What brought you here?"

"My father was a prospector. *Mejicano*. My mother was Lipan Apache. I was born in Agua Prieta, and my parents ran a goat farm. When my mother left and went back to her tribe, Papa gave up the farm and started prospecting for gold. He found little but rocks and dust and the carcasses of soldiers killed by Apaches. When I was ten he took me to Tucson and left me there on the doorstep of the Butterfield stage manager."

Camilla extended her right leg, moving the injured foot around in a circle, wincing slightly as she stared at her beaded moccasin. "The manager was not a nice man, if you get my drift"—the girl snorted her distaste for the man—"so I took to the streets. I met a gambler—a nice enough gringo, as far as gringos go—and followed him to Laramie.

He was shot there while using a privy behind a whorehouse by a man he'd cheated at stud."

Camilla glanced at Cuno, her lips shaping a grim smile. "When his money started running out and they kicked me out of the hotel I was in, I started looking for work. That is when Mr. Lassiter came to town, looking for a girl to help with the children and chores on his ranch. It was a good job. The Lassiters were good folks."

Cuno swallowed his last bit of jerky and washed it down with coffee, resting his elbow on his knee as he looked down at the girl staring up at him obliquely. "Where will you go after the fort?" he asked her.

"I will see to the children. Then . . ." Camilla shook her head. "We haven't even gotten to the fort yet. I think we will do well by getting out of this cave without becoming *el oso loco*'s last big meal before he turns in for the winter."

"Haven't heard him out there for a while. Could be he got sleepy, decided to bed down for the evening at least."

As Cuno stared at the narrow passageway leading to the front of the cave and the opening, Camilla clamped her hand down on his thigh quickly and spoke with frightened urgency. "Do not go tonight. Don't leave me."

Cuno turned to her, frowning. She must have thought he was considering going after his horse in the dark. "I'm not gonna . . ."

He let his voice trail off, felt himself falling into her wide brown eyes. He leaned toward her and ran the first two fingers of his right hand along the straight, firm line of her jaw, over the long, pale scar to her ear. Her eyes grew wider as he stared into them, and when he lowered his mouth to hers, her lips opened for him.

He pressed his lips to hers and wrapped his arms around her, drawing her taut against him, and he could feel her breasts heave beneath her clothes as they kissed hungrily. She groaned softly and ran her hands up his back and into his hair, holding his kiss and pressing her chest against his, as though she were afraid he'd let her go.

Her mouth was ripe and sweet-tasting, and her tongue

darted in and out of his mouth, entangling with his, and he could feel his body warming from inside, his loins swelling. Suddenly, he pulled her away from him and jerked his tunic out of his pants. As he lifted the garment over his head, she went to work shucking out of her own clothes, both of them sitting across from each other in the low-ceilinged cave, flushed and breathing hard with a furious, elemental desire.

Cuno tossed aside his gun belt and kicked out of his boots, wrestled his breeches and then his longhandles down his legs. He sat naked in the firelight, waiting for her to finish shucking out of her clothing. His pale body, rounded and strapped with hard muscles, his belly flat and ribbed as a washboard, his blond hair falling to his shoulders, was copper-colored in the dancing flames. His dong jutted, fully engorged, from between his heavy, hairless thighs.

His chest rose and fell as he watched Camilla, naked from the waist down, lift her camisole over her head and toss it away, her hair tumbling back down across her face and shoulders, her brown eyes peering out from behind the long, coarse, black strands. Her legs, angled before the fire, knees slightly bent, were long and smooth, the calves and thighs nicely muscled, her feet long and slender. A small, silver crucifix hung from a rawhide thong between her full, round, light brown breasts framed by her hair.

Cuno grabbed her by the shoulders and drew her to him. He kissed her again hungrily, and then she lowered her head to his crotch, licking and nuzzling his jutting, throbbing member, her hair dancing across his chest. She lay back on his bedroll, propping herself on her elbows, and spread her knees. She stared up at him smokily, expectantly, through her screening hair.

As her breasts rose and fell, nudging the silver crucifix from side to side, the brown nipples jutting, Cuno positioned himself before her spread legs, laid his hands against the sides of her face, and, pressing the hair back from her cheeks, felt her guide him into her hot, wet core.

"Oh," she said as he drove in slowly, deeply, arching his back and neck and squeezing his eyes closed, savoring the moment. "Oh . . . *Cristo*!"

Later, they snuggled together inside the bedroll. Cuno had built up the fire from the pile he'd gathered from the slope. They didn't say anything, only nuzzled each other, caressed, and kissed in the dolor of a spent passion. The fire popped and crackled, occasionally hissing when sap hit the flames.

Cuno ran his hand slowly up her smooth thigh from her knee and across her belly. Then he lifted his hand to her face and ran the back of his index finger from her left ear to her chin. She took his hand in hers and ran his finger along the scar.

"Wanna know how I came by this?" she said, half shutting her eyes as she caressed the scar with his finger.

Cuno rested his chin on her shoulder. "Streets of Tucson? The gambler?"

"The gambler's wife. She was Coyotero." Camilla spat the word like a bad chunk of meat. Her sudden smile took him aback, her lips spreading back from her fine, white teeth, firelight dancing in her exquisite eyes. "She'll never do *that* again!"

In his dreamy state, the bear and the Indians a thousand miles from his thoughts, it took Cuno a few seconds to comprehend her meaning. Then he chuckled as he ran his hand down her neck and into her cleavage, beside the leather thong and along the ripe curve of her breast to the nipple. "Remind me not to get on your bad side."

"Sí." She chuckled and rolled toward him, cupping his balls in her hand. Instantly, he began coming alive again. "I will remind you!"

Cuno groaned, pushed her back down on the blanket once more, and rolled between her knees, which she spread for him eagerly.

Cuno woke every two hours or so to throw more wood on the fire, keeping it built up all night while Camilla slept, curled in his blankets. To stay warm, he'd donned his clothes, and he slept with his head on his coat rolled up at the base of the cave wall, lying with his hip touching the girl's, his hat pulled down over his eyes.

When pearl light shone in the sky above the smoke hole, he put coffee on the fire to cook, then knelt down beside Camilla, asleep on her side, knees draw up, her hair fanned over her face. He was about to touch her shoulder but stopped suddenly when he heard a soft rasp as she drew a long, slow breath, then a lower-pitched sigh as she let it out. A few strands of her hair puffed slightly out from her lips then lay flat again as she breathed in.

He knelt there for nearly a minute, listening to the girl breathe in her sleep, her shoulders moving slightly with each breath. It was a peaceful, homey sound. He'd forgotten the simple, subtle joy of hearing someone breathing peacefully beside him as he'd once heard July breathing as she'd slept beside him in their little ranch cabin, their baby growing ever so slowly inside her.

Waking before his young wife in the predawn hours, when their room was all mist and blurred edges, he'd often imagined her breath becoming the baby's breath, and her exhalations the same as the baby's filling the room around him.

Cuno leaned down, slid the blanket away from Camilla's bare shoulder, and gently pressed his lips against the smooth, warm flesh. He kept his lips pressed to the girl's shoulder and squeezed his eyes closed, the keen pang of bittersweet grief swelling inside him.

Camilla's breathing changed suddenly as she drew a deep draught of air into her lungs and groaned sleepily, turning a little to look up at him, the corners of her mouth lifting as she raised her elbows above her head, stretching.

Then she gasped and her eyes snapped wide with a start as she lowered her hands to draw the blanket up to her neck, looking around the firelit cave, her dark eyes filling suddenly with the realization that the night was over and another day of peril was just beginning.

Cuno set his hand on her shoulder. "Everything's all right. Early yet. I'm gonna go out and try to find my horse."

"I will go with you."

Cuno shook his head. "You best stay off that ankle. I'll be back for you soon, with or without the paint." Cuno laid his hand against her cheek. "We'll be all right. Don't leave the cave. I haven't heard the bear, but that don't mean he's not still on the lurk out there."

As he rose and turned, she said, "Cuno, be careful."

He nodded and ducked through the narrow passageway, then dropped to his hands and knees as he entered the small foyer-like area and continued to the oval opening. The bear had dug a sizable crater beneath the opening, and Cuno thought he could still smell the beast's fetor.

He poked his head out slowly. The sharp cold air, tinged with a piney tang, nipped his cheeks as he drew it into his lungs, and he shuddered at the sudden chill pressing against him after the fire's soothing warmth.

There was no breeze. The shrubs and rocks, coated with a ghostly white frost, stood stark against the pale gray light filtering down from the eastern sky.

A few stars still burned. Down the hill, the valley lay unmoving, black and gray and ominous. Utter silence except for the occasional, glassy murmur of the stream sliding over the ice-coated stones.

Neither seeing or hearing the bear, Cuno moved out onto the rocky slope and gained his feet. The sand and gravel in front of the cave had been torn up by the bear's claws, branches strewn as though by a wind storm.

For a time Cuno hunkered down behind a high, angling escarpment jutting from the slope just ahead and right of the cave opening, pricking his ears to listen. He raked his gaze slowly back and forth across the valley floor, squinting at the dark pines clustered on the far side and fronting the other stream angling along the base of the far wall.

No shadows moved.

No sound but the occasional distant yip of coyotes. Grass blades scratched in a vagrant breeze.

Cuno started zigzagging down the slope, one hand on his .45. When he gained the valley bottom, he crossed the stream, keeping his boots dry by negotiating the icy rocks, and headed north after his horse.

"Come out, come out, wherever you are, *el oso loco*," Cuno sang under his breath, swinging his head slowly from left to right. His boots crunched the frost-furred grass. "Do it now . . . before I get too damn far away from the cave . . ."

23

THE SUN WAS well up though hidden by low, gunmetal clouds, and Cuno had seen no sign of the bear.

A chill wind blew leaves across his path as he continued along the slowly rising, gently curving canyon floor with the stream on his left and a low rock ridge on his right, with a steep, boulder-strewn slope rolling up beyond it to stand several thousand feet above the canyon floor.

Mares' tails of dark clouds caught and tore on the bizarre stone formations jutting from the ridge crest.

Occasionally Cuno saw the mark of a shod hoof in the gravelly turf, and believed it to be one of Renegade's. They were the only prints he saw, and he'd seen Renegade hightail it in this direction. For all Cuno knew, the paint could be in Wyoming Territory by now and still heading north.

When he figured he'd walked a good two miles, taking occasional sips from the stream, he sensed another presence. The hair under his coat collar pricked, and he stopped at the edge of the trees lining the stream and, one hand on his revolver's grips, looked around at the valley stretched out before him, dun grass and gray-green sage blowing in the chill wind.

The bear could be anywhere in here. A rogue male, he'd no doubt staked out a broad territory, and woe be to interlopers.

A branch snapped behind Cuno. He jerked with a start and, whipping his Colt up and thumbing back the hammer, wheeled, crouching and aiming the gun straight out in front of him.

His heart skipped a beat and then he depressed the Colt's hammer and dropped the gun by his side. The paint clomped toward him through the trees, angling away from the stream, hooves thumping and crunching the dry brush and dead leaves, water dripping from his snout.

"Damn, boy," Cuno said, blowing out a long, relieved breath. "Scared the hell out of me."

Renegade stopped a few feet away, his eyes still wary, and snorted and bobbed his head and twitched his ears—as glad to see Cuno as Cuno was to see him. The young freighter moved up to the horse and, that uneasy feeling continuing to lift the hairs beneath his collar, glanced around warily as he reset the saddle on the paint's back, tightening the latigo and adjusting the breast strap, then slipping the bridle bit back into Renegade's mouth. He adjusted the boot, as well, relieved to see that the Winchester was still inside.

The horse, too, looked around, occasionally holding still and staring up canyon, ears pricked and tail slightly arched.

"What is it, boy?" One hand on the horse's neck, Cuno turned to stare in the same direction the paint was staring. The horse seemed to be holding his breath.

Cuno cast his gaze through the trees and into the open canyon beyond, angling it north. There was nothing but trees, grass, sage, rock, and the low, gray sky that seemed to grow darker by the minute.

A wooden rattle sounded, obscured by the whoosh of the wind in the treetops.

Silence.

Another wooden rattle. There was yet another sound that Cuno couldn't identify, and the amalgam of sounds seemed to be getting louder and coming out of the north, whipped and torn by the wind.

Cuno turned and placed a hand on the side of Renegade's neck. "Come on, boy." Gently, he swung the horse around and led him back toward the stream. He continued casting wary looks over his shoulder as he led the paint across the shallow creek tumbling ice chunks over the rocks, and stopped behind a sharp-edged, slant-topped boulder as large as a cabin standing at the base of the ridge wall. He tied the horse to a cedar jutting from a fissure in the rock.

"Stay, fella."

Cuno patted the horse's snout, the signal to keep quiet. Shucking his Winchester from the saddle boot, he quietly racked a fresh shell into the chamber, then off-cocked the hammer and stole out from around the rock to make his way back across the stream. Staring north through the trees, he left the stream and continued toward the clearing beyond, weaving around pines, scattered aspens, and brush snags.

The rattling grew steadily louder. A wagon clattering over rocks. Near the edge of the woods, Cuno hunkered down behind a large ash bole and a boulder just beyond it, and edged his gaze around the left side of the bole and peered between the tree and the boulder.

A hundred yards away, a horseback rider sat on a low rise—a bulky figure on a short-legged horse and cradling what appeared to be a rifle in his arms. Horse and rider were merely silhouettes from this distance and in this light.

The rider peered straight ahead of Cuno, unmoving, and Cuno tensed, drawing his head back closer to the tree, exposing only one eye as he continued staring northward.

His heartbeat quickened.

Had the rider seen him? He didn't want to be seen until he knew who was doing the seeing.

The man turned his head slowly from right to left, then back again. Suddenly, he swung his head sharply to one side, looking behind him as he raised the rifle high with one hand. He turned forward again, pressed his knees to his horse's sides, and horse and rider trotted off the ridge crest toward Cuno, the horse's hooves thudding dully on the grassy turf, occasionally kicking a rock.

The rider was within fifty yards of the young freighter when the clattering behind him continued and then a team of horses appeared atop the rise he'd just left. As they continued over the top of the rise and started down the other side, a wagon appeared. The man in the driver's box whipped the reins across the horses' backs, grunting and bellowing words Cuno couldn't hear above the wind and the creaking of the bending trees.

No, not horses.

The team came on, and the gray light slid across the animals to reveal four mules in collars and hames. Not just any mules.

Cuno's mules.

And they were attached to Cuno's Conestoga, which rumbled after the trotting mules, barking over rocks and crunching sage shrubs as the driver continued flicking the reins over the backs of the steaming team and grunting and spewing the guttural, consonant-hard words of an Indian tongue.

A wave of nausea washed through the young freighter as he stared in shock toward the wagon clattering down the slope and the lead rider who was also an Indian dressed in deerskins, with a deerskin hood on his head. Black hair pushed out of his hood to dangle over his shoulders.

The rifle in his arms was a Winchester carbine. His horse was a stout-legged cream painted for war. As the man passed in front of Cuno, about sixty yards out from Cuno's position, the profile of his broad, hooked nose shone, dark as tanned leather against the gray ridge on the other side of him.

His horse's hooves clomped on the cold, hard ground.

Behind him, the wagon pushed forward, and Cuno anxiously swept the green-painted box with his eyes. That's when he saw something trailing behind.

No, not something. *Someone.* Two people—one jogging along behind with a rope tied around his waist, the other end of the rope tied to the wagon box.

The dark brown hair and build of the boy bespoke Karl Lassiter. Hatless, the kid wore no gloves, and his coat flapped open at his chest, revealing his flannel work shirt and suspenders. He ran with a shambling, loose-footed gait, several times nearly falling even as Cuno watched him, the boy's face expressionless, head wobbling around on his shoulders as though his neck were broken.

Beside and slightly behind him a body was being dragged from a rope attached to the side of the wagon nearest Cuno. As the wagon rattled and squawked straight out from the tree and the covering boulder, Cuno inspected the figure quickly as it fishtailed along the ground behind the wagon, bouncing over hummocks and rocks, jerking and pitching and swaying.

He sucked a sharp breath when he saw the balding head over which thin strands of silver hair slid in the wind. The gray-bearded face turned toward him, eyes squeezed shut. Serenity's arms were thrust out in front of him, his tied hands clutching the taut rope angling forward and up toward the wagon box.

The oldster lifted his head slightly to peer up at the wagon, then bellowed something Cuno couldn't make out as he feebly tried to gain his feet, digging the toes of his high-topped boots into the ground. But it slid under him too quickly for the graybeard to gain a purchase.

He screamed again as he fell, hitting the ground and bouncing, his voice shrill with rage and misery. Then his thin, bent body fell slack once more, and his bearded cheek dropped to his shoulder. The wagon rattled on past Cuno, dragging his old friend's limp figure along behind it.

On the far side of Serenity, Karl continued to stumble along, half jogging, half falling, his lace-up boots crunching grass and sage clumps.

Cuno's heart hammered with rage. He squeezed his rifle and moved toward the other side of the tree to deliver two quick, killing shots to the wagon driver and the lead rider. Seeing something out the tail of his left eye, he stayed his attack and edged another look around the left side of the tree.

Another rider jogged his horse down the slope about fifty yards behind Serenity and Karl Lassiter. Holding his reins high against his chest, he was bundled in deerskin breeches and a buffalo coat, with elkskin moccasins rising nearly to his knees. A rifle hung down his back from a braided leather lanyard, and from the barrel dangled what looked like a tuft of feathers or maybe a light-colored human scalp.

The man wore nothing on his head, and his long, black hair was streaked with gray. The slope of his shoulders also marked him as old. His horse was a big palomino stallion with a savage fire in its eyes, and it had a large, red circle painted on its left hip, with several smaller geometric shapes of different colors painted inside it.

Two more followed this man, riding abreast, and then two more and three more and four more . . . until Cuno counted nine more Utes trailing the wagon in various-sized clumps. All were armed with either bows and arrows, with quivers hanging down their backs, or Winchester or Spencer rifles. One brave held a big Sharps buffalo gun across his shoulder, the broad stock decorated with copper rivets limning a star.

Gritting his teeth with frustration, Cuno edged a look around the other side of the tree. The wagon dwindled into the gray distance down canyon, every second drawing it farther and farther away.

The old Indian, who, judging by his age and the splendor of his horse, figured to be Leaping Wolf himself, jogged along behind with the other, younger warriors bringing up the rear, bouncing and jouncing in their saddles, a couple conversing in their clipped, harsh-sounding tongue.

Holding his rifle straight up and down in front of him,

Cuno pressed his left shoulder to the tree, every muscle in his body drawn tense as razor wire. He hoped against hope that Renegade remembered his training and, despite the whiff of savage, wild-smelling Indian on the chill breeze, did not loose an involuntary whinny.

If one of these grim warriors spied Cuno, the young freighter wouldn't have a chance against the group, and he'd have no chance to help Serenity and the others. He didn't know why they were being kept alive—Cuno had only a glimpse of Michelle and Margaret huddled under hides in the back of the wagon—but Leaping Wolf likely didn't aim to keep them alive for long.

Cuno stared down canyon as the last of the warriors became a thin, brown, jostling smudge in the far distance. The clattering of the wagon dwindled off into silence, leaving only the ceaseless rush of the wind in the trees.

Cuno rose slowly, his heart still thudding and his mind racing, his eyes still staring down canyon where the procession had been absorbed into the gray, wintery distance. Blinking as though trying to awaken from a nightmare but realizing the nightmare was real, he stepped back away from the tree.

He moved quietly back toward the stream, crouching, afraid one of the Indians or their horses might still hear him. Preoccupied with the image of Serenity being dragged so mercilessly behind the wagon, he stepped carelessly and, his boot slipping off an ice-encrusted stone, he nearly fell in the water as he crossed the stream.

"All right, damnit," he told himself when he'd gained the other side, dropping to one knee, doffing his hat and running a brusque hand through his long hair. "Settle down. Take your time. You gotta think this through slow and careful-like."

He had to follow the group, see where they were going. He had to do it carefully so they didn't see him, so their horses didn't smell him. As badly as he wanted to gallop into the bunch, guns blazing, he had to bide his time and wait for the moment when he had the best chance of helping Serenity and the others, though his odds—one against eleven—would likely never be anything but long.

Any other way would only get him and the others killed for certain.

He strode over to where Renegade stood behind the boulder, wide-eyed and tense and craning his neck to stare back in the direction in which the Indians were headed.

"I know, partner," Cuno said as he stepped into the leather. "Don't like tailin' Injuns any better than you, but that's what we're gonna do."

He put the horse across the stream, through the trees, and, staying close to the edge of the woods, headed back in the direction he'd come, trotting and staring straight ahead. The Utes might roll a scout off their flank at any time, and he had to be ready to dart back into the trees.

He pushed Renegade hard for a half mile, staying close to the trees and riding with his Winchester resting across his saddlebow.

When he caught the first vague glimpse of the group's flanking riders—three braves riding side by side, two fairly close, the other farther away to the left—he slowed the horse to a trot. He kept pace with the group, slipping no closer nor farther behind.

He stared tensely at the backs of the three flanking riders. At any time one could swing a look behind. If so, Cuno had to stop Renegade quickly and rein the horse behind any available cover. Fortunately, there were plenty of shrubs, trees, and stony escarpments along the canyon floor, and the air was beginning to be obscured by light, wind-tossed snowflakes, limiting his chances of being spotted.

When the group began moving toward the section of canyon in which Cuno had left Camilla, the bowstring of tension in his back drew even tauter. Suppose the girl was outside the cave or, figuring the hoof clomps of the lead Ute was Cuno, came running down the slope only to find herself at the mercy of Leaping Wolf's savage warriors . . .

There was no chance that he could somehow sneak past

the Indians and warn her. He had to hope she was as savvy and cautious as she seemed to be and would stay hidden.

As Renegade continued clomping forward, shaking his head at the snow, another worry raked Cuno. Camilla was probably keeping the fire up inside the cave. There was a chance the Utes would see the smoke issuing from the hole at the top of the scarp. If so, they'd have her out of there in seconds, and with her bad ankle she'd have little chance of escape.

They'd either kill her or add her to their prison roll.

Cuno slid his gaze back and forth between the Indians and the north wall of the canyon, scrutinizing the pine tops for Camilla's wood smoke. The Indians must be approaching the cave; Cuno recognized the terrain ahead, the main stream curling along the ridge to his right, the secondary stream branching across the canyon floor and angling over to the opposite wall.

He couldn't see the scarp in which the cave lay, but Leaping Wolf was likely just now passing it on his palomino.

Cuno slid his gaze back to the left and winced.

Above the pine tops, about where the wagon was now passing, a ragged puff of dark gray smoke shone in the light gray air. Faint, but visible. And if the Utes didn't see it, they might smell it.

Just as Cuno slid his eyes back to the Indian party ahead, muttering a prayer that the procession would keep riding, the flanking riders suddenly started to grow slightly larger before him.

Cuno halted Renegade, lifting the horse's head. As the horse skitter-hopped sideways, Cuno saw that the party had stopped. One of the flanking riders turned his own horse sideways while the horse farthest left danced around, swishing its tail anxiously.

Cuno pulled back and up on the paint's reins, and the horse snorted with annoyance as it started backing up. When the Indians were mere blurs ahead, nearly concealed by a slight bend in the canyon, Cuno pulled Renegade behind an escarpment jutting from the north wall and dismounted.

Quickly, he tied the horse to a pine branch, grabbed his Winchester and his binoculars, stole forward about ten yards, and dropped to a knee. He laid the rifle across his thigh and raised the field glasses, adjusting the focus until the Utes swam into relatively clear view ahead in the gray, snow-stitched distance.

"Ah, shit!" he hissed sharply.

In the magnified field of vision, one of the warriors, wearing a white man's yellow-and-black mackinaw, pulled his horse sharply left and trotted toward the slope in which the cave lay.

The brave had either seen the smoke or seen Cuno's and Camilla's tracks along the creek.

24

PEERING THROUGH HIS spyglass with one hand, Cuno fingered his rifle with the other.

Frigid sweat trickled down his back beneath his buckskin tunic and cotton undershirt.

The Indian in the yellow-and-black mackinaw stopped his horse at the edge of the stream directly below the cave entrance, which Cuno couldn't see from this angle and distance. The brave dropped from the back of his coyote dun and crouched on his haunches as he reached down with one hand, as though fingering sign in the grass and gravel before him.

Soon, Cuno thought, he'd see the tracks leading to the base of the ridge, and he'd look up and see the smoke.

Then he'd go up and drag Camilla out of the cave.

Again, Cuno fingered the rifle. He couldn't sit here and watch them kill her. Just throw her in the wagon with the others, he silently beseeched. Don't kill her. Don't beat her. Don't rape her.

The other Indians sat their ponies behind him, including Leaping Wolf, who sat his palomino a little ways beyond, hipped around to regard the Indian squatting near the creek.

The wagon was continuing forward, the wind drowning its rumble.

Cuno could just barely make out Karl Lassiter jogging along behind it. Serenity was out of sight amidst the grass and sage.

Suddenly, the brave near the creek rose and leapt fluidly back atop his horse, heeling the dun back over to the group. He threw an arm out toward the far side of the canyon and then threw it out beside him, tracing a broad semicircle, as though indicating something large.

Ahead of him, Leaping Wolf turned to stare across the canyon. The old man lifted his head to scan the ridge above the southern stream, then heeled his horse forward after the wagon. The other braves followed suit, all looking around the canyon as though expecting the bear—whose sign they must have spotted, not Camilla's—to charge out from the trees.

Only partial relief eased the tension in Cuno's back.

He continued to glass the Indians as they moved on down the canyon. When they were a hundred yards beyond their stopping place, he strode back to Renegade, dropped the glasses back in their saddle pouch, and mounted up.

He gigged the paint ahead, following the bending ridge wall on his left. When he gained the stream sliding blackly over the ice-edged rocks, the large, downy snowflakes melting into it silently, he saw what the Indian had crouched over.

A big pile of chocolate-colored bear plop beaded with wine-red chokecherries. Easily the size of a dinner plate, and a good three inches high. The fetor made Cuno's lungs contract. Even in the cold air it smelled like something three days dead.

Cuno resisted the urge to call out for Camilla. The Indians were too close. Dropping out of the saddle, he tied Renegade to a spindly cottonwood branch—he didn't want to lose the horse again in case the bruin returned—and climbed the slope to the mouth of the cave.

"Camilla?" he said softly.

Dropping to his knees, he stuck his head in the dark, oval opening. Smoke wafted inside the cavern rife with the smell of pine. He poked his head a little farther inside and raised his voice.

"Camilla?"

Nothing. Faintly, the air sifted through the narrow passageway behind the small, low portico. Cuno crawled inside the cave, made his way to the far right, then stood and, crouching, made his way through the passageway to the back room in which the fire snapped and popped softly.

Cuno froze with one hand on his gun handle.

A man stood on the other side of the fire, a grin revealing large, white teeth between thick, bearded lips. He held a cocked Peacemaker revolver to the underside of Camilla's jaw. The girl stood partly in front of the man, shielding him, held there by one of the man's hands clamped soundly across her mouth.

Her brown eyes were bright with fear.

"Drop the hogleg, amigo, or your girlfriend buys a pill."

The man was roughly Cuno's height. He wore a heavy wolf coat that dropped to mid-thigh, wooly chaps, and a wool cap under his battered Stetson. He had bushy, dark brown brows and cobalt blue eyes, a thick wedge of a nose cleaving his face.

"Who the hell are you?"

"Mason. Sheriff Dusty Mason from Willow City. Seen your handiwork back west a ways—the three marshals you left deader'n last year's Christmas turkey."

Cuno stared at him, his blood freezing.

"I was supposed to meet up with 'em, and we was gonna take down some claim jumpers together." Mason held the Schofield taut against Camilla's chin, the hammer cocked, his gloved hand shaking slightly. "Damn near did meet up with 'em, but that was just before you killed 'em. I heard the shots. After I found the bodies, I tracked you . . . all the way to here, you murderin' son of a bitch."

"They were after the women," Cuno said, trying hard to keep his exasperation from his voice. "They drew first."

"Shut up and toss down that hogleg or she buys one. Damn, you're younger'n I figured. Tough to figure a cold-blooded killer."

"Nothin' cold-blooded about it, Sheriff."

Cuno glanced at Camilla, at the five-inch barrel of cold, blue steel shoved up against her jaw. He glanced at the sheriff again and narrowed his eyes with entreaty as he hooked his thumb over his shoulder. "There's Injuns out there. They've got my party. They're draggin' my partner behind my wagon. If I don't catch up to 'em soon—"

"I saw them Injuns." Frustration and befuddlement flashed through the sheriff's cobalt eyes. "Seen all dozen of 'em. Nothin' to do about that, and the way I figure it, your partner gets what he deserves. But I *can* arrest *you* for the killin's of three lawmen and for sellin' Winchesters to the Utes."

The accusation nearly rocked Cuno back on his heels. *"What?"*

"I saw them bright new Winchesters they was carryin'. Seen 'em on another party farther west, before me and the marshals split up to track the claim jumpers. Pretty damn plain someone's been sellin' guns to Leapin' Wolf's band, and I ain't seen any other freight wagons in these mountains for well over a year."

"Listen, mister . . ."

"I ain't gonna ask you again," Mason snarled, canting his edgy gaze toward Camilla. "If she shakes so damn hard she trips my trigger, it's her fault, not mine!"

"Hold on, hold on." With two fingers, Cuno slowly slid his .45 from its holster, thrust it out in front of him where Mason could get a good look at it, then, crouching low, dropped it with a thud. Just as slowly, holding both hands in front of him, palms out, he straightened.

"Got another one on ya?"

"No."

"How 'bout a knife?"

"No," Cuno lied.

He had a bowie in his boot. Let the sheriff find it for

himself, if Cuno didn't find a chance to use it on the man first. He had no qualms about killing the sheriff. It was either Mason or Serenity and the children. But he needed to do it fast.

Mason slid his hand away from Camilla's mouth, leaving a white oval where his hand had been. He shoved her to his left, and she stumbled away, glaring at him, hardening her jaws with fury.

"Go over there and sit down, senorita. One move out of you and your gringo friend gets drilled through his heart."

Keeping his Schofield leveled on Cuno, Mason reached inside his open coat and behind him. He pulled out a set of handcuffs and tossed them over the fire. They fell on the dusty, rocky floor at Cuno's feet.

"Put those on good and tight. Then you, me, and the girl are goin' for a ride to Fort Jessup. Wouldn't make it back to Willow City before the storm moves in. Besides, killin' federal badge toters and sellin' rifles to Injuns is a *federal* offense."

Rage sweeping him like a wildfire, Cuno said through gritted teeth, "I didn't sell any rifles to Indians. I sold those—"

"Put 'em on and be quick about it!" Mason glanced at Camilla. "Go over and stand by your boyfriend. Either one of you tries anything, I'll shoot you both. Got no qualms about killin' women. These rampaging Utes got my nerves tangled, and all I *really* want's a drink and a warm *bed*!"

As Camilla sidled around the fire, limping slightly on her bad ankle and keeping her eyes on the lawman, Cuno stooped, picked up the cuffs, and reluctantly set his right wrist in a ring. Desperately, his thoughts flailed around for a way out of this current dilemma. Finding none, desperation made his heart hammer and his temples pound.

"You're makin' a mistake, Mason. Those federals got what they deserved, and I didn't sell any rifles to the Utes."

"Tell it to the judge."

A log popped in the fire between Mason and Cuno, and the lawman stumbled back with a start, snapping his eyes wide. Embarrassed, he aimed the Schofield straight out from his shoulder as he shouted, *"Put them cuffs on, goddamnit—I'm through triflin' with you!"*

Cuno glanced at Camilla, then dropped his gaze to his right wrist as he closed the cuff around it. He set his other wrist in the other cuff and, closing it, hearing the click, he felt his cheek twitch and his knees turn to putty, as though the door to an inescapable trap had just been closed and bolted behind him.

"You first, senorita," Mason ordered, wagging his gun at the passageway. "Head on out. Then you, freighter."

Camilla turned slowly and, favoring the ankle she'd twisted while fleeing the bear, ducked into the passageway. Cuno turned to follow her, dropping to his knees and crawling awkwardly, unable to use his cuffed hands. Camilla was crawling out the low entrance ahead of him when he heard Mason behind him, the lawman's boots scuffing the cave floor, spurs ringing, his nervous breaths echoing around the cavern.

Cuno could feel the bowie snugged down in the sheath he'd sewn into the side of his boot well. If he could get to it, he'd use it. He'd cut the lawman's throat if he had to . . . if it was the only way he could shed the man and get back on Serenity's trail.

He poked his head out the cave entrance. Camilla had turned toward him on her hands and knees and, wrapping her right hand around a good-sized rock, looked at Cuno meaningfully as she slowly rose to her feet.

Cuno shook his head. Her chances of being able to knock the lawman out with the rock were slim, and the attempt might well get her killed. Frowning and pursing her lips, Camilla dropped the stone.

"Step back away from the entrance," Mason ordered as he poked his head out the cave entry. "Give me a good ten feet, and face me. Don't try makin' a run for it. I'm right handy with this here hogleg."

When Cuno and Camilla had stepped back away from the entry, Mason crawled out on one hand and his knees.

Keeping the Schofield aimed at Cuno's chest, the lawman heaved himself up with a wince, his bearded face flushed and sweating, steam rising around his head.

"Whew!" he said, chuckling nervously. "Right close quarters in there." He looked down the slope to where Renegade stood in some tall grass along the stream, staring skeptically up the ridge. Snow was beginning to stick to the horse's back and saddle.

Mason looked at Cuno. "Where's the girl's hoss?"

"Only got the one."

"Head down to him, then. Mine's in a box canyon 'bout a half mile north." Mason grinned. "Me and the girl'll ride your horse till we come to mine. You'll lead the way . . . on foot."

Cuno stared at the lawman.

Mason read the dark intent in the young freighter's eyes. "Remember—you try anything, I'll drill you both. Got no time for nonsense."

"Yeah, I know," Cuno grumbled as he turned and, Camilla walking beside him, started down the slope. "You just want a drink and a warm bed."

Cuno sidestepped down the slope that was slippery from the fresh snow dusting the grass and slide rock. It was an awkward maneuver, for he couldn't distribute his weight with his arms, and he almost fell several times. It didn't help that he was distracted by the urgent need to escape the lawman. Somehow, he had to get the knife out of his boot. If an opportunity didn't show itself sooner, he'd look for his chance when they were changing horses up canyon.

He took another step, almost slipped on a flat rock. Catching himself, he heard a loud grunt behind him. He turned his head to peer over his shoulder. Both of Mason's boots were sliding out from beneath him, his hands flying skyward.

Mason's revolver roared, stabbing smoke and flames straight up at a couple of low-arching pine boughs. The lawman hit the slope on his back, and his revolver clattered against the rocks about four feet above his head.

Cuno dropped to both knees.

The sheriff, face etched with pain, twisted around and dug a boot heel into the slope while flinging his right hand upslope toward his revolver. Cuno wrapped his cuffed hands around the man's left foot and jerked him straight down the slope, so that his hand missed the gun by a foot.

Cuno was atop the man in a second, straddling the man's torso bundled in the wolf coat.

As Mason cursed and grunted and flung his left hand upslope and behind him like a broken wing, flailing for the gun, Cuno raised his cuffed hands back behind his shoulder like a club, his biceps drawing the sleeves of his mackinaw taut, then swung them forward and down. He smashed the knuckles of his gloved left hand soundly against the lawman's bearded left cheek.

Mason's head whipped up and sideways, and his eyes fluttered.

Cuno swung his clenched fists up behind his left shoulder, and rammed them down against Mason's right cheek. There was a solid thud. The man's head slammed back against the slide rock.

The sheriff winced, bunching his untrimmed beard, the cuts on both cheeks showing in the dull light. He lifted his head slightly, the muscles in his face drawn slack, and then his lids fluttered down over his eyes, and his body fell slack against the ground.

Out like a blown lamp.

Blood from one of the cuts trickled down from the nub of his cheek and into his beard.

Camilla stood beside Cuno, staring down in shock, her earflaps jostling in the wind with her hair.

"Dig around in his pockets for his key," Cuno said, breathing hard as he straightened, his boots straddling the lawman's legs.

While Camilla fished around in the lawman's coat pockets, Cuno looked around. The sky was about as gray as it could get without turning night-dark. It was a black-and-gray world, the snow fluttering like goose down. There were no animals around. Some of the snow was starting to lay, but not enough to hinder travel.

When Camilla found the key, she fumbled around for a time, her bare fingers numb from the cold, before the cuffs ratcheted open. Cuno flung them aside, then opened the lawman's coat. His pearl-gripped .45 was wedged behind Mason's cartridge belt.

Cuno lifted the lower right flap of his own coat, slipped the revolver into its holster, then scooped up the lawman's Schofied and stuffed it behind his cartridge belt. Taking Camilla by the arm, he started back down the hill toward Renegade.

"He is not dead," Camilla warned, glancing back at the lawman.

"No."

"You shouldn't kill him?"

"Yeah, I should," Cuno grunted. But he couldn't.

He helped Camilla down the last part of the slope and threw her up onto Renegade's back. He ripped the reins from the pine branch, then climbed up in front of her.

He clucked to the horse.

As Camilla leaned taut against him and wrapped her arms around his waist, he heeled the paint into a wind-shredding gallop up canyon. He'd lost precious time, and Serenity might already be dead.

But he'd get Michelle and the kids back from the murdering Leaping Wolf if he got himself killed in the bargain.

25

A SHRILL CRY cut through the hushed, chill air of the canyon.

Cuno halted Renegade and looked around as another scream sounded—a shrill exclamation of unbearable pain and terror that echoed off the rolling, shrub-tufted hills to his right and off the steep, sandstone wall looming on his left, the crest of which was swallowed by heavy clouds.

With the echoes in the eerily quiet, snow-stitched air, it was hard to get a fix on where the screams were originating. Cuno turned to peer along his back trail, toward the high saddle barely visible in the gray distance.

He and Camilla had crossed the saddle over an hour ago, riding as fast as Cuno dared push Renegade on the uncertain terrain. At the bottom of the saddle they'd followed the canyon that they were still following now south by southwest, the tracks of the wagon and the Indian ponies clearly marking the brush, sand, rocks, and the dusting of wet snow.

Another scream rose. It sounded as though it were uncoiling from the bottom of a deep, stone-walled well. It pricked the hair beneath Cuno's collar, and tightened his gut. He looked around quickly, shuttling his gaze back and forth across the canyon, from the base of the high ridge on his left, along which a stony, dry creek bed snaked, stippled with leafless trees and tangled brush, to the ravine-sliced hills rising more gently on his right.

He could feel Camilla's heart beating in her chest pressed against his back as she, too, swept their surroundings with her eyes.

"It's ahead of us," Cuno said, lifting his right boot over the saddle horn and dropping straight down to the ground.

He couldn't tell if the scream, which continued with frustrating, horrifying regularity about every fifteen seconds, belonged to a man or a woman. That he'd drawn to within a few hundred yards of the Utes had been plain in their sign, the snow only having just barely dusted their tracks since they'd passed. Within the last ten minutes, he'd spied steaming horse apples.

"What are you going to do?" Camilla said, scooting up into the saddle.

Cuno tossed her the reins. He dug around under his coat for Mason's Schofield. He filled the .44 from shells on his own belt, spun the wheel, and extended the gun to Camilla grips first.

She frowned at the gun, slowly wrapped her mittened hand around the handle.

"Hole up down in that creek bottom. If I'm not back for you in an hour, you're on your own. The Indians are ahead, so you'll need to find a way around them to Jessup. Shouldn't be but a few miles from here."

Staring gravely at Cuno, Camilla shoved the gun down in a pocket of her bulky coat. "There are too many Indios, Cuno. You don't have a chance against them."

He shucked his Winchester from the boot beneath the girl's right thigh. "Maybe I'll get lucky."

He racked a shell in the Winchester's breech, off-cocked the hammer, and set the barrel on his shoulder as he swung around and started down canyon.

"Hold on."

Cuno turned. The girl reined Renegade up beside him. She grabbed his coat collar with one hand, then leaned down and kissed his lips, drawing him toward her tightly. She didn't say anything as she released his collar and straightened. Her solemn, brown-eyed gaze held his.

Cuno turned and began tramping west, his insides recoiling at each echoing blast of the chilling scream. Behind him he heard Camilla put Renegade down the slope toward the streambed, the horse's shod hoofs ringing dully off snow-furred rocks and crunching frozen brush and branches.

He walked a hundred yards, rounding a sharp zigzag between two granite scarps, the screams growing shriller and more frequent. They were joined by a softer sound that Cuno gradually came to recognize as little Margaret Lassiter's crying. There were other sounds, too—the harsh voices of the Indians drowned by occasional bursts of hearty laughter.

Continuing down canyon, holding his rifle up high across his chest, following the screams and the sobs and the laughter, Cuno soon found himself climbing a low scarp of raw granite. The formation had bubbled up out of the ground several millennia ago, and it now bristled with a couple of stunt cedars and a tiny juniper that grew out of a crack in the top.

The surface was slick with melting snow.

Cuno crabbed forward amongst the shrubs and, keeping his head low, stared into a broad horseshoe of the creek bed down the other side. The wagon was parked there along the bed, amongst sprawling cottonwoods and aspens. Nearly a dozen or so Indian ponies were there, as well, ground-tied and nibbling at the tall, yellow grass growing up around the trees. Several of the ponies stopped foraging to jerk their heads up at each tooth-gnashing scream that rose above Margaret's continuous sobs.

What caught the brunt of Cuno's attention, and set his heart to turning somersaults in his chest, was the figure tied between two trees on the far side of the creek bed, at the base of the irregular ridge wall. A hand was tied to a branch above and on either side of him. The figure looked like a field-dressed deer that had been hung up to bleed out and season.

Only, it wasn't a deer.

It was a man.

What made him look like a field-dressed deer was the blood that covered his short, slender, bony, near-naked body from the top of his bald head to the toes of his bare feet. Several Indians stood or sat in a ragged circle around the man and a nearby fire, while one of the warriors circled him slowly, performing a mock victory dance, hopping from foot to foot while wielding a bloody knife in his right hand.

As the warrior came around the right side of the tree, laughing with the others, he lunged toward the bloody figure once more, crouching low and slashing at the graybeard's right thigh with the knife.

Serenity lifted his head sharply, eyes squeezed tight, and sent a shrill, agonized scream careening around the canyon and causing one of the horses to sidestep abruptly and whinny. The scream continued to echo as Serenity dropped his chin to his bloody chest, his gray beard spotted crimson.

"You sons o' bitches," Cuno raked out as he thumbed the Winchester's hammer back to full cock.

As he drew his index finger taut against the trigger, he glanced around quickly. The children—Margaret, Karl, and Jack Lassiter—were sitting on the ground near Cuno's Conestoga, hands tied behind their backs. All three, including Margaret, sat leaning forward over their laps, heads down. Margaret's and Jack's heads bobbed as they cried. Karl stared dully at something on the ground a few feet in front of him.

Seeing no sign of Michelle, Cuno winced once more as the man with the knife slashed Serenity from behind, and the old man sent another shrill scream bouncing around the canyon like an enraged bird trying to make its way out of hell. From the amount of blood, from the viscera protruding from his middle, and the plaintive, diminishing pitch of his screams, the old man was nearly dead. His knees were bent, his arms bulging out of his shoulder sockets.

"Gutless bastards," Cuno raked out again. "Preying on an old man and kids!" He snugged his cheek to his rifle stalk while drawing a bead on the man with the knife. Breathing hard, his chest on fire, he gritted his teeth and tasted the salt of tears on his tongue.

The knife-wielding Ute shuffled to Serenity's right side, turning his back on Cuno. When he turned around again, bobbing his head to the beat of the chant on his brown lips, he was behind Serenity once more.

He held the bloody knife above Serenity's head, as though showing the blade to the others gathered around the fire. Suddenly, his face collapsed in a savage scowl. He stooped down behind Serenity, thrusting toward the old man with the knife.

"Forgive me, pard." Cuno's voice cracked as he took up the slack in his trigger finger, and the Winchester belched smoke and flames.

The rifle's whip-crack echoed loudly, and all the warriors around the fire jerked with starts. The man behind Serenity straightened quickly, frowning as he thrust his head over the old man's spindly shoulder to stare into his face. His lower jaw dropped slightly as he saw the blood spurting from the hole in the dead center of the old man's forehead.

The Winchester belched again, before the echoes of the first report had even started to diminish. The slug punched through the knife-wielding Ute's right eye, and the brave screamed shrilly as he staggered back behind Serenity's twitching body, dropping the knife and cupping both hands to his face.

Cuno leapt to a knee and quickly replaced the spent cartridges in the Winchester's receiver, while the Utes were still looking around in shock and trying to figure out where the shots had come from. When he'd punched the second slug into the rifle, he calmly but quickly raised the stock to his shoulder, his jaws set hard, his blue, tear-glazed eyes stony beneath mantled, blond brows.

The Utes were grunting and bellowing and reaching for their rifles or bows amongst the trees in which the smoke from the fire hung like a blue fog. Cuno picked out one of the bolting figures—a short, stocky brave in an open bear coat and wearing a red bandanna angled low over his ears—and fired. The brave yelped and flew back and sideways, clamping a hand to his left side, just above his hip, and sending a bright, horrified gaze toward Cuno's rocky perch.

As the spent, smoking cartridge flew up over Cuno's right shoulder to clatter down the scarp, Cuno rammed his cocking lever home, picked out another skin-clad figure, and fired. The brave, who'd been jerking one of the new Winchesters to his shoulder, was punched straight back into the fire, where he fell on his ass, wailing like a bobcat in a bear trap and flopping like a landed fish, throwing the Winchester clear.

Cuno clipped another brave in the thigh and another in the shoulder before he blew the top of another brave's head off a half second after the brave had loosed an arrow. The arrow bounced off the scarp around Cuno's boots, and then rifles began hammering from the trees below, which were even more obscured now because of the smoke sent up by the brave roasting in the fire pit.

Cuno bolted forward, leapt onto a ledge about five feet down from the top of the scarp, and fired two quick rounds as slugs and arrows whistled around him, one bullet carving a loin-tingling line along his left side, halfway between his shoulder and his hip, about a half inch deep. He leapt from the ledge to a boulder on his left, fired another round, hearing a grunt as the round hit its target, then leapt from the boulder to the ground as more slugs and arrows cut the space he'd just vacated.

Shouts, howls, groans, and screams rose from the trees fifty feet in front of him as the braves—those that weren't down and dead or flopping around wounded—ran toward him, most wielding Winchester or Spencer rifles while a couple others wielded bows and arrows.

One threw a feathered spear, which Cuno ducked before hearing the missile thump point down in the ground six feet behind him. Cuno racked a fresh shell and drilled the brave who'd thrown the spear just as he'd turned to run back toward the riverbed.

Ejecting the spent brass and seating fresh, Cuno slid his rifle barrel left and pulled the trigger. Another brave grabbed his shoulder and staggered sideways, firing a Spencer carbine straight out from his right hip and blowing a hole through the top of his right moccasin.

The brave scrunched up his face and yowled as he leapt straight up in the air and hit the ground on his butt, throwing the Spencer out behind him.

Cuno narrowed his eyes and gritted his teeth, continuing steadily forward in spite of the bullets and arrows careening around him, blowing up sand and gravel, spanging wickedly off the scarp behind him, and taking painful nicks out of his flesh.

He moved like a man possessed, jaws hard, tears streaking his cold, red cheeks.

26

A BRAVE RAN up toward Cuno and dove behind a fallen cottonwood. When the brave lifted his head and extended a Winchester over the top of the log, Cuno drew a hasty bead on the brave's forehead and fired.

The brave screamed as his forehead turned red and slumped forward against the log, nodding and twitching as though he were trying to heave the tree out of his way.

Two rifles barked from inside the billowing smoke, and Cuno winced and stumbled sideways as one slug carved a hot line across his right cheek, nicking his ear, and the other plowed into his thigh, setting his entire leg on fire.

He triggered the Winchester in the direction in which one of the rifles had flashed, but his hammer hit the firing pin with a dull ping, empty.

Tossing the Winchester aside as another slug nipped his left shin, Cuno grabbed his .45 and stumbled forward, limping on his numb right leg. He dove forward and right, hit the ground on his shoulder, and rolled.

Two slugs thundered into a large rock behind him.

Flat on his belly, chin up, he aimed the .45 out and up. A brave in a knee-length bear coat was racking a fresh shell into his Spencer repeater, down on one knee ten yards in front of Cuno, his coat hanging off his shoulder.

Cuno's .45 roared and leapt in his hand.

The slug hammered the breech of the brave's Spencer with a sizzling roar, ricocheting and plowing into the brave's right cheek. The brave threw the rifle straight out away from him as though it had grown suddenly hot in his hands and snapped his eyes wide with shock, blood pouring from the ragged hole in his face.

A rifle barked ahead and left. The slug slammed into the rocks just ahead of Cuno, showering his face with shards. Cuno fired back through the smoke where he'd seen the gun's red flash. His slug slammed into a tree with an angry bark. There was a grunt, and then footsteps rose, dwindling quickly as someone ran away.

A breeze cleared some of the smoke, revealing one of the braves he'd wounded lying on his back and grunting Ute curses as he hugged a bloody knee to his chest. Cuno ratcheted back the Colt's hammer and aimed.

The brave turned his head toward Cuno. His eyes snapped wide, and he opened his mouth to scream, but before the howl had left his lips, Cuno's .45 roared, and his slug drilled a neat round hole through the brave's forehead, snapping his head back the other way.

The brave's hands dropped from his knee, and his leg sagged down to the ground, his mouth opening and closing quickly, as though he were trying desperately to scream.

More grunts and groans rose to Cuno's left, and he turned to see the foot-shot brave crabbing belly down toward a revolver jutting from a wide, leather band around a dead warrior's bloody waist. Grunting against his own aches and against the throbbing in his right thigh, from which blood welled to soak his deerskin breeches, Cuno pushed himself to his knees.

He took a deep breath and, gritting his teeth, climbed to his feet. Looking around, he saw only dead bodies including the one in the fire pit, and the three Lassiter children still sitting by the wagon ahead and left. Their eyes were on him, filled with awe and terror, the boys' lips and cheeks cut and bruised from the beatings they'd received from the merciless Utes.

Cuno held a hand up to them, then, gritting his teeth and cursing under his breath, limped toward where the Ute brave was wrapping his hand around the Colt Navy jutting from the dead man's hip.

Cuno's shadow fell over him. The brave turned his head just in time to receive Cuno's bullet through his heart. As the brave, quivering, slumped over the other dead man, Cuno quickly thumbed open his .45's loading gate, and replaced the spent shells with fresh from his cartridge belt.

There were nine dead Indians around him. From atop the escarpment, he'd hastily counted eleven—the same number he'd counted when the caravan had passed him earlier.

Spinning the Colt's cylinder, he moved forward, left of the fire, not looking at Serenity's bloody body hanging slack between the trees, and deeper into the dry, rocky riverbed lightly dusted with fresh, wet snow. He hadn't realized until now that the clouds had lifted, and the sun was shining through the gaps—a wan, late-day sun making the snow-limned branches glow.

Another dead Indian lay ahead, belly down at the end of a long, broad blood trail. One of the new Winchesters that Cuno, Serenity, and Dallas Snowberger had unwittingly hauled out from Crow Feather lay in the snow and gravel beside him.

Far back in the trees to his right, beyond the wagon and the Indian ponies, a couple of his mules were braying.

Beneath the brays rose another, softer, rhythmic sound. It was coming from his left.

Sucking a sharp breath against the throbbing pain in his bloody thigh, Cuno headed toward the source of the oddly beguiling sound that somehow seemed to originate from either the ground or the sky. He followed a slow bend in the streambed, limping, sometimes slipping on the slick rocks, the sheer, red ridge wall curving toward him on his right.

The sun suddenly seemed brighter and more golden as it fell through the branches. Gauzy, sunlit snowflakes continued to fall, as well, but melted immediately upon landing. The breeze swirled the smoke fetid with the smell of burning animal hide and human flesh.

Cuno stopped and lifted his cocked .45 straight out in front of him. Something rose from his belly to constrict his chest.

Thirty yards away, a cream-colored figure was staked out on the ground, spread-eagle on her back. It wasn't hard to see that it was a woman. A blonde with smooth, porcelain-pale skin that had gone faintly blue from the cold. Her long, loose blond hair slid around in the wind, glowing in the cold, golden sunlight.

Ahead of her was a boulder. A man in a thick fur coat sat atop the boulder, facing the naked figure on the ground before him. His long, coarse black hair was liberally streaked with gray. His deep-sunk eyes were open, but he was staring somewhere to Cuno's right and above him as Cuno approached slowly while squeezing the cocked Colt in his hand.

A Winchester rifle leaned against the rock the man was perched on, to the man's left. A curly, silver scalp dangled from the barrel by a leather thong.

Leaping Wolf's lips moved and his feet rose and fell rhythmically as he chanted and danced while sitting at the head of his victim, lightly placing each foot down flat before lifting it again at various distances above the ground.

A bizarre, seated death dance, or a dance of sacrifice, Cuno thought.

Was the old man offering Michelle to the gods in exchange for the return of his own daughter, killed by Trent's waddies?

The old man held a knife in his right hand, resting on his

fur-clad lap. The man looked down at the knife now and raised it face high, holding the hide-wrapped handle so that the flat of the blade faced out away from him. He didn't look at the knife but continued staring into the distance beyond Cuno, his wizened face with broad, brown nose hanging slack against his high, broad cheekbones, his eyes red-rimmed and haggard.

The old man rose suddenly from the rock.

Cuno stopped fifteen feet away. "Leaping Wolf."

Not reacting to him, the old man dropped to his knees in front of Michelle's head. The girl lifted her eyes to him, her lips, her entire body shivering from the cold. The chief continued to chant as he passed the knife over the girl's naked breasts and flat, white belly in a slow, swirling motion.

"Hold it," Cuno said, hearing the tremble in his pain-racked voice.

As the old man raised the knife in both hands above Michelle's chest, the girl's mouth and eyes snapped wide, and she loosed a loud, shrill scream, arching her back and neck and fighting at the stakes and leather ties holding her firmly against the ground.

Cuno's Colt barked. Leaping Wolf jerked back slightly, continuing to hold the knife in both hands, blade down, over Michelle's chest.

The old man looked at Cuno and frowned slightly, as though seeing the intruder for the first time.

The Colt roared again, smoke wafting in the cold, late-day sunshine.

Leaping Wolf jerked back against the rock, falling to his butt, knees raised before him, both holes in his chest sprouting blood through his heavy bear coat. He dropped the knife, which tumbled onto the rocks beside him, and his hands fell to his lap. His head sagged slowly back against the side of the boulder.

His lips moved, and he said something—"Sundra-No-May-He"—which Cuno suspected was the Ute name of his daughter, and then he gave a twitch. His head fell slightly sideways and, his eyes turning hard as black stones while still staring off somewhere behind Cuno, he gave a long, last sigh and died.

Quickly, Cuno holstered his Colt and dropped beside Michelle's shivering body. She looked up at him but said nothing as her teeth chattered and her blue lips trembled. Cuno grunted and sighed as he plucked his bowie from the sheath in his right boot, then, stretching out his right leg and keeping one hand clamped over the wound, he quickly sliced through the leather ties holding the girl's limbs to the buried stakes.

As he worked, he glimpsed the Winchester leaning against the rock, and a sour expression passed across his face. The bloody scalp dangling from the barrel—thick, curly, silver hair rustling in the breeze—was Logan Trent's. Cuno fought the imagined image of Trent's grisly murder from his mind, and continued working to free the man's daughter.

When he had her free, she continued lying there, trembling.

"Come on," he said, hunkering down and sliding his left arm beneath her shoulders, frustration raking him. She needed to get up and get warm, but she didn't seem able to or willing to move. "Come on, goddamnit . . ."

He glanced at Leaping Wolf leaning back against the boulder, his head tipped nearly to his shoulder. Cuno slid his arm back out from beneath Michelle, then slid himself, wounded leg still extended, up beside the dead Ute chief. Nausea and fatigue blurred his vision and lightened his head and, as he lifted the bowie to the man's coat, he nearly passed out.

Grabbing a handful of snow and rubbing it across his face to brace himself, he cut the bone buttons from the dead man's bloody coat, then clumsily ripped it off his withered shoulders. He set the knife down, tossed the coat over Michelle, wrapped it around her shoulders, then again dropped low beside her and snaked his left arm beneath her shoulders.

She was trembling violently, blue eyes lit with an other-worldly horror.

"Come on, now." Cuno's voice was weak. Again he shook his head, feeling the melting snow sliding down his cheeks. "Gotta help me, now . . . damnit. Gotta get you . . . back . . . to the fire . . ."

He groaned loudly as he dug his right boot heel into the ground and, pushing up with his left knee, started heaving himself to his feet.

A clatter of rocks and a crunch of brush stopped him, and he sank back down to a haunch, the girl in his arms. An Indian had stumbled out of the trees—a big man wearing a deerskin tunic, his hair pulled back in a feathered braid. The side of his broad forehead was bloody, as was his lower left leg. He held a Spencer repeater to his shoulder as he limped toward Cuno and Michelle, a frigid smile stretched taut across his chiseled, brown, war-painted face.

Cuno sank back against Leaping Wolf's still-raised knees, his heart leaping heavily. He slid his hand from around the girl to his side, but his coat flap was pulled down over his .45.

He stared, transfixed, as the wounded brave shuffled toward him, extending the Spencer straight out from his right shoulder, the man's cheek snugged up against the stock. The brave's cheeks slid even farther back from his large, white teeth, and his eyes narrowed as he stared down the rifle barrel at Cuno's head.

A gun barked. Cuno jumped. The girl in his arms jerked and sobbed.

There was an echoing screech and a puff of rock shards and snow just beyond the Indian. The brave jerked his head up from the rifle, frowning.

The gun barked again. There was a thumping sound as dust puffed from the brave's heavy deerskin tunic. He dropped the rifle to his side and stumbled sideways, staring in shock down the dry creek bed behind Cuno.

Faintly, Cuno heard the click of a pistol being cocked.

There was another bark, and more dust puffed from the

brave's tunic—higher this time. He grunted, dropped the rifle, which clattered onto the slick rocks, then twisted around, stumbled over the rifle, and fell belly down on the snow-covered, sun-dappled stones.

Blood quickly welled out from under his still form.

Cuno looked over his right shoulder. Camilla knelt on both knees about fifteen yards down the riverbed, at the edge of the trees. She held the sheriff's revolver in both hands straight out in front of her face. Smoke curled from the barrel.

Her dark eyes were grave.

She lowered the gun, pushed to her feet, and holding the pistol in one hand down low by her side, hitched up her skirts and ran to where Cuno sat with Michelle Trent's quivering, fur-clad form in his arms.

"Ay-yi!" Camilla looked at the blood pumping from the hole in his thigh. It had dribbled down his leg to melt the snow, sending up little snakes of steam.

She ripped off her neckerchief and quickly wrapped it around his leg, gritting her teeth as she tied it tight. Cuno threw his head back, bunching his lips as the pain blazed through him.

"How bad?" Camilla asked.

"Don't think it hit the bone." Cuno raised Michelle in his arms. "Take her over to the fire. She needs to get warm. The Lassiter kids are there—looked all right a few minutes ago." He chuffed without mirth. "As good as could be expected, I reckon . . ."

As Camilla crouched to wrap one of Michelle's arms around her neck, the Mexican girl flicked her gaze to Cuno nervously, her brown eyes filled with worry.

"I'm gonna sit here a bit," Cuno said. "I'll be along."

"I will be back for you." Straightening and holding Michelle up beside her, Camilla began making her way up the creek bed. "Come, Michelle," she told the blonde, easing her along, Michelle's bare feet slipping and dragging across the stones. "We must get you warm."

Cuno dragged himself to the side of the boulder and

leaned his back against it, keeping his wounded leg straight out in front of him, the other one bent so that his boot heel rested against the inside of his calf. He looked at the dead brave, and he smiled.

Camilla.

His vision dimmed, and he rested his head back against the boulder, nudging his hat low on his forehead.

Someone jerked his shoulder, and he opened his eyes. Camilla crouched on her haunches before him. Behind her, the orange sun was falling behind the trees.

She gave a relieved sigh, narrowing her eyes slightly. "I thought you were dead."

"I'll be all right. You got the blood stopped." Cuno leaned forward and grabbed the girl's arm, pulling her toward him. "Just help me back to the wagon."

With the girl's help, he climbed to his feet and wrapped his arm around her neck, leaning against her as she guided him across the stones, heading toward the fire flashing orange through the darkening trees.

Breathing through his teeth and trying to distract himself from the pain in his torn leg, he looked at Camilla, her long hair tickling his cheek. "Don't think I caught your last name."

"Be quiet. Save your strength, crazy gringo boy." Camilla chuffed and shook her head as she held him close about the waist. "Cordova."

"Camilla Cordova. Has a nice ring to it."

"Shh."

They angled across the creek bed and into the soggy, smoky woods. As they approached the fire, Cuno cast a reluctant gaze toward the two trees where Serenity had been staked. There were only the two leather thongs that had held his wrists, dangling against the damp tree trunks.

Looking around, he saw a blanketed form on the ground near the wagon's front wheel. A tuft of thin, silver hair blew around the top of the blanketed bundle in the breeze. Cuno stopped as a wave of grief welled up through his pain and weakness, and a large, dry knot grew in his throat.

"I am sorry," Camilla said, looking up at Cuno from under his arm.

Cuno blinked back tears, cleared his throat. "Serenity . . ." He shook his head, ground his jaws with renewed fury at Leaping Wolf's blind vengeance. "He didn't deserve to die like that."

Michelle Trent and Margaret Lassiter lay side by side by the fire, curled up under several heavy blankets and buffalo robes. Neither girl moved. Michelle didn't appear to be trembling anymore. She and Margaret had drifted into deep slumbers, thoroughly spent. A bloodstained leg of Margaret's doll protruded from an edge of a robe.

Karl and Jack Lassiter were carting one of the dead Indians out of the camp, both boys' faces set grimly as they each took an ankle and dragged the corpse down canyon, away from the mules and horses.

"You sit here," Camilla said as Cuno leaned back on his hands, his legs hanging over the edge of the tailgate. "I will get some whiskey and clean those wou—"

"Hello the camp!"

Cuno palmed his .45 instantly, rocking back the hammer.

At the same time, Camilla plucked her own revolver from her coat pocket and swung around, cocking her Schofield with both thumbs and holding it out in front of her.

Cuno's pulse quickened once again as he watched a horseback rider move out from behind the escarpment west of the camp and ride toward the wagon. The man held a rifle up against his bearded cheek, reins trailing down and away from the receiver. The nubs of his cheeks were bloodsmeared.

He came on slow, the white-stockinged dun loose-kneed and blowing, as though it had been ridden hard.

"You should have killed him," Camilla said tightly.

"Drop them irons," Sheriff Mason ordered as he drew to a halt about ten yards from the wagon.

Cuno grimaced at another pain spasm shooting up and

down his leg. He continued to hold his .45 straight out in front of him, his hand trembling from weakness, but he glanced at Camilla beside him.

"Do as he says."

Camilla frowned at him indignantly.

"Do it."

The girl returned her gaze to Mason sitting his saddle before them, staring down the barrel of his Winchester saddle-ring carbine. The vapor from his breath puffed around his face silhouetted against the colorful western sky behind him.

Camilla depressed the Schofield's hammer and flung the gun away angrily.

"You, too, freighter," Mason said, holding the rifle steady on Cuno.

"On one condition."

Mason was silent—a dark figure against a branding-iron sky.

"You get her and these kids to the fort," Cuno said.

Mason stared at him, his eyes two faintly glistening circles above the Winchester's receiver and cocked hammer. The man lifted his head away from the rifle and, keeping the gun trained on Cuno, swung slowly down from the saddle.

Dropping the horse's reins, Mason walked toward the wagon, extending the rifle in one hand. His spurs chinged. Wooly chaps flapped against his legs.

"You got a deal," the sheriff growled. "But I'll be takin' you in, too . . . under arrest for the dead lawmen and the rifles."

Camilla sucked a sharp breath and turned to Cuno.

Cuno returned her look. He tried to smile reassuringly, but as nausea swept through him and gauzy darkness closed down around him from within, he wasn't sure he'd gotten his lips to move.

He could feel cold blood trickling down from the nicks and cuts on his cheeks.

Turning back to Mason, who stood four feet away from

him, he depressed his Colt's hammer and flipped the gun straight up in the air. He caught it by the barrel and thrust it out before him, grips first.

"Fair enough."

Peter Brandvold was born and raised in North Dakota. He currently resides in Colorado. His website is www.peterbrandvold.com. You can drop him an e-mail at peterbrandvold@gmail.com.

PETER BRANDVOLD

series featuring Sheriff Ben Stillman

ONCE A MARSHAL

ONCE MORE WITH A .44

ONCE A LAWMAN

ONCE HELL FREEZES OVER

ONCE A RENEGADE

ONCE UPON A DEAD MAN

ONCE LATE WITH A .38

PETER BRANDVOLD

"Make room on your shelf of favorites:
Peter Brandvold will be staking out a claim there."
—Frank Roderus

THE DEVIL'S LAIR

STARING DOWN THE DEVIL

RIDING WITH THE DEVIL'S MISTRESS

.45-CALIBER MANHUNT

.45-CALIBER FURY

.45-CALIBER REVENGE

ROGUE LAWMAN #2: DEADLY PREY

ROGUE LAWMAN

"Recommended to anyone who loves the West
as I do. A very good read."
—Jack Ballas

"Takes off like a shot, never giving the reader a
chance to set the book down."
—Douglas Hirt

PETER BRANDVOLD

DEALT THE DEVIL'S HAND

With a bloodthirsty posse prepared to pump him full of hot lead, bounty hunter Lou Prophet tries to steer clear of the sweet young thing who's making him think twice about his drifter lifestyle.

THE DEVIL AND LOU PROPHET

Call him manhunter, tracker, or bounty hunter. Lou Prophet loved his work—it kept him in wine and women, and was never dull. His latest job sounds particularly attractive: he's to escort to the courthouse a showgirl who's a prime witness in a murder trial. But some very dangerous men are moving in to make sure the pair never reach the courthouse alive.

M33AS0907